RECALLED TO LIFE

By Dan Burns

This is a work of fiction. Names, characters, places and incidents are either the product of the authors' imagination or are used fictitiously. Any resemblance to actual persons, living or dead, events, or locales is entirely coincidental.

Published in the United States by ***Eckhartz Press***

ISBN: 978-0-9894029-0-3
Printed in the United States of America

Cover art by *Susan Rackish Janssen*
Cover design by *Siena Esposito*
Interior design by *Vasil Nazar*

First Edition

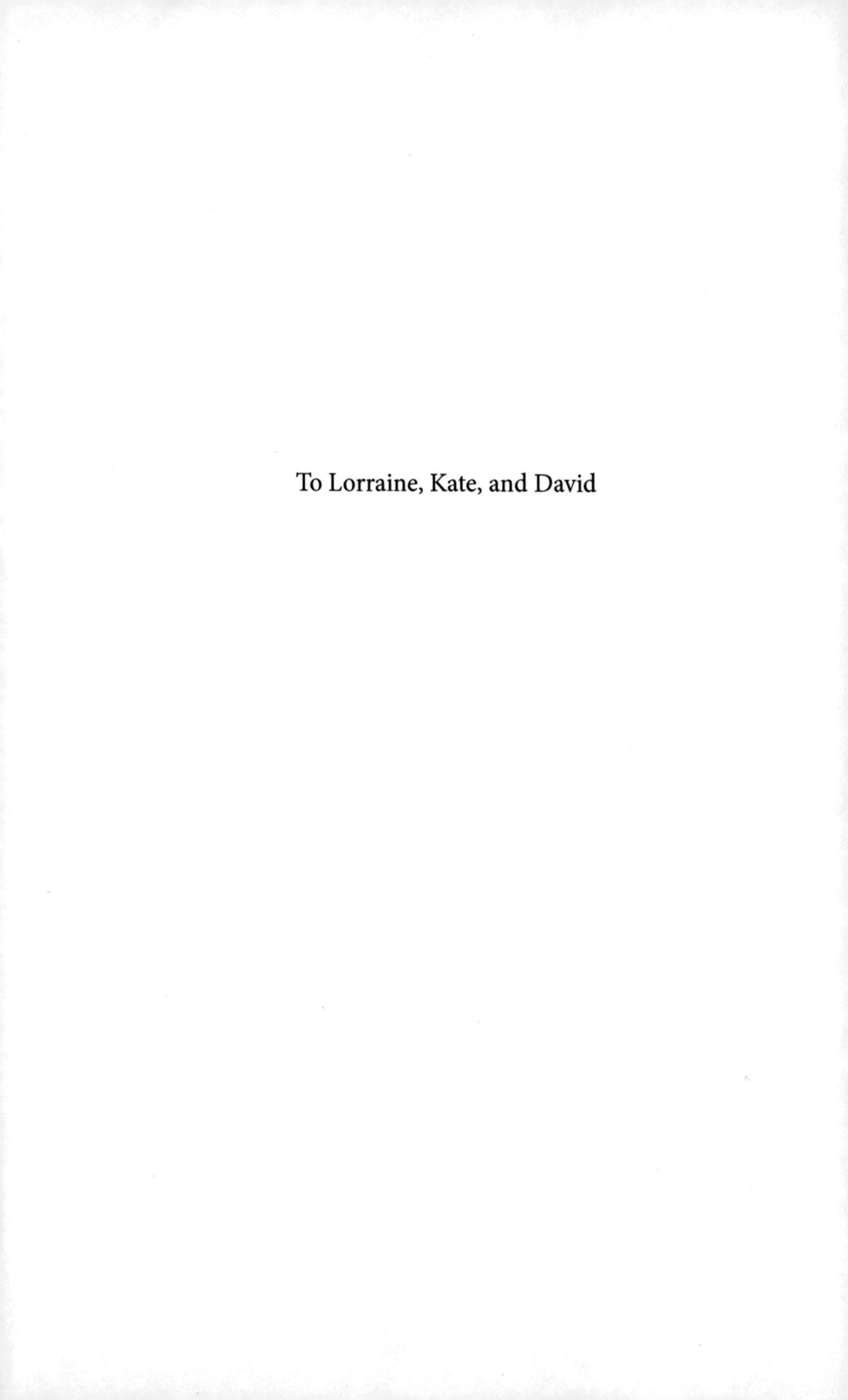

To Lorraine, Kate, and David

"The world, like a great iris of an even more gigantic eye, which has also just opened and stretched out to encompass everything, stared back at him."

"And suddenly everything, absolutely everything, was there."

— Ray Bradbury, *Dandelion Wine*

1

All the clock hands and timepiece gears and digital counters in the world became weary, slowed, then stopped altogether, if only for a moment. That's how Peter O'Hara felt at this moment in time, on this special day. Standing alone under the shade of a blooming catalpa tree, the wind blowing calm and cool on a late spring afternoon, Peter was at peace.

If you were so inclined to be a half hour early for the release of students from the Briar Avenue Public School on this day, on the east side of Briar Avenue, directly in front of the main entrance, you would see him standing there, smiling and content. You wouldn't think anything of the fact that he was standing there alone, and you would be as comfortable as he was. You would feel like you knew him and would be tempted to walk over and speak to him. The street would be silent, the landscape still, and you would feel like Peter did, lost in time.

Peter O'Hara was a captive of life and of his career, yet he was also a willing captive of his family and his son in particular. There was nothing more important to him than his family, but it often didn't seem that way. He pledged to himself that no matter what life orchestrated on this particular day, he would turn it off, shut it out, say good-bye, and walk away. For, on this day, there was nothing that could, or would, stop Peter from picking up his son from school.

Nothing.

* * *

It was a Monday, and it was a fine and special day. Peter knew it, and his son would realize the significance of the day shortly. Peter had been planning the day for some time but had kept the details to himself. He was good at keeping secrets. As he stood in front of the school and waited, he felt better than he had ever felt in his life. Today he would reveal the secret, and it would certainly make one extraordinary little man very happy.

He had managed the routine for this day with expert care, leaving nothing to chance. In his schedule for the day, Peter made a point to get to the school at least an hour early. His primary motivation was to ensure that he would not be late, regardless of the circumstances or the traffic. When he was at the office, it seemed there was always someone who had an issue, a question, or a problem that only he could address, and no matter what time of the day or day of the year, the smartest people on the planet could not predict the traffic that would be waiting for him on his way from his office in downtown Chicago to the suburbs. He planned to leave the office at exactly one o'clock and knew that even with a few last-minute interruptions and a traffic jam of epic proportions, he could be at the school by three, guaranteed. His plan worked well. On this day the interruptions were few and the traffic was light. He arrived at the school a half hour early, which allowed him to enjoy the quiet time alone while he waited for his son. It was unusual, but for a brief moment he had not a care in the world.

From his vantage point, Peter viewed the full expanse of the neighborhood grade school. He had missed the sight of the building and was glad that he was back. It was last year that his son Jake had asked if he could ride the school bus with his friends, thereby eliminating the need for Peter and his wife to juggle the drop-off and pick-up schedules. Jake said he wanted some independence—a statement coming from an eight-year-old. Peter smiled as he thought of it. He and his wife had struggled with the decision, wanting to give Jake his independence but also wanting to keep him close and protected. They agreed to give it a try, and neither he nor his wife had been back to pick Jake up since. Though Peter missed the car rides with his son, the decision worked out well, and work quickly filled the void.

Peter appreciated the architecture of the building. He studied its lines and imagined the craft of the artisans who had laid the brick and stone some eighty years ago. The bricks were dark, reddish-brown, and rough-edged, set in a natural mortar and accented by blocks of ancient limestone at every edge and opening. He looked at the building, searching for a message from the architect who designed it. The building captivated him, the form and structure pulling him in. The school grounds surrounding the massive building were manicured and quiet, providing Peter a solitary refuge. He looked on, lost in his thoughts, aware of nothing but the building and the quiet surroundings.

If you were at the school to pick up your son or daughter on this day, you would likely have noticed Peter. He was in his late thirties, slim and fit, and his shoulder-length hair was raven-colored. He smiled with little effort and looked relaxed while he waited, and though you might not be able to pinpoint why, you would likely want to find out who he was. His gaze was thoughtful and inquisitive, fixed at a point along the roofline of the school. He looked like a cross between a successful artist and a CEO, a fitting description since he was a senior architect and associate partner at one of the leading architectural firms in the country.

He definitely looked the part. Most noticeable was his standard-issue uniform, which was unlike what most of the other parents were wearing as they arrived. His perfectly tailored suit hung on him like fine drapery, and his shirt was a blinding white. He took creative liberty with his tie selections, yet they always contributed to the overall palette and presentation. He was of average height, but he stood tall and prominent, much like the buildings he designed.

After waiting just a short time, Peter's solitude was broken when his phone beeped. It was a muffled and barely audible sound, but it got his attention. He sighed, looked at his watch indifferently, and ran a hand through his hair. He thought about his next move, and his body tensed. Any remaining trace of his smile faded. He thought for a few seconds more then reached into his jacket pocket, pulled out the phone, and pressed a button. Peter listened to a voice message that seemed to go on much too long. He became agitated, a brief Jekyll and Hyde moment. He hung up, shook his head in disgust, and returned his gaze to the building, hoping to forget the message and the interruption altogether. He took a deep breath and straightened. After a few minutes, the transformation reversed itself, and he was calm again.

The school was situated in the center of town, bordered on four sides by established, tree-lined residential streets. As the end of the school day neared, the streets came alive with the rush and roar of a crowd, as though an enormous floodgate had been opened at one end. The school was a high-powered magnet, drawing people in from every corner of town for the daily ritual. The once-empty streets became crowded with parked and idling cars filled with waiting parents, grandparents, and babysitters

Peter heard the faint sound of a bell ringing from inside the school. His heart quickened much in the same way that it had when he had been a student there himself, knowing that freedom was just a moment away. As if on cue, the front doors opened wide, and children spilled out, a flood of arms waving, legs sprinting, and countless voices ringing out at elevated pitches. Quiet changed to pandemonium. Children ran everywhere, car engines started, and parents emerged as if from nowhere. He looked around and noticed for the first time the deluge of cars that had gathered in the streets.

He found himself in a swarm of anxious bystanders and looked out of place. He didn't notice. Instead, he focused on the main doorway of the school, straining over the mass of heads gathered in front of him. *Where did they all come from?* he wondered. Most of the other parents were on their phones and talking with an unnecessary level of aggression and volume, like they were in the midst of preventing the launch of a nuclear weapon. Many had bags over their shoulders containing the requisite gear for their child's after-school activities. Peter was free of such an anchor. They all seemed overly restless and looked at their watches time and again, as though there was absolutely no second to spare. Their modus operandi was simple: get the kid, shove a snack in his mouth, hurry him into the car, and speed off to whatever was next. It looked exhausting.

In order to maintain his line of sight, Peter swayed back and forth between the bouncing people lined up in front of him. He spotted his son Jake as he exited the building and waved a hand to get his attention. Jake noticed and sprinted toward his smiling father, weaving with swift determination through a maze of parents and other children. He did his best to squeeze through the numerous human barricades without touching anyone. He made his way to his father and stopped short in front of him.

Surprised, Jake leaned in closely while looking around, as if someone might be listening. "Dad, what are you doing here?"

"It's nice to see you too," Peter said. "I thought I would surprise you."

Jake looked at him curiously. "A surprise?"

Peter had him hooked. It was that simple. "How would you like to go see Grandpa?"

Jake's eyes opened wide, and his face beamed with excitement. "Really? You mean it?" His mouth remained open, and his eyebrows peaked as he waited for an answer.

"I mean it. It's time." Peter took Jake's backpack, put his arm around his shoulder, and navigated him through the maze of people as they hurried to the car.

* * *

For the next twenty minutes, Peter and Jake drove down a seemingly endless patchwork of whispering and peaceful tree-lined streets. If you weren't from the area, you would think that all the streets looked very much the same. Each had two lanes with well-established oak trees at both sides of the curb that rose up and connected in the form of a grand arch forty feet above the street. The houses, representative of an earlier century, were moderate, colorful, and cherished. Most were set back fifty feet on unassuming lots. Children played in the front yards, riding bikes, chasing dogs, and letting go of all the pent up energy that still remained from earlier in the day and the previous winter. Yes, you would think that all the streets looked the same, and you would realize that is how it was meant to be. You would think it would be a nice place to live.

As he drove, Peter's expression was serious and fixed and contemplative, although he wasn't thinking about anything in particular. The first part of the plan had gone better than he had expected; his mind was on a break, enjoying the intermission. He was glad to be in the car, sitting next to his son in quiet confines away from the madness in front of the school. He was conscious only of the roadway and its many signs and distractions, and the second part of the plan eluded him for the moment.

Sitting next to him, Jake was quiet, looking out the side window at the world passing him by. He was eight years old and small for his age. The circumstance of his current height didn't bother him, except for the few times he got pushed around at school. He knew it was *just a matter of time until the forces of biology and heredity kicked in and elevated your stature*. Those were his father's words, not his, but he still believed them. Jake wore jeans, gym shoes, a long-sleeved T-shirt, and a sleeveless vest. Atop his head was his favorite Red Sox baseball cap that his father had bought for him years ago on a business trip through Boston. The team was a good thousand miles away, but Jake claimed it was *his* team. He wore the hat even though it was a stark contradiction to the Cubs or Sox hats that his friends wore. He had the same dark hair as his father, yet by all other accounts you would not know they were related. He had big, green eyes and a small and slender nose.

A thin scar was visible above his left eye. The scar was an add-on feature obtained at a friend's birthday party two years ago when he was a bit too eager to rush in for the candy while one of the boys was still swinging wild at an un-dead piñata. He had a reserved and wondrous quality to him, keeping to himself more times than not while always observing with a keen eye the life that transpired around him. Jake seemed not to have a single concern, and at the same time you could tell that he cared, a trait most evident in the way he *looked* at something. He was conscientious, thoughtful, and considerate. You could see all of that in his eyes, an unusual and uncanny quality for an eight-year-old. He stared out the car window and took in the sights and sounds around him.

"I called your mother to let her know we wouldn't be home until dinner," Peter said.

Jake appeared not to hear and said nothing. There was nothing more that needed to be said. A slight smile formed at the corner of his mouth as he continued his gaze out the window.

They drove on in comfortable silence as they made their way to the other side of town.

* * *

As they arrived at their destination, Peter pulled the car over to the curb and shut off the engine. Jake unbuckled his seatbelt and was out of the car before Peter could say a word. Peter got out and joined Jake on the sidewalk where they stood side by side, looking up to a grand, pillared entryway. Set atop two stone columns made of stacked nineteenth-century granite and looming fifteen feet above the ground was an arch of intricate and distressed ironwork, across which, in block lettering, THE SHADY ACRES HOME was displayed. Jake stared at the sign in wonder. He turned to his father, who nodded back to him. Peter put his arm around Jake, and they walked through the entryway and up a long brick-paved driveway.

In the distance was a massive, ivy-covered, red brick building. It looked imposing and stately, like it might have housed the founding fathers. The chipped, faded green, slate roof had weathered a thousand pounding storms, and the rain that flowed down its slopes had been captured by copper gutters with a veined patina you would think had been brushed on by the meticulous hand of an artist. The painted trim of the building was cracked but intact, its original light beige color bleached white from the harsh sun. You might think the building had seen better days. Possibly the better days were yet to come.

The building rested amid a primeval stand of trees, mostly red and white oaks that towered over and shadowed the struggling maples, and there were a few black walnut gems interspersed in an arbitrary pattern. The forest was untouched and unspoiled by man, greed, and the need for change, the only exception being a simple network of crushed stone walking paths that allowed for casual navigation through the ten-acre property.

At the end of the drive, they came to a stairway that led up to the building's entrance. There were only five cement steps, but they went off some ten feet in each direction. Collectively they were large enough to hold a fair-sized choir. The steps were worn at the center from the visitors of the last century, and Peter and Jake added to the wear as they ascended the stairs. They entered the front door of the building and walked into an open, high-ceilinged room flooded with daylight. The windows were bare, the light was harsh, and the cream marble floors contrasted with the dark and aged woodwork. Their footsteps echoed in the empty room, one that could accommodate a museum exhibit. Directly ahead of them was a massive, wood desk that stood four feet high, behind which a young man in a security uniform sat. In a different building you might think you were standing before a judge arguing your parking ticket. The young man behind the desk was Sam Cartwright, a local college student, twenty years old with reddish-brown hair flattened by the day's stress. His complexion reflected years of struggle with acne and adolescence. His single-issue blue security guard shirt hadn't been pressed in a while, and its cleanliness was questionable.

Peter and Jake approached the desk.

"Well, good afternoon, Mr. O'Hara," Sam Cartwright said.

Peter was slightly distracted by the unusual music coming from an unidentified source, but he reacted to the booming voice, a voice that didn't match the face from which it came. "Oh, hi, umm," was all Peter could muster and his words trailed off.

Sam stood up behind the desk, and with a pleasing and overly accommodating demeanor he said, "The name's Sam, Sam Cartwright. I was here when you came to visit last week." He looked and waited, hoping for a sign, any sign, of recognition.

Peter remembered their last meeting and at the same time felt the young man should sit down and relax. "Of course. It's nice to see you again. Sam, this is my son, Jake. He's here to visit his grandfather."

Sam smiled with confidence and conviction and rested his hands on his hips like he owned the place. "Hi, Jake. Have you been here before?" Sam was trying too hard, and though he didn't know it, he was wasting his time.

Jake didn't even realize that the young man was speaking to him. He looked up and all around, scouting and surveying the room and taking it all in. His nose twitched, and he made a face. Something didn't smell quite right.

"This is his first time here," Peter said.

"Well, Jake, welcome to Shady Acres," Sam said.

Jake was preoccupied, on a mission of his own. He grabbed his father's hand, turned, and started walking.

Peter held firm and pulled him back. "Hey, wait a minute.

I need to sign the guest log." He scribbled on a sheet of paper fastened to a clipboard then slid the clipboard across the counter toward Sam. "Thanks. We know where we're going."

Peter took Jake by the hand and led him down a very long, dimly lit, deserted hallway. There were framed, painted portraits of old, stone-faced men and women along each wall, and Jake likely felt that the oil and canvas caretakers dated back to prehistoric times. Jake glanced at a few of them with an inquiring eye as he tried to make sense of their relevance, but he lost interest quickly. He had something else on his mind. Sam watched them both as they disappeared around the corner at the end of the hall.

They walked in a U-shaped pattern around the building and came to a stop at the room marked 146. Between them, the tarnished brass numerals were visible on the closed door. Peter looked at Jake. His side profile reflected concern and caution. Jake turned to his father. His eyes grew wide as he smiled, brimming with excitement. Peter couldn't remember that last time Jake was so excited. They nodded to each other.

Peter knocked and, without waiting, opened the door wide. The heavy slab creaked on its hinges. They stood for a moment and looked in on an unassuming room, small and brightly lit by the afternoon sun through the three large windows that made up the wall opposite the door. The room was furnished with antiques from various eras with little concern for matching styles. A full-sized bed and a single night stand, both made of dark mahogany, were flush against the right wall. To the left, there was a simple, oak dresser in a natural and much lighter finish, on top of which a dusty television sat. The faint sound of classical music came from a large, floor-model radio in the near corner. You could almost hear the radio tubes humming. In front of the windows was a high-backed chair with only the back visible.

They walked into the room with trepidation in their steps. Peter grabbed hold of two wooden folding chairs that leaned against the wall behind the door. He reached back to close the door, and they proceeded to the chair by the window. They were conscious of the sound their footsteps made on the hard, parquet floor; the wood creaked under the pressure of their weight. They came around the side of the chair to find an old man looking with fixed eyes to the afternoon scene unfolding outside.

The old man was Jack O'Hara, Peter's father. He sat, motionless, save a barely noticeable rising of his chest. His head was leaned back and to the right against the high wing-back of the chair, and his eyeglasses rested halfway down the bridge of his nose. His mouth was closed, and his dry lips barely connected. He was breathing softly, the air whistling through his nostrils. He had not noticed that anyone had entered his room.

Peter unfolded the chairs in front of Jack and arranged them to his liking. He stepped forward, leaned down, and kissed his father on the forehead. "Hey, Pop. It's Peter." He straightened and stepped back as Jake made his way forward, timid.

"It's alright," Peter said.

"Hi, Grandpa," Jake said, the words catching in his throat as they came out. He seemed to think about saying it again but held back. He extended an arm slowly and touched his grandfather on the arm. He reacted with surprise at how soft and warm the skin felt. Jake stood there for a long moment, looking and wondering.

Peter and Jake sat down, their backs to the windows and facing Jack, who hadn't moved. He was quiet and unaware of their presence. Jake really wasn't sure what to do, so he rested his folded hands in his lap and chewed his bottom lip.

Peter reached over and placed a hand on Jake's knee. "It'll be all right," he said. Calm and collected, Peter got up to take off his suit jacket. He hung it on the back of his chair then sat back down. In a voice that was louder than necessary, he said, "Pop, remember the last time I was here, I told you I was being considered for that associate partner position?" He waited a few seconds, although he didn't expect a response. "Well, I found out today that I got it."

Jake snapped his head toward his father. "You got a new job? Why didn't you tell me? Do you get a new office? Did you get a raise?" He struggled to get all of the words out at once as he bounced up and down on his chair.

Jack said nothing and remained motionless.

Peter put his hand back on Jake's knee. "Take it easy. I just found out myself, and yes to the office *and* the raise."

"I bet that *pud*, Marc, is disappointed," Jake said with unexpected conviction.

"*Pud*? Who taught you to talk like that?"

"You," Jake said sheepishly.

Peter smiled, somewhat proud, but glad that his wife wasn't around. "How many times do I have to tell you to stop listening to me?"

Jake grinned, and his pride in his father returned. "Dad, tell me what happened."

"Well, there's not much to say. There were three of us being considered over the last year, and they really seemed to like my last design. You remember. I showed you."

Jake searched his memory vault. "I remember. The Murphy Building?"

"The Murray Building."

"Yeah, the Murray Building, that's what I said."

Peter grinned. "Anyway, the partners spoke to the customers I worked with and got a lot of great comments. The partners like happy customers. They bring more business to the firm."

"And . . ." Jake said, leaning in and wanting more. "What else?"

"That's about it. I got the news this morning." Peter explained it to Jake with the same enthusiasm he would show if he had just won two dollars on a lottery ticket—no big deal. He had planned for the promotion and had expected it for so long that it was a little anticlimactic.

That wasn't the case with Jake, who was wide-eyed, smiling, and still squirming in his seat.

Jack was a wax figure in his chair.

As though flipping a switch, Jake changed the topic. He got comfortable and suddenly couldn't contain his excitement any longer. He moved forward in his chair and leaned in to talk to his grandfather. "Grandpa, I have to tell you about the game-winning hit I made last week." He looked at his grandfather's face and waited for a sign. Nothing.

He turned to his father and looked for a sign.

"It's okay," Peter said. "It's a good story, and I'm sure he's listening."

Jake turned back, scratched an itch behind his ear, and continued. "Uh, it was the bottom of the ninth, two outs, man on third, the game tied. It was my turn to bat, and . . . ah . . . I was a little nervous." He got up to show his stance, holding an imaginary bat and digging his worn gym shoes into the wood tiles to secure his footing. The rubber sole against the clean floor made a loud screeching noise, and Jake looked around to see if anyone noticed. He looked to his father, who shrugged.

Jake pulled up his pants by the belt loops and built momentum as he continued, "The coach told me to swing away at the first pitch, and that's what I did." He swung his imaginary bat through the air. "POW! Right up the middle, and our man on third scored to win the game." He raised his arms and ran in a small circle around the chairs. "Wooooo," he hollered. He gave his father a high-five then stopped to look at his grandfather, who showed no reaction at all. Undeterred and still smiling from his game-winning hit, Jake sat down.

Peter was glad to hear the story again and to see it told with such animation. Jake never talked much about baseball, his team, or the games he played in, so this was a treat. This was the first time he actually saw Jake's pride in the fact that he played the game. Jake's love of being outdoors and his effort far exceeded any natural athletic ability. It seemed like he saw baseball simply as a game, as something to do, but that didn't bother Peter. It certainly didn't bother Jake. They both just wanted it to be fun.

Over the next hour, Peter and Jake took turns telling their stories to Jack. They covered topics like work, school, Mom, favorite meals, sports, and planned activities for the summer. As Peter prepared for his next revelation, he leaned in toward Jack and looked into his blank stare. While Peter spoke, Jake looked on with his chin resting on folded hands. They both watched Jack closely for any sign of contact, of life. When Peter spoke, he became quite animated in his storytelling, arms waving and hands gesturing for effect. Jake watched his father as though he was the greatest storyteller ever.

Jake got another turn and stood up. "Grandpa, do you want to hear about the fish I caught?" This time he didn't wait for an answer. "Dad took me to the lake, a, a while ago." He couldn't remember exactly when, and he looked to his father, confused.

"Last year."

"Last year?" Jake said, surprised it was that long ago. "Anyway, you should have seen it—it was a monster!" With words and gestures, Jake told his grandfather about the monster fish. He showed how he set the hook, lifting hard on his imaginary fishing rod, then showed how he fought the fish in a battle of wills. When the fight was over and Jake was victorious, he held his hands up eighteen inches apart to show the size of the catch. Peter and Jake both smiled with pride.

The stories completed, they sat quietly and looked at Jack.

Jack looked straight through and past them with no movement and no emotion.

On his last birthday, Jack had turned seventy years old. He looked eighty. He had lost most of his hair except for two small, cotton ball patches of wispy, white strands above each ear. He had more hair on his eyebrows and coming out of his nose and ears. His face was pale, and his skin was blotchy. Though he was clean-shaven and looked fresh, he appeared uncomfortable, slouched in his chair as he gazed over the top of his eyeglasses. He wore a pressed, collared, white shirt that seemed to have been aged from the sun. It hung loosely on him and was tucked into dark slacks, with the waistband material bunched up under a tight belt. The whistling breath through his nostrils had softened to just a whisper, and his eyes were lost and watery.

Peter sighed, stood up, and folded his chair. "Well, I think it's time to go. Can you help me with that chair?"

Jake rose, folded his chair, and followed his father to put it back behind the door.

As they walked back toward Jack, Peter said, "Jake, I know it seems like Grandpa's out of it, but he can't help it."

"It's okay," Jake said. "I just like talking to him."

"You know, I truly believe that he can hear everything we're saying. I don't know why or how; it's just a feeling I have. That's why I come here. I need to keep him updated on everything that's going on so that when he's ready to come home, it will be like he never left."

Jake shrugged in agreement. "Is he all right?"

"He's fine," Peter said, realizing that wasn't quite accurate but not wanting to worry his son any further. He walked back around in front of Jack, leaned down, and kissed his father's forehead. "I'll see you later, Pop. I'll be back next week."

"Me too?" Jake asked.

"We'll see," Peter said as he stepped back.

Jake stepped up and leaned forward to hug Jack, squeezing his arms in behind Jack's neck. He pulled himself forward and, while leaning, he rested his forehead against the chair back, which kept him from falling onto Jack and that put them cheek to cheek with each other. Jake whispered softly into his grandfather's ear as his father looked on. Then he released his grip and stood upright.

Without saying anything further, they both turned and walked out of the room.

* * *

Peter and Jake exited the building and stopped momentarily at the top of the steps. They looked out at the wooded landscape, at nothing in particular. Peter took Jake by the hand, and they descended the steps and walked back down the stone driveway.

Peter said, "What did you whisper to Grandpa?"

"Uh, oh, nothing. I just said good-bye, that's all."

Peter didn't believe him. "Just good-bye, huh?"

They both smiled and walked hand in hand down the long driveway.

Halfway to the car, Jake stopped and looked up at his father. "Thanks, Dad, for bringing me here."

"It was time," Peter said. "I'm sorry it couldn't have been sooner."

"That's okay."

"You know, Grandpa is family, and in the end that's all we've got." After the words were spoken, Peter thought it sounded a little *deep* and wondered if Jake understood.

Jake thought about it for a moment. "Yep, family's all we got," he said, trying to sound like his father.

They both smiled, happy and content, lost in the moment. Jake stepped forward and hugged his father tightly. Peter gave him a firm squeeze and looked down at him. "C'mon, we don't want to keep Mom waiting."

Jake reluctantly loosened his grip and stepped back. He took his father by the hand, and they walked on through the pillared entryway, got back into their car, and drove away.

It was a day that would remain fresh and significant in their memories for the rest of their years.

* * *

The following morning, Peter made his pilgrimage downtown as he did on most days. If he left by seven, he could be at the office by eight-thirty at the latest. If he left later, his arrival time was anyone's guess. He enjoyed the solitude of the drive, even if it was for just a short time. His car was his refuge, and though it was eight years old, it was reliable and comfortable. He drove in silence when he wanted to, yet the stereo could accommodate his love for pure and clear classical music at a volume only he could tolerate. He was the only one in the family who cared for that type of music, and his car was his orchestra hall.

Peter's favorite perk from the firm was his reserved parking space in the garage next door to the office building where he worked. It was a big deal to him because the parking garage was always full, and his space was on the first floor, just as he pulled in, which saved him from the dizzying turns he would have to take to try to find a spot on a higher floor. He was always trying to save a minute whenever he could, and the parking space was a real time saver. He parked the car and was out of the garage in under a minute, walking the half-block down Michigan Avenue to the office building.

The entrance was clearly marked with a marble slab chiseled with JACKSON, PARKER & FINCH, ARCHITECTS. The building was a contemporary work of art, combining brushed steel with blue and silver glass panels. It was sleek, straight, and perfect, rising twenty stories into the downtown skyline. It wasn't the tallest building, but it was one of the most striking, exhibiting an exquisite grace in a field under pressure to build bigger and taller.

Once he came out of the garage and hit the sidewalk, Peter was all business. It wasn't a conscious effort but felt more like he was on autopilot. Peter approached the entry of the building with a quickened pace and a definite sense of direction. He disappeared into the revolving doors without missing a stride.

He rode the high-tech elevator up to the twentieth floor and felt the ride up to heaven would likely be just as smooth. Jackson, Parker & Finch resided on the top three floors of the building. They had that right, since they had designed, financed, and constructed the building. Aside from the first floor, which accommodated a variety of small retail shops and a reserved but sleek promenade, the remaining floors were filled with numerous businesses and professional offices, all of which paled in comparison to the success and prestige of the firm.

Peter exited the elevator, dressed in a perfectly tailored suit made of a wool fabric the color of night. He checked his appearance as he stepped out, and though he was hurried, he felt confident and focused, ready to accept the new day as a fresh start. He walked past an empty reception desk and down a long aisle, greeting several early-starters along the way. There were only a dozen workers on the floor at that time of the morning, but there was already a buzz of activity.

The aisle was bordered by continuous rows of half-wall cubicles in a palette of muted earth-tone fabrics and finishes. In some of the cubicles, the tops of heads were visible. The office area was decorated like an art gallery. The walls were lined with a collection of exquisitely framed artwork of colored angles, unconventional lines, and renderings of commercial buildings of all shapes and sizes. Delicately illuminated by recessed and obscured spotlights, the creations were displayed to spur creativity and to serve as an exhibition of the firm's best work. The open space was naturally bright from the light coming in through the spotless glass walls, and every visible surface was free of even the slightest hint of dust.

As Peter reached the end of the aisle, he passed his assistant, April, who occupied the cubicle just outside of his office. She always made a point to be at the office before he arrived, and Peter liked that about her. It seemed that whenever he needed something, anything, she was there for him. Peter thought of her as a miracle-worker, able to somehow navigate through the daily administrative, political, and logistical barricades with swift and effective dignity. She was good at her job, and every day Peter tried to let her know that he appreciated her efforts, one way or another. She had auburn, curly, shoulder-length hair and was petite. She had perfect ivory teeth, and her skin resembled fine china.

"Good morning," Peter said as he came around her cubicle-desk and faced her.

"Good morning, Peter. Say, Mr. Parker just stopped by looking for you."

Peter grinned. "Mr. Parker? His name is Tim. We grew up in the same neighborhood, for Christ's sake. Remember? And I thought we dispensed with all the formality a long time ago. How long have we been working together anyway?"

"I know. I'm sorry, but he makes me call him Mr. Parker. He said he would be back in a few minutes."

The door to his office was open, and Peter turned and walked in while April was still talking. He seemed to do that often without realizing he was being rude. It would have annoyed April if anyone else had done that to her, but with Peter she let it go. He looked at his watch as he approached his desk, behind which was a wall of windows from waist height to ceiling. Beyond the glass was a view of the perfect downtown cityscape, a unique amalgam of brick, concrete, steel, and glass set before the perfect, blue-green backdrop of Lake Michigan. The sky was clear, blue, and perfect, and Peter stood there looking out and realizing how lucky he was.

He set his briefcase down and looked for something on his desk. It was the desk of a busy person, meaning that it was messy. There were rolled-up drawings, piles of documents to review, and stacks of unread books, many of which he might never get to. It wasn't like him, the messiness, but he just couldn't keep up with everyone who came in and left something. He couldn't keep up with the stuff *he* left. Someday, he would have to allocate a few extra hours to catch up and put a system in place to control it all. Someday.

After a few seconds of looking around, Peter became frustrated. He shouted, "April, do you have any idea where the Gattling proposal is?"

"It's over on the work table, lower-left corner," she shouted back, like she knew the question was coming.

Peter looked from where he was standing and immediately spotted it. He walked to the work table, picked it up, and leafed through the first few pages.

While he read, Tim Parker entered his office, walking in like he owned the place. Tim was the boss, one of the partners of the firm, and he dressed the part. He looked at the suit Peter was wearing, noticed a slight resemblance, and seemed to pout. His short hair was perfectly parted, not a single hair out of place. Its color was too dark and unusual to be natural.

"Peter, just the man I'm looking for. Do you have . . ."

Before Tim could finish asking, Peter closed the proposal and handed it to him. "The Gattling proposal. Here you go—updated based upon our meeting yesterday."

"You've reviewed it?" Tim asked. It was more of a statement than a question.

"Uh, yeah. It's ready to go," Peter replied, part lie, part truth.

"Great. Meet me in my office in ten minutes so we can go over some of the details before Gattling gets here. You know how he is: big building, big investment, lots of questions. His new building is going to be his legacy, and he wants it to be perfect."

"Let me check on a few things, and I'll be right over," Peter said.

Tim leafed through the proposal as he left the office. Without turning around, he said in a stern voice, "Don't keep me waiting."

The phone on Peter's desk rang. He paid no attention and turned back to the work table, shuffling papers and trying to get organized for the day. It seemed he wasn't making too much progress.

April stuck her head in the doorway. "Sorry to bother you, Peter, but there's a call for you."

"Not now. Take a message."

She shifted in the doorway, uneasy. "I think you should take it. It's Dr. Halper, your father's physician. He said it's urgent. You can take it on line two."

Peter stopped what he was doing and felt a noticeable heart palpitation with a twinge of anxiety. A look of concern swept over him. He hurried to his desk, sat, and took a deep breath. He pressed a button on the phone console and picked up the handset.

"Hello, Doctor, this is Peter. How's my father?" He listened intently, growing more troubled as the doctor spoke. Peter raised his voice. "What?" He listened again, and his expression turned to disbelief. "How can that be? How did this happen?" He listened once more, rose from his chair, and walked around the desk. "I'll leave right now. I should be there in an hour."

He set the phone down and bolted for the door. He was in a zone, aware of nothing but the internal replaying of words from his phone conversation, words that, when strung together in the proper order, just did not make any sense. The meaning the words conveyed surpassed all sense of logic and reason. Once at the doorway, Peter broke free of his mental exercise and turned around, looking for something. He hurried back, grabbed his briefcase, and headed out the office doorway.

He hurried past April without looking and hoped that maybe she wouldn't notice.

"Peter?" she said.

He kept walking and turned toward her. "Listen, I need to leave. Tell Tim I have a family emergency to take care of."

"But . . ." She tried to be understanding but firm.

"What?"

"What about the meeting with Mr. Gattling?" she said.

Peter continued down the aisle and after a few more strides, he said over his shoulder, "Ask Marc if he can cover for me."

She didn't say anything, but she was noticeably uncomfortable with the suggestion.

At once and coming from different directions, Tim and Marc Jackson made their way toward April's cubicle. Marc arrived first, which was good for him and unfortunate for April. Marc was average in every sense: personality traits, physical stature—you name it. He lacked confidence and moved with a spine that was a bit too flexible. He had a goofy-looking smirk on his face, one that always seemed to be present and always made you wish you didn't see it. He waved a hand and said in a loud voice, "No problem, buddy. I'll take care of it." With a curious expression, he watched Peter walk away then leaned in toward April and talked out the side of his mouth. "What am I taking care of?" Indifferent, he looked at April for an answer, but she didn't respond as she turned to look at Tim, who stood before her now as well.

Tim looked at April then turned to Marc. He looked at Marc as though he wanted to strangle him. Marc noticed, straightened up, and tried to be normal.

Tim turned to the hallway. "Where do you think you're going?" he shouted to Peter in a commanding tone, his vocal volume at six.

Peter turned around, flustered and at a loss for words. He was halfway down the aisle, his mind elsewhere. "I've got an . . . emergency. I've gotta go. Marc can cover for me."

Tim notched the volume up to eight. "Marc CANNOT cover for you. Gattling thinks he's an—" Tim stopped himself. He looked at Marc, overcome with disgust. Now angry, he turned back to Peter. "Don't do this. Gattling is expecting you," he said, vocal volume at nine.

"I'm really sorry. I've gotta go." Peter turned and walked away.

Tim struggled for words as his blood pressure rose and his face flushed. He was alone, like a man left to fend for himself in the desert. He grunted and pushed his voice to ten. "You have a responsibility to this project and to this firm." He swallowed hard. "You have a responsibility to *me*!" A vein in his neck bulged.

Peter was now at the end of the aisle, and Tim realized he was talking to no one. The buzz in the office had ceased, and Tim scanned the room. The office staff sat unmoving, uncomfortable, and silent. Everyone looked at Tim.

Tim reached into his pants pocket and pulled out a roll of antacids. He peeled off a few then tossed them into his mouth and chewed fast, hoping that relief would soon follow. The chalky paste in his mouth was almost too much to bear, and he grimaced as the cement lingered in his dry mouth. He smacked his lips a few times and scraped the goo off the roof of his mouth with his tongue. He looked around for something to wash it down with but was out of luck. His spit would have to do. He looked again at Marc, irritated. "Are you really Phillip's nephew? Our *senior partner's* nephew?"

Marc turned into a soldier and saluted. "Heir to the throne, in the flesh." As soon as he did it, he realized the mistake, lowered his hand, and shrugged.

Tim shook his head and huffed. "Unbelievable," was all he could muster. He turned and headed back to his office.

Marc looked at April, who shrugged. Marc shrugged in return. It was nonverbal communication, but it was effective at surmising the situation. Peter was gone, and Marc was clueless. With caution and an uneasy slither, Marc hurried off to catch up with Tim.

2

Peter was in his car, anxiously trying to drive while ending a phone conversation. "All right, I'll see you there," he said. He terminated the call and dialed another. His impatience grew while he waited for an answer. His body movements, the sound of the engine, and the shifting of the car were indicative of someone driving aggressively, somewhat recklessly, and at a high speed.

His wife Melanie answered his call. He spoke into the phone, excited and louder than necessary. "Mel, it's me."

"Oh, hi. Is everything all right?" She wasn't used to hearing from him in the morning.

"Yeah, fine."

"Then, what a nice surprise," she said.

"I'm on my way to see Pop. Dr. Halper called about fifteen minutes ago, and you'll never believe what he said."

"Is he all right?"

"Pop's *awake*. The doctor said he's awake, up and walking around."

"My God."

"I know, I don't believe it either, but that's what the doctor said. Pop's up and around and asking to see Jake."

Melanie said nothing.

"He's lucid, talking, and actually being a little belligerent. Can you believe it—belligerent?" Peter's anxiety broke. He grinned and shook his head. "Anyway, I'm on my way to see him. I called Jackie, and she's going to meet me there. I'll call you after we meet with the doctor."

Silence.

"Mel?"

"Okay, sure. Sorry, I'm just so surprised. I never expected to have this conversation."

"Listen, I've got to go."

"Drive careful," she said. "And I love you."

"I will. Love you too. Bye." He hung up and slid the phone into his jacket pocket. Peter relaxed, slowed the car, and settled into his seat, a little more at ease with the day. He grinned and shook his head again in disbelief.

* * *

It took Peter a full hour to make it to Shady Acres. The traffic was heavy and frustrating, typical for that time of the morning. After signing in at the security desk, he headed down the hallway in the opposite direction from his father's room. Halfway down the hallway, he stopped at a closed door with a gold plate on it, the office of Dr. Edward Halper.

Inside, Dr. Halper was sitting behind his desk, reading a file. He periodically glanced over the top of thick, dark-rimmed glasses as he read. Even from behind his desk, he looked short and appeared tired and stressed. Either he had worked a night shift, or it had been a tough morning. He wore the traditional physician's white coat with a loaded pocket protector in the front pocket and a white shirt, closer to a shade of gray now from age, with a dark paisley tie. The collar was unbuttoned and open, revealing some chest hair. He might have been fifty years old, or maybe forty, depending on the day and the circumstances. He read a document in the file, sighed, read some more, and sighed again.

Peter's sister, Jackie, sat across from him. Her jacket was draped over her folded hands, resting in her lap. She sighed as well as she ran a hand through her dark, boyish haircut. Her resemblance to Peter was noticeable. She was confident but quiet, and right now, she was trying to get a read on Dr. Halper.

Jackie O'Hara was Peter's only sibling, three years younger and protected since she was born. When she got older, was on her own, and her parents no longer had the ability to look after her regularly, Peter took over. Actually, Peter was always there, from when she was teased in grade school up until her recent marital challenges. Peter and Melanie had helped Jackie through the tough times and the counseling, and she made it through fairly unscathed. Peter made it a point to provide his own form of counseling for her husband. Her marriage was back on solid footing, and her life was getting back to normal.

Like Peter, she was very focused and determined, and as Peter knew his calling was in the business world, Jackie knew her calling was in having a family and raising children. She had a plan, a timeline, and though she was a little behind schedule, she and her husband were *trying*. She knew it was only a matter of time until everything fell into place.

Jackie and her husband, Mike, lived on a small, organic farm about forty miles outside of the town where she grew up. At the university, she studied literature and ancient cultures, which garnered mixed comments from her parents. When she switched to agricultural studies in her junior year, the comments were united. Her parents wondered how she would ever put such schooling to "good use." Unfortunately, neither of them was able to visit her once she and Mike bought the farm and started raising chickens and growing vegetables. Though their house was only forty miles away, to her parents it felt like she lived in another state. Peter was the only one who supported her decision to change majors. He told her to find something she was passionate about. Farming was, indeed, her passion, and it seemed to be Mike's passion as well, even if he did need to work at the local auto plant to supplement their income.

Peter knocked on the door.

"Come in," Dr. Halper said, looking up from his file. He pushed his glasses up on the bridge of his nose.

The door opened, and Peter walked in, closing the door behind him.

Dr. Halper rose and stood behind his desk. "Peter, I'm glad you could come so quickly. I was just reviewing the latest assessment results with Jackie."

Peter walked over to Jackie and kissed her on the cheek. She smiled and shrugged, and he saw a glint of confusion in her eyes. "Hey, Jackie, thanks for coming." He reached across the desk and shook hands with Dr. Halper, then he stepped back and sat down next to Jackie. He asked the doctor anxiously, "So, where's my father?"

"He's in the Gathering Hall," Dr. Halper said.

"And is he all right?" Peter asked.

Dr. Halper adjusted his glasses again and said, "He was watching television for a while, but he got antsy and started walking around and trying to talk to everyone. As you've seen when you've been here, there's not a lot of socializing that goes on, no matter how hard we try. The other residents are not reacting to him very well."

Peter looked at Jackie, gave her a nudge, and smiled. "Pop's socializing, can you believe it?"

The doctor continued, "Peter and Jackie, I wanted to talk to you both before you see your father."

"That's fine, but can we do it quickly?" Peter's impatience was evident.

"Doctor, what really happened?" Jackie asked. "For so long now, we were led to believe that he would never come out of . . ." She paused. "His condition. And now this?"

Dr. Halper fidgeted, shuffled papers, and cleared his throat. "I'll try to make it as clear as possible." There was a long pause and more fidgeting.

"And?" Peter asked, trying to pull him along.

"I have no idea," Dr. Halper said. He sounded and looked perplexed.

"Well, that's reassuring," Peter said sarcastically.

The doctor reacted quickly, saying, "You have to understand. This is an unusual situation. We're dealing with the human brain." His sentences were clipped and canned. "There's so much about it we still don't understand. And in your father's case—"

Peter was compelled to interrupt. "All right, we've heard all the *brain* dissertations before and, frankly, we don't know what to believe anymore. Are you saying you have no explanation as to why our father has remarkably just popped out of his . . ." He gestured with both hands to make quotation marks in the air. "*Coma* after all this time?"

Dr. Halper composed himself and straightened his tie. He looked up from his desk and struggled for confidence. "I know you want an explanation."

"I'd like an answer," Peter said.

"Very well." The doctor rose from his chair and walked around his desk toward the windows. He pondered for a moment, like he was getting ready to lecture a group of medical students. "Let me tell you what I know. Peter, after you and your son left yesterday, one of the staff members went in to help your father with his dinner. Nothing was unusual. At eight o'clock yesterday evening, your father was in the Gathering Hall with everyone else. Nurse Benson dispensed medication, as she does every night, then she and the rest of the staff helped everyone back to their rooms. Again, nothing was unusual. Your father was in bed and asleep at nine.

"When we went into his room this morning to help him get ready for the day, he was already awake, showered, dressed, and standing there like he was waiting for us. His suitcase, which was still in his closet from when you first brought him here, was out on his bed, and he was busy packing it."

Jackie listened intently.

Peter was bored with the explanation. "Okay, so you don't know anything. Can we see him now?"

"Peter, I can understand how you feel."

"Really?" Peter shot back as he started to get up. Jackie put a hand on his arm and kept him down.

Dr. Halper said, "Peter, this is a *good* thing. He's back with us. And while I realize this is unexpected, he's back!" He was spinning the situation.

Peter gently removed Jackie's hand from his arm and stood up. "I know, but *you* have to understand. I saw him yesterday and nearly every week since we brought him here, and there was nothing, always nothing. He'd just sit there, oblivious to the world.

And now? I can't believe it."

"Doctor, can we see him now?" Jackie asked.

"Of course, but first let me say this: we need to remember that he's lost quite a bit of time, quite a bit of his life. A lot has happened during that time. While he may seem perfectly fine, we have to be careful about how we address the past."

Jackie looked up at Peter, concerned. "We'll be careful."

Dr. Halper walked over to them. Peter walked toward the door, opened it, and held it open while Jackie and Dr. Halper exited. He followed, and the door closed behind him.

Peter and Jackie led the way down the hallway and entered the Gathering Hall with Dr. Halper trailing closely behind. The room was immense and open, with high ceilings and richly paneled walls. It might have once been a library or a place where old men gathered to smoke, drink, and talk business. A large stone fireplace was visible in the far corner, the opening large enough to stand in but dark, cold, and quiet. The furnishings were old but well kept. The sofas and loveseats were covered in worn, brown leather, and the chairs were covered in a variety of tapestry-like upholsteries.

One wall was comprised mostly of windows, rising from the sill up to the ceiling. The windows were draped along the top and down the sides with heavy, green fabric edged with gold tassels. The windows hadn't been cleaned in a while, but the morning sun still shone through, the external metal grillwork barely visible from the inside. A single television was in the room, its volume very loud. A dozen or so people were in the area, some sitting around the television, some dispersed to other corners of the room. Looking around, you could see that they all pretty much kept to themselves and seemed to like it that way. No one was speaking, except for Jack, who was sitting directly in front of the television, leaning forward in his chair and talking to the news commentator like he was an old friend.

Peter started to cross the room. “Pop?”

Jackie hurried to catch up.

As if by instinct, Jack turned, paused, and looked in the direction of the recognizable voice. He bolted up from his chair and started toward them. He used a cane and moved stiffly, with a slight limp, but came at them at a fast pace. Peter and Jackie couldn’t believe what they were witnessing.

Jack was elated, and he went to Jackie first. “Jackie, I’m so glad to see you!” He hugged her quickly then moved to Peter. “Peter, you’re a sight for sore eyes.” He grabbed Peter’s hand and shook it excitedly, then he patted him on the side of the arm a couple of times. “Good to see you, boy. I thought you would never get here. Where’s your mother? Say, I never noticed the gray hair before. What’s the matter, work getting the best of you? You can fill me in later. Actually, it looks good on you. Come on, let’s get out of here.” Jack grabbed Peter by the arm and tried to turn him around. Jackie looked nervous, and Peter wasn’t sure what to do.

“Pop . . .”

Dr. Halper stepped forward to intervene. “Mr. O’Hara, we’d like it if you could stay with us a little longer.”

Jack was quick to respond. “Thanks, Doc, but no. I’m ready to go home.” He leaned in closer to Peter. “What the hell kind of place is this?”

Dr. Halper said, “Mr. O’Hara, you’ve been a very sick man, we just want to make sure that you have a clean bill of health before you leave.”

“Trust me, Doc, I’m ready.” Holding firmly onto his cane, Jack slapped himself on the chest with his free hand, with pride and conviction. "I'm fine—healthy as a horse. I've never felt better in my life."

He turned to Peter. "Come on, let's go. I want to see your mother. You know how she gets when I'm away for any extended period of time. How long has it been? A week? By the way, how did you come across this place? What's wrong with Hillgrove Community? I like the people there. And what about O'Malley? I never really thought much about his doctoring skills, but I'd gotten used to that old son of a bitch."

He turned back toward Dr. Halper. "No offense, Doc."

Dr. Halper smiled, uneasy. His white coat hung loose and was slipping off one shoulder.

Jack continued, "Anyway, this place seems a little ritzy. Are you sure my insurance will cover all of this extravagance?" He waved his cane around to show the room. His other hand was firmly holding on to Peter's arm, and he was trying to push Peter out of the room.

"But, Pop—listen," Peter said.

"Dad, we need to talk to you," Jackie added, cautious.

"Sweetie, we can talk when we get home. I'm fine. Really. I just need to get out of here."

"Mr. O'Hara, I'm going to have to insist," Dr. Halper said.

Jack's reaction was instant. Now authoritative and firm, he said, "Insist? How about I insist that you be a nice doctor and sign me out of this cheap, little dance hall you're running here."

Dr. Halper straightened, offended. "Mr. O'Hara."

Jack paid no attention. "Peter, I don't know what happened, but this is no place for me. Nobody talks. I made the rounds today." He seemed to relax some as he pulled up his pants, turned around, and started to point like a tour guide. "See Mr. Morris over there, in the red sweater? Nice man, but he sleeps all the time. See the Irishman? You can't miss him, the one with the rusty hair? His name's Riley, the only other Irishman here. I'm sure he's nice too, but I can't talk to him because he won't stop moving long enough to have a conversation. Miss Agnes over there in the blue dress, I think she actually tried to hit on me this morning, except that she kept calling me Percy. Jerry, the skinny kid, he came over to watch TV with me."

Jack waved a hand and shouted, "Hey! Jerry!"

The skinny young man by the TV turned and waved back with an exaggerated grin. Jerry sure was skinny, so much so that if he turned sideways, you might not see him. This morning he was still in his pajamas, which consisted of baggy gray lounging pants and an even baggier white T-shirt. He sat in a leather club chair in his bare feet and watched television like it was his very own living room. He yelled, "C'mon back, Jack. Our show's just gettin' started." He thought about what he said then said it again, more to himself, "C'mon back, Jack." He snickered.

Jack continued to look at Jerry as he said, "He's the perfect watching partner. I had that remote control smoking because I was flipping through the channels so fast and not a peep out of him. He's respectful and quiet; I like that. All it took was one game of backgammon earlier, and we were pals. He's a good kid. Seems he's had a little trouble coping, but who doesn't at one time or another. He got up this morning and was dead-set on not getting dressed until lunchtime. The staff didn't care for that too much, but they let us vote on it—very democratic. It was unanimous. As far as I'm concerned, he can wear his pajamas all day if he wants. Who am I to say?"

He looked to Peter then turned back toward Jerry. "Funny thing about that TV too; there's got to be two hundred channels and nothing to watch. They're all shows I never heard of before. Over two hundred channels, two-fifty-two, to be exact, and no *Price Is Right*. Earlier I had to settle for some blowhard sharing his personal political opinions. At least it was someone to talk to, to argue with. Anyway, it's a beautiful place, all fine and dandy, but it's not for me."

He turned back to Peter and Jackie, and as he leaned in, he said, "Actually, I have to say, the food is not too bad here. I had these cheesy eggs this morning that were unbelievable. Bacon, toast, fresh-squeezed orange juice—the works. They even let you have dessert at breakfast. Yes, the food I will miss." He quickly added, "Don't tell your mother I said that."

"Mr. O'Hara, could we all sit down and talk?" Dr. Halper motioned to some chairs lined up along the nearby wall.

"Thanks, Doc, but I'm all done talking for today. Jerry wore me out." Jack chuckled to himself as he looked over to Jerry, who was sitting in front of the television, hands folded in his lap, quiet as could be. "It's time for me to go. What time is it anyway? I want to catch *The Price Is Right* with your mother."

"But, Pop," Peter said.

"I said it's time to go!" Jack demanded, anger rising in his voice. A few heads turned, now interested. Jack realized his outburst and tried to calm himself. He put a hand on his chest, took one deep breath and then another.

Jackie was scared.

Saddened, Peter stepped up to Jack and put his hands on the sides of his arms, holding him gently. "Pop, it's been four years."

Jack's expression turned from confidence and control to

uncertainty and fear. You could see him trying to process what Peter had just said, then he just shrugged it off. "What are you talking about? Four years? That's ridiculous. Who stays in the hospital for four years?" He looked around as he said it and quickly realized that he was not in a hospital. Confusion about his surroundings overcame him.

Peter said, "Pop, it's really good to see you. You look great. Actually, I can't believe *how* great you look. But you've been very sick. You've been here a long time, and a lot has happened." He paused a moment, looked at Jackie, and turned back toward Jack. "This is your home now."

"What?" Jack said, puzzled.

"Pop, why don't you show us to your room, and we can talk there for a little while."

Jack wilted some. He was confused, trying to figure out what was going on, but he couldn't make sense of it. He looked at Peter, then Jackie, with lost eyes. Peter took Jack by the arm, and they began to walk out of the room. He reached back to grab Jackie by the hand, and the three of them walked out of the room and down the hallway without saying another word. Dr. Halper watched, then he turned and walked in the opposite direction. The rest of the room's occupants did not notice them leaving.

* * *

They were back in Jack's room, minutes later. Jack was in his high-backed chair, quiet, nervous, and somewhat restless. Peter and Jackie sat on folding chairs facing him, both with their hands folded in their laps. Peter talked first, then Jackie took a turn. Back and forth they went. They explained to their father what had happened when he got sick the most recent time, about how it came upon him abruptly, without any warning. They told him about his first two weeks at Hillgrove Community and how they had to look at other facilities after learning of the long-term prognosis for his condition and recovery.

This time hadn't been like the others, they told him. This time, the doctors at Hillgrove Community had made it perfectly and painfully clear that Jack would not be going back home, ever. They told Jack about the painstaking process of looking for a facility and their good fortune to get a referral to Shady Acres by another family they had met at Hillgrove Community, a family that had been through a similar predicament. Peter and Jackie were convinced that someone had been looking down upon them at the time, as Shady Acres seemed to be the perfect place. The move happened fast, and each of their lives continued on, though not so much for Jack.

Jack listened for a long while, attentive and still curious, then he waved his hand at them in disbelief as he tried to get comfortable in his chair. He wanted to make sense of the situation, but it just wasn't sinking in. In fact, it was preposterous to him. "Aw, get out of here. That's crazy," was all he could say.

The noon hour was fast approaching, but it seemed much later in the day given the fading daylight. It was raining outside, and heavy drops splattered hard against the windows while the gloom from beyond seeped in, even though there wasn't room for much more. The three of them sat for a long while, silent and tense, thinking about what was next.

"So your mother's not coming?" Jack asked.

Peter and Jackie leaned forward on their chairs, and they each simultaneously rested a hand on one of Jack's knees. Their distress was obvious. Jack noticed and braced himself.

Jackie started this time. “Dad, about a year ago, Mom got sick.” That’s all it took. She got emotional at the first word, tears welling up in her eyes, the words coming out in small chunks. She reached into her purse for a handkerchief and dabbed at her cheeks and eyes until she could speak again.

“Jackie, what is it?” Jack asked, wanting clarity.

Peter leaned back and rested his hand on Jackie’s arm, calming her. “Pop, Mom went through a lot. Every day for three years she came here to visit, to make sure you were well taken care of. Every day, after breakfast, she got in the car and drove over here. You know how much she hated to drive. She would drive over and sit and talk with you. She would bring over those science fiction books that you like and read to you for hours.” He got up, walked over to the nightstand, and picked up a book. He showed it to Jack. “*The Andromeda Strain*. It’s your favorite, right?”

Jack didn’t say anything.

“Pop, she talked with the staff and the doctors every day, certainly more than they would have liked. She was always looking for another doctor or another staff member who knew something more or something different that might shed some light, anything, on your condition and how to get you better. She must have gone through a dozen doctors. She was persistent with the daily staff, always wanting to know in detail what happened since she had left the day before. She was strong, always positive, and she kept us all together like you did. She was convinced you would be coming home, that it was just a matter of time.” Emotion set in, and Peter paused to collect himself.

Jack listened, fixed on Peter’s every word.

Peter cleared his throat and said, “Last year, she got really sick, and it progressed so fast.” He braced himself.

Jackie raised the handkerchief to her mouth to hold in her emotions. A tear dripped down her cheek.

Jack looked at Jackie, now fearful, then looked to Peter. "Peter?" he said.

Peter tried to find the right words.

"Peter?"

"Pop, Mom passed away a year ago."

Jack stared at him in disbelief. He didn't want it to register, but eventually, he realized what Peter had said. He slumped forward in his chair, broke down, and started to weep. A heavy sadness fell over all of them. It was the first time Peter and Jackie had seen their father cry, and it was heartbreaking. Time crawled as they sat in silence for a long while.

Dr. Halper entered the room and stood in the doorway, not wanting to interrupt. His impatience won over, however, and he interrupted nonetheless. "Hello. Is everything okay?" He looked in at the shadows and listened to the silence. The rain had slowed, but the day was even darker. He struggled to see them.

Peter and Jackie stood quickly, seeming to appreciate the interruption. "We were just getting ready to leave," Peter said. Jackie added, "I do need to be going. It's a long drive home." The momentum had shifted, and now they eagerly wanted to say good-bye to Jack and to the moment. Jack didn't get up; he couldn't. He was lost in his thoughts as he looked out through the rain-washed windows. He was deeply troubled and scared, and his clarity from earlier in the day was now clouded.

Peter and Jackie each leaned in to kiss Jack on the top of the head, then they turned to leave the room. Halfway to the door, Peter turned around and waved and said, "I'll see you tomorrow, Pop."

They left the room, passing Dr. Halper as he nodded with understanding.

"Jack, are you all right?" The doctor looked in at the shadow in the chair. "Jack?"

"Yeah, fine. Just fine," Jack said.

"Need anything?"

"No."

"I'll check in later. Hit the buzzer if you need something." Dr. Halper stepped back from the doorway and closed the door behind him, leaving Jack to himself and the misery of the room's company.

* * *

The hours passed deliberately, and it was so quiet that Jack could hear the ticking of his watch; each tick and tock was spaced so that he thought it must be running slowly. Later that evening, he was still sitting in his chair, looking out the window and trying to make sense of the madness of the day. Half a day had passed him by, and he hadn't moved. He couldn't move.

He struggled to put the pieces together, so jagged and irregular that they would never really fit, even if he forced them. He pushed back into the recesses of his mind for any hint of the cause or the catalyst that got him to this time, to this place. All he could remember was sitting in his den at home, the feelings of regret sinking in, the heart palpitations mounting, and the sweat dripping from his forehead. He remembered that the radio was on, providing background noise, and the light from his desk lamp was burning his eyes. He remembered wanting to sleep, but not being tired, and how he fought with every ounce of his will to resist the coming wave of fog. Eventually, with no choice in the matter, he surrendered to the heavy weight and the unbearable pain. With his eyes wide open, the darkness overcame him. His last memory was the sound of the gentle words from his wife that seemed to come from a place far, far away: *Jack! Please, God—no!*

Outside his room at Shady Acres, the sun had set, and inside the room the day was darkening still, if that was possible. No lights were on, and the shadows from the street had invited themselves into his room, flashing across the walls and lurking. Jack watched for a while. He actually welcomed the shadows, for they kept him from feeling alone. He *was* alone, he realized. He was a man in despair. His eyes darted around, almost frantic, and his hands gripped the arms of his chair tightly. His mind raced and searched, and he pleaded for an answer that would not come. As was now becoming a regular event for the day, his emotions got caught up in his throat. Before today, he could remember not a single time that he had cried, and he thought about that as a single tear dripped down his cheek.

3

A week later, on Sunday afternoon, Peter and Melanie stood along the baseline fence at Jake's baseball game, watching and cheering with the other proud parents. It was Jake's second season playing baseball, and they all had come to relish their game time together. The game schedule started in early spring and continued, uninterrupted, until the end of the school year in June. For those months, they were completely committed to the cause. They had come to the realization early on, when Jake started playing the year before, that their weekends were to be for one thing and one thing only: baseball.

The field was green, plush, and well manicured. The scent of fresh-cut grass lingered in the air. The field was bordered by the school to the west and was buffered from the rest of the neighborhood by a dense grove of trees surrounding the other three sides. The field itself was the envy of most other schools in the area with its newly built grandstands that seated a crowd of two hundred along each baseline and plenty of open areas for standing onlookers. The local chamber of commerce had sponsored the erection of the high-tech scoreboard beyond the fence in center field, and the PTA had spearheaded the two-year fundraising effort for the simple but effective lights that rose high above the grandstands on each side of the field.

They took their baseball seriously at the Briar Avenue School.

It was encouraged nearly to the point of mandate, and almost all the children participated. Times had changed when it came to sports in this small town. The school promoted competition, but full participation and sportsmanship had come to matter more. After much debate and discussion, the school did away with tryouts and cuts for all the athletic programs. It was a close call, but the school board won over the dissenters with a vow to maintain the competitive spirit without crushing the hopes and dreams of the young children who wanted to participate but would likely not have made the cut. As a result, there were three leagues, each representing different ages and levels of ability. There were eighteen teams in all with a full schedule of games throughout each weekend of the three-month season.

Two teams were on the field, the Panthers and the Flyers, and the game was in progress. Jake was a Panther and proud of it. There were shouts, cheers, and unrelated discussions in the background, and the coaches were yelling to their players in a full chorus. Jake was in right field, pounding his glove, and waiting for something to happen. Given his size, he looked like a speck on a vast landscape. You wouldn't have thought Jake was the athletic type, but as he ran around on the baseball field you could see he was quite agile and comfortable. More than anything, he was confident. He was in the "B" league, having been moved up since last season, and he was working hard to make it up to the "A" league next season. He didn't especially care to be stuck in right field, as he felt he was better suited for shortstop, but he would do what the coach asked, knowing his time would come.

Melanie looked out at the unfolding game, and next to her, Peter watched her instead of the game. She was as tall as he was, with strong and striking features. Her long, straight, dark hair glistened in the bright sun. She had delicate eyes that could keep you at bay but could arrest you at the same time, green and brilliant, accented by dark and tempting eyebrows.

It was Melanie's eyes that had captured Peter in the first place. They were both at a college party when Peter first noticed her, noticed those eyes and the mystery they conveyed from across the room. He stared at her for a long time, waiting and wanting to make eye contact. He felt sure that no additional effort would be necessary after their eyes connected. She had come to the party with some friends, but she had her own agenda. She stood alone, smoking a cigarette and studying the dance floor like an anthropologist. He thought she was perfect, except for maybe for the smoking, but he could hardly judge as the ember of his own cigarette glowed in front of him as he took a long drag.

His friends had tried to pull him away for a late-night burger run, but he ignored them outright. He knew what he wanted, and he wasn't going to let the opportunity pass. Her eyes finally met his, and there was an instant connection. The relationship was immediate. He didn't know it at the time, but Melanie knew what she wanted as well. They talked well into the next morning, and as they shared coffee, eggs, and toast at a local diner, neither of them found it unusual to be talking about careers, houses, and children. Their love and the beginning of their life together started that day. *It was all in the eyes*, Peter had thought to himself many times, and it was now with those eyes that she was looking out on the field at their son.

For Melanie, there was no place else she would rather be than at the game and at this stage of her life. She was happy, content with her life, and she felt fortunate and maybe guilty sometimes for being so happy. Not many of her past colleagues or college friends could say the same. She had heard the gripes and war stories about failed marriages and unfulfilling, lackluster careers, and she was glad to now be an outsider. After college, she pursued a successful career as a journalist with a national newspaper. Though she was good at her craft, she became disenchanted with the corporate environment and office politics that crept in and infringed on her efforts. She was a writer at her core, and after a few years she realized she didn't need the accolades or the baggage that came with her corporate job. All she wanted to do was write, and she often found herself frustrated with the people, the process, and the unnecessary nonsense. All of these were roadblocks that hindered her from doing the one thing that actually meant something to her: writing.

It wasn't until Jake entered the first grade that she floated the idea to Peter about the *possibility* of changing careers, that she was considering the *possibility* of pursuing a deeply rooted and much-considered dream of being a novelist. She had used the word *possibility* once too often with Peter, and he had stopped her short, telling her to forget the *possibility* and just go ahead and do it. He didn't care what it might mean to their financial situation or anything else; he just wanted her to be happy. He'd heard of the dream many times before, and he knew from her passion and the details of her plans and approach that she was ready for the change and would be good at the new role.

The day after they talked about it, she walked into her editor's office and explained her decision. Surprisingly, her editor understood and suggested that Melanie take an unpaid leave of absence, just in case there was a change of heart or circumstance. Melanie obliged, knowing it was the prudent thing to do, but she also knew that she would never return. So she was now a novelist, working on her second book and loving every minute of it. She spent her mornings writing and was there for her husband and son when they arrived home at the end of the day. She was living her dream.

Peter watched her, smiling, and eventually she noticed.

Melanie turned to him and smiled coyly. "What?"

"Nothing, just watching the game," he said as he turned back toward the field.

Peter's phone rang, ruining the moment. With a quick draw, he pulled the phone from his pocket, looked at the display, and recognized the caller. "Sorry, I need to take this. It's Dr. Halper."

He turned and walked back behind the stands where it was quieter. "Hello, Dr. Halper," he said.

"Hello, Peter. I hope I'm not interrupting, but do you have a minute to talk?"

"Sure."

"Peter, over the last five days we've completed a full battery of tests, and the results are all positive. That's the good news.

"Good."

"Physically, your father is quite healthy. He could use a little more exercise—couldn't we all—and certainly a little more physical therapy now that he's fully mobile again, but he's in remarkably good shape, given his situation. Truthfully, I never expected he would be up and walking again, not like this. I guess I still don't have a medical explanation for his changed mental state . . ." He trailed off and stopped.

"And?" Peter asked.

"He's fine, just fine. All the test results show a perfectly functioning brain. Aside from his loss of memory during his time here and the time he spent at Hillgrove Community, both his long and short-term memories seem to be fully intact."

"That's good to hear."

"It's quite remarkable, actually. I spoke with him today, and he's doing very well. He needed a little time to deal with, you know, to mourn the passing of your mother, but I think he's adjusting to it, accepting it. He has a very positive outlook, and he's quite talkative. It's a remarkable case."

"That's great news," Peter said, not sure where the discussion was going and really not comfortable with the doctor talking about his father as a *case*.

"There is one other item I need to speak with you about," Dr. Halper said.

"Yes?"

There was a moment of silence, then Dr. Halper said, "There's no easy way for me to say this."

"What is it?"

"Given your father's current condition, we're not going to be able to keep him here at Shady Acres."

There was a roar from the crowd, and Peter struggled to hear. He put a finger in his open ear to block out the noise. "You said you can't keep him? What are you talking about?"

"Peter, this isn't a retirement community. It's a specialized facility. There's nothing physically or mentally wrong with your father, and there's nothing more we can do for him here."

"Don't you think that's a little abrupt?

"Sorry?"

"After treating my father for four years, you're just going to send him on his way? You can't even explain what's happened, but you're comfortable that he's ready to leave?" The agitation in Peter's voice was clear.

"I think he'll be fine," Dr. Halper said. The statement was weak.

"Really? Based on what? You don't think there's a possibility he'll relapse?"

Silence.

"Doctor?"

"Peter, there are other circumstances to consider as well."

"Circumstances?"

"With regular treatment and services no longer necessary, we can't get the subsidy for his care. You know the monthly expense, and it just wouldn't be cost-effective for you to keep him here."

Peter shook his head. "I should have known."

Dr. Halper replied quickly, trying to justify his position, "There's also the matter of his current behavior. Peter, he's acting and functioning as a normal human being, like you or me, and he needs social interaction. He's going around to all the residents and trying to talk to them. I understand his desire to do that, but the other residents aren't used to it. I've received a number of complaints."

There was another long pause, but Peter knew more was coming.

"And I just don't think your father is comfortable here."

"So, how much time do we have?" Peter asked, cutting to the chase.

"We'd like to keep him under observation for another week."

"A week . . . That's just great." Peter reached back to rub the knot that had formed in his neck. He couldn't find anything else to say, so he just hung up without saying good-bye and shook his head, expressing a combination of frustration and disbelief.

He walked back to Melanie at the fence, his hands in his pockets as he studied the tops of his shoes. His mind was elsewhere as he approached her, and he didn't notice the clapping and cheering resulting from the Panthers' first scored run of the game. He walked up and stood alongside her, saying nothing.

She turned to look at him, noticed his expression, and reacted with concern. "What is it? What's the matter?" she asked.

"He said Pop is just fine, physically fit and mentally sharp." The words came out in a monotone stream. "All his test results show he's one hundred percent healthy."

"Well, that's good news, right?"

"Yeah," he said, looking off into the distance beyond the field with a blank stare.

"So why that *look*?"

Peter thought about the question. Others in the past had mentioned this so-called *look*, and he didn't know what to make of it.

"Peter?"

"Dr. Halper needs to release Pop in a week," he said.

"Oh."

They both looked to each other, hoping for an answer, and when one didn't come, they turned to look out to the field as the game continued. This was no longer time for cheering, only pondering, wondering, and searching. In their concern, Melanie and Peter were swept away to another place. Their minds raced through options, analyzing the implications. Life was happening in real time, and they plotted the future.

The baseball game faded into the background of life.

* * *

Jake approached his parents at the fence, one hand holding the bat that rested on his shoulder and the other flipping his mitt in the air and catching it. He maintained the concentration of a scientist. He almost walked right into the fence but caught himself in time. “Good game, huh?”

“*Great* game,” Melanie said.

“How about that hit?”

Peter and Melanie looked at each other, stumped.

“My hit—fourth inning, off the pitcher’s leg?”

“Yeah, that was a good one,” Peter said unconvincingly.

“You missed it?”

He was caught. “Sorry, buddy, I had to take a call.”

“I thought you said *no phones at baseball*?”

“I know, but it was Grandpa’s doctor.”

“Is he all right?”

“He’s fine. The doctor said Grandpa’s talking about you all the time. He said he can’t wait to see you again.”

That made Jake smile. “When?”

“Soon,” Melanie said. “We’ll check the calendar when we get home.”

“You were looking good out there in right field,” Peter said.

“Dad, only one ball came to me, and it went right through my legs. You missed that too?”

“I saw that,” Melanie said.

Jake smiled at his mother, then he turned to his father and gave him a half-serious and stern look.

“I promise it won’t happen again,” Peter said.

Jake could see the disappointment in his father’s face. “It’s okay.” He quickly changed the subject to take advantage of the situation. “How ’bout some ice cream?”

Peter couldn’t say no, and he turned to Melanie.

She quickly conceded. “All right. You just promise to keep

practicing and improving and letting us come here every week to watch you play."

"Deal," Jake said.

They held hands and joined the crowd in its mass migration to the parking lot, off to ice cream and to the remainder of the weekend together.

* * *

Peter was at the office earlier than usual the next morning to get a jump on the overloaded schedule for the day. Visible through his office windows was a rising blood-orange sun, which was just coming up over the horizon in the distance and bringing the heat of the day to the hushed city. He relished early mornings and solitude, the new beginning that each day brought. Even if he had only a few minutes to himself, quiet and uninterrupted, his day was better as a result. It wouldn't be long before the office came alive and the day took on a life of its own.

Sitting at his desk, he looked at his watch, looked at the phone, and looked at his watch again. He wanted to call his sister Jackie before the day got away from him, but he didn't want to wake her or her husband. Just because he was up didn't mean the rest of the world was. His deliberation was swift, and he calculated the odds. He picked up the phone and dialed the call.

"Jackie, it's Peter. Did I wake you?"

"No, no. I've been up a while, and Mike left for the plant early today. Is everything all right?" she asked, her voice still plagued by early-morning hoarseness.

"Dr. Halper called me yesterday to update me on all of Pop's test results."

"What did he say?"

"Everything's fine. All the test results were fine."

"You don't sound too happy about it," Jackie said.

"No, no. It's great news. Jackie, there is a small problem, though." Peter paused.

"What is it?"

"They need to release him in a week."

"A week?"

"Dr. Halper can't justify keeping him any longer."

There was silence at both ends of the line. The quiet hung like an ominous cloud.

Jackie said, "But the house . . ."

The issue of what to do with their parents' home had challenged Peter, Jackie, and their spouses, for many months—years, actually. After learning of his father's long-term prognosis, a year into Jack's stay at Shady Acres, Peter brought up the topic of the house with his mother. It was a fairly large house and a lot for her to manage, especially since his father had always handled everything. He suggested to her that maybe a smaller place or one of the new apartments in town might be more suitable, but his mother would have none of it. She had lived in that house for all of her married years, and she said very clearly that it was where she would die. More importantly, she said the house had to be there for her husband when he came home, and he *would* be coming home. She was sure of it.

So life went on. Even though the house was fully paid for, there were still numerous expenses associated with the upkeep of the property. The responsibility for managing the expenses and the actual maintenance fell on Peter. The expenses weren't the issue; it was the time. It was always about the time. Peter found it necessary to go to the house more frequently just to check on it and visit with his mother, and every visit resulted in a punch list of additional things to do: clean the gutters, follow up with the lawn service, call the plumber—or someone—to see if they could remedy the endless seepage that found its way into the basement.

With every visit, the list grew and grew, eventually to the point that Peter could never catch up. It might have been easier if he had time to spare, but he didn't. It was unreasonable to expect Jackie to take care of the house, even though she offered to drive the forty miles periodically to meet with a contractor that Peter had scheduled. His mother always insisted that she could take care of the house, but Peter and Jackie were both concerned that things might not get taken care of appropriately or that she might be taken advantage of by a thief posing as a do-gooder. So, Peter just took care of it all, and neither his mother nor Jackie fought him about it.

When their mother passed away, Peter and Jackie made a quick decision about what to do with the house. They would sell it and sell it quickly. The decision was the easy part. Even hiring a local real estate agent and getting the house ready to show to prospective buyers was fairly painless. Knowing that the burden of the house would soon be lifted was enough to get everyone energized. The house went up for sale a month later, and after only two months they had a signed contract.

That's when the pain hit. Going to the house to pack everything up, decades of accumulation of history and memories, was a task they both dreaded. But they forged ahead and arranged weekend packing parties. Jackie and Mike drove in on Saturday and stayed at the house overnight. Peter, Melanie, and Jake met them there. They agreed they would work as long as they could stand it, would try not to get too emotional, and would celebrate with pizza at the end of the day.

Everyone was fairly civil about the process, which was one of the bright spots. Not every family can be conscientious and democratic when it comes to dividing up the family property. But the O'Hara family did their best. On their first weekend they went through everything, each person making a specific request for one item they would like as a keepsake. Jackie started, then Peter, then on to Melanie and Mike and even Jake, who wanted only one thing: Grandpa's baseball cards. He vowed to take care of them until his grandfather came home. They went around the circle time and again until everything that *mattered* had been decided upon.

Subsequent weekends focused on packing everything else up, the only concern being what to do with Jack's things: his clothing, his books, and the endless knickknacks he had accumulated over the years. What if he *did* finally come home? They agreed to not debate the idea. Instead, they simply boxed everything up and stored it in Peter's basement, which was already filled to the brim. They would cross the bridge of deciding what to do with Jack's things when they came to it later.

The sale on the house had closed six months ago. It was ancient history, and Peter and Jackie had nearly forgotten about it until this day.

"I knew we shouldn't have sold the house," Jackie said.

Peter didn't expect that. "But we agreed."

"Yeah, but . . ."

"There was no other choice. It was the only logical and responsible thing to do."

"We could have waited."

"No, we couldn't have," he said firmly.

"But what do we do now?"

Peter said, "Given the circumstances, I wish we still had his house too, but there's nothing we can do about that now." He needed to get back on track and promptly changed the subject. "Listen, I'd like your help to start calling around to some retirement communities to see if we can find a place for him, quickly. I did some research last night and came up with a list of places for us to consider. I'll send it to you. You take the first half; I'll take the second half."

She didn't respond right away.

"Jackie?"

"Okay, I'll get started right away this morning."

"Thanks, Jackie. You're the best. I'll talk to you later."

"Bye." Jackie hung up.

Peter set the phone handset down on the console and stared at it for a long while, thinking. He couldn't control the urge to revisit and re-analyze past decisions, but after only a minute he realized the thoughts were unproductive. He picked up the phone and dialed another call.

"Good morning, is this Windward Hills? My name is Peter O'Hara. I'd like to set up an appointment to tour your facility."

* * *

Later that afternoon, on his way back to the office from a meeting with a client, Peter drove while listening to someone on the phone. "Four o'clock this afternoon? Can we do it any later?" Disappointed, he said, "All right, I'll see you at four." He hung up the phone, frazzled.

He tried to keep the appointment at the scheduled time,

but a meeting with Tim ran long, as they usually did. He made it there at five-twenty, about the time he originally thought he would get there. Tom Farnsworth, the managing director of the Sunset Ridge Senior Living Community, was not happy to have been kept waiting. Peter could feel the man's discontent before the formal introduction took place.

Farnsworth was middle-aged and round; his thin hair stuck to his sweaty forehead. His suit fit snugly, and he looked like he'd had a rough day. He let Peter know that immediately. Farnsworth was not a pleasant man, and Peter sensed that his demeanor carried over into how the facilities were managed. They never left Farnsworth's office, and that was fine with Peter. He didn't need to see anything else. The meeting lasted only ten minutes. Peter excused himself and made his way home.

* * *

He was back at the office the next morning, early again. By nine o'clock he had put in an hour of good work and was having a stand-up meeting around his work table with his team. The stand-up meeting ensured that they stayed on topic and kept the meeting brief. There were seven of them in attendance, and they discussed the latest changes to the Gattling Project. Ken was responsible for keeping the project plan up to date and communicating their status. Jill and Tom were responsible for all designs and drawings. Aaron led the engineering team, while Karen and Matt handled all contractor and vendor management. They were a small team, but each person was hand picked. They all worked well together. Ten minutes into the agenda, Peter's phone rang, and he hurried over to his desk to answer it. It was unusual for Peter to answer his own phone, and the team noticed.

"Peter O'Hara," he said.

"Hi. This is Judy Colin from The Meadows. You left a message inquiring about our facility?"

"Yes, thank you for returning my call. I'm interested in considering your facility for my father, Jack O'Hara." He sat down behind his desk and continued the call, fully engaged. He flipped through some sheets of paper from a file folder he had open in front of him and made check marks and notes while listening intently.

His team waited a few minutes as they watched and listened. They wondered if they should continue on with their agenda or wait; if they should stay or go. After a minute of uncomfortable eavesdropping, they filed out in a solemn procession, accepting that their meeting was over and their goal unattained.

Ken was the last in line to leave the office, and he stopped as he reached the doorway. He turned back to Peter, who was lost in another task. He wanted to ask if they would re-convene later, but he let it pass. Peter was elsewhere. As Ken cleared the doorway, Tim Parker stepped in.

Peter was still on the phone and hadn't noticed the traffic. He heard someone clear his throat in a loud and exaggerated manner that annoyed him. He looked up, ready with an evil eye for one of his employees, and that's when he saw Tim.

Tim said nothing and made no gestures, yet his expression told Peter that he wanted to say something and have his full attention. He had an evil eye himself.

Peter turned his focus back to the person on the phone. "Excuse me, could you hold a minute?" He set the phone down on the desk and raised his eyebrows. "Good morning," he said.

Tim said, "Can I see you in my office?"

"Sure. Let me finish this call and I'll be right in."

"We'll meet now. I'm already late for a meeting."

Peter was surprised at Tim's abrupt attitude. Then again, he wasn't. He picked up the phone. "I'm sorry. Could I call you back? Great. Could you send me the prices you were quoting? Thanks, I'll get back to you shortly."

Tim was still standing in the doorway, annoyed at having to wait even those few seconds. Peter hung up the phone, rose from his desk, and walked to the doorway.

"Personal problems?" Tim asked.

"It's nothing," Peter said.

Tim stood expressionless as Peter walked up and stopped before him. Tim stared like a scolding third-grade teacher, then he turned and walked down the hall. Peter was surprised again at the reaction, but the thought dissipated as he followed Tim out of the office and down the hallway.

They entered Tim's office, which was easily five times the size of Peter's. Every time Peter walked in, he wondered why it was necessary for anyone to have an office that large. The office had the same skyline view as his own, just more windows. A lot more windows. Not only that, but the expensive furnishings bordered on obnoxious. The centerpiece of the office was a huge desk that one could get lost behind. It was eight feet wide, four feet deep, and made of solid walnut from an archaic forest, milled and carved by craftsmen who cared. The desk defined Tim.

"Come in, Peter, and have a seat," Tim said in a cold, monotone voice. He directed Peter to one of three chairs in front of the desk.

As Peter approached, he noticed how small the chairs were. They seemed almost pre-schoolish in size, dwarfed by the enormous desk. It was the first time he noticed the disproportion.

He sat down in the middle chair, and it felt like upholstered stone. He sensed Tim had something serious he wanted to talk about and tried to control the conversation by speaking first. "You're in early."

"I'm in at six-thirty every morning," Tim said as he walked around his desk and sat in a massive, leather, high-backed chair.

Peter looked and felt uncomfortable. He squirmed a little in his tiny, hard chair and said nothing.

"Peter, I'm concerned. I've noticed a change in you over the last couple of days. Is everything okay at home?"

It wasn't like Tim to get so personal, and Peter waved off the inquiry. Or was it a statement? "Fine, just fine," he said.

Tim sat silently, hoping Peter would say more, but Peter wasn't forthcoming. With his elbows propped on the arms of his chair, Tim rested his chin on his folded hands, stone-faced. He stared at Peter.

Peter sat motionless then raised his eyebrows. "Is there anything else?" He was busy and really didn't have time for this.

Tim unfolded his hands and adjusted his tie and suit jacket. He said, "You left me hanging the other day. I had to take the Gattling meeting with Marc. You know, I promoted you over him for a number of very good reasons, not the least of which is that I think he's incompetent. You're a rising star here. Don't make me regret my decision."

Is he serious? Peter wondered. "Tim, I appreciate your confidence in me—I do—and I'm grateful for everything you've done. I can assure you, it won't happen again."

"You just seem unfocused, distracted. What is it?" Tim tried to sound sincere.

"It's nothing, really. Everything's fine."

Tim realized that Peter would not be sharing any more information, and he became frustrated. "Gattling was disappointed you didn't show. He's one of the reasons you're in this position. He likes you and wants you to be the point person on his project. He's expecting to see you when he's back in town next. I'll get you the date and time once it's scheduled. Don't miss it, and don't be late."

Peter nodded.

"By the way, what's going on with your team?" Tim said. "I heard grumbling as they were leaving your office. You know, it took us a long time to put that team together for you. Don't screw it up. Do you hear me?"

Peter felt Tim was treating him like a child but tried to shrug it off. "Tim, c'mon. It's me. Don't worry. Everything's fine. My having to run out the other day—it was a fluke. It won't happen again."

Tim didn't say anything and continued to stare at Peter. Like before, he appeared to want more but knew the well was likely dry. He asked anyway. "That's it?"

"That's it," Peter said. Case closed.

"All right. I won't pry. I trust you will act like a professional in the future and respect your responsibilities to this firm. If you have personal issues, deal with them on your own time."

"Of course. Is there anything else? I've got a meeting with engineering."

"No, that's all," Tim said. He retained his look of concern and watched as Peter rose from his chair and walked out of the office.

* * *

The day passed in fast-forward, and Peter found himself alone at the deserted office late that night. Only traces of people remained. He sat at his desk with his chair turned and looked out the windows aimlessly. His office was dimly lit by a desk lamp that provided a soothing glow. He sat back in his chair and reclined with his legs extended, crossed at the ankles. His folded hands rested in his lap. He wore a solemn expression and had much on his mind. Looking out at the night sky, it seemed just minutes ago that Peter was relishing the start of the new day, and now it was gone, wasted. He sat there for a while, wondering what he really had to show for the day and for the effort.

He got up and threw a few things into his briefcase: files, paperwork, and reading he needed to get to. Yet he knew they would likely be in the exact same position when he returned to the office the following day. He turned off the desk light and left his office, leaving the day behind him.

* * *

Peter arrived home that evening around eleven after an uneventful drive from the city. At that particular hour of the day, traffic was light. It seemed to him that he was the only person who had to work late. He came in the back door and was greeted by Murphy, a mutt they had rescued from an animal shelter three years ago. Jake had seen an ad in the newspaper and had worked Peter and Melanie hard for a week straight. He was relentless, and this came after more than a two-year effort to justify the need for a family dog. Murphy was a collie-shepherd mix, gentle and mild-tempered, and he was a dog that everyone loved at first sight. Melanie came up with the name, a name she remembered fondly from a picture book she used to read to Jake. He liked the name just fine, but he really didn't care. He would take a dog by any name. Peter set his briefcase on the counter and knelt down to pet the dog. For him, there was nothing better than being greeted when he got home, and when Melanie and Jake were not around, Murphy was a more than suitable substitute.

Peter went to the refrigerator, grabbed a beer, and walked over to sit at the kitchen table. He knew Jake was already asleep and assumed that Melanie was up in bed, reading. Murphy was settled in for the night in his dog bed in the corner. The lights were dim, and it was quiet as Peter sat alone. It felt to him like he had been alone most of the day. He was tired and distraught. He ran a hand through his hair, searching for the best parts of the day, becoming frustrated when nothing came to mind.

He heard footsteps coming down the front hall steps, and the footsteps turned down the hallway toward the kitchen.

Melanie shuffled in, her furry slippers sliding across the tile floor with a *swoosh*. "I didn't hear you come in," she said. She walked over to Peter, bent down, and while holding his face with both hands, kissed him hard on the lips. She stepped back, smiled, and noticed his beer. He looked up and smiled halfheartedly. "Mind if you join you?" she asked.

He didn't say anything.

She walked over to the refrigerator and opened the door. "Peter?"

"Oh, sure."

She grabbed a beer and closed the door. She opened a kitchen drawer, pulled out a bottle opener, and removed the bottle cap. She set the opener and the cap down on the counter.

To Peter it seemed like deliberate slow-motion. "Need a hand?" The words came out laced with sarcasm.

"I'm good." She walked over and sat next to him at the table. "How about a little more light?"

"I kind of like it this way. It seems quieter." He shook his head and turned to her. "It's been quite a week. Cheers."

They clanked bottles and drank.

"How are you holding up?" she asked.

"Fine."

"Anything I can do to help?"

He shook his head, not much in the mood for talking but knowing he needed to. He rubbed the back of his neck and looked across the table at nothing in particular.

She stood up behind him and began to rub his shoulders. He sighed softly at the touch of her fingers and leaned his head back, closed his eyes, and worked his head around on his neck like a Ken doll. Unable to relax, he gave up and snapped forward.

"Jackie and I, we have a list of fifteen places in and around the area here, places that we might be able to move Pop into. We've called most of them, and the initial contact hasn't been very positive. We've visited six and have two more visits scheduled for tomorrow. It's a daunting process."

"Are there any good options?"

"Nothing that's quite right." Peter took another drink and he thought for a moment. "I went to see Pop this afternoon; that's why I had to work late. He went ballistic. He said we were trying to *put him away* and was still harping on the fact that we *sold his house out from under him*. I tried to explain, tried to get his input on what we should do, but he wants nothing to do with it. He keeps saying he just wants to go home."

He took another swallow. Melanie kept to herself.

"It's no use. No matter what we do, he won't be happy. It's a no-win situation." Peter wanted to change the subject but said nothing further.

Melanie moved to sit back down.

"How's Jake?" he asked.

"He's fine. He missed you at his practice game after school today."

Peter had completely forgotten about the game.

"You promised," she said.

"Yeah, I know. I hate letting him down. I wanted to be there, but I really needed to go see Pop. And I'm behind on my work. Looks like I can't make anyone happy there either." He let out a gust of exasperation. "Tim called me into his office this morning, said he's concerned about me and my lack of focus. He's thinking he might be regretting his decision of promoting me over Marc. *Idiot.* I'd like to see how he'd be right now with Marc leading the Gattling Project."

"The coach told Jake he needs to practice his fielding."

Peter only heard *fielding*. "What?"

"Jake needs to work on his fielding. It seems another ball got through his mitt."

"Yeah," he said, distracted.

"Peter?"

"I'll work on it with him this weekend." He wondered where the time would come from and how he would squeeze it in. The weekend was days away, an eternity, so he let the thought slip from his mind.

"Don't worry. This will all pass," she said. "A week from now, your father will be settled in somewhere, and life will be back to normal."

Peter took a drink; he wasn't convinced.

"Right?" she said.

They both sat and looked at each other, quiet. He said, "I had an idea. I know I really have no right to ask this, but . . ." He paused, not sure how to proceed.

"What?" she asked.

There was no easy way, so he just said it. "How would you feel about Pop moving in with us here?" He got it out and was relieved.

Melanie was a little surprised. "How would *you* feel about it?

"I don't know. I kind of think we need to have him around here," Peter said as he settled in. "We were so close when I was younger. I was attached to him at the hip until I became a teenager. I was always following him around, wanted to be like him, no matter what he was doing." Peter thought back over that time. "I remember most Saturdays I'd go with him to the office, sit at the desk right next to him, and pretend I was a businessman. I'd write letters to my mother on the company stationary and file things for him and staple papers together. He always let me lick the stamps for the mailings that had to go out, and he probably thought I was nuts when I told him that I liked the taste. I didn't, but mailing the letters was *my* thing, *my* responsibility. After a few hours, he'd take me to lunch and tell me about his business. I really didn't understand much of what he was talking about, but it didn't matter."

Melanie watched him as he told the story and saw the slight smile appear on his face.

"Then, you know, adolescence, off to college, a career, you, Jake. He and I lost touch."

"It was more than losing touch."

The smile faded. "I know." He took a long draw from his beer. "It's been a long time and I've gotten past it. I'd like to get to know him again. More important, I want Jake to know him. That's why

I finally took him for a visit. And you know he thinks the world of you. I figure he could stay in the guest room upstairs. He could have his own bedroom and bath. He couldn't be too much trouble, could he?" Peter wondered if he believed that, couldn't believe he had said it in the first place.

Melanie smiled, and Peter laughed out loud.

Then he turned serious again. "It could be a temporary option for us. We get him home, settled, and ease him back into his new life. He'll have family around, and it will give us time to find a more permanent solution."

"Will he be all right, being alone by himself most of the day?"

Peter wanted to say something but held back.

She knew exactly what he was thinking. "I've got a deadline. I've got to finish this book."

"I wasn't implying that you'd have to take care of him," he said. "I really think he'll be fine by himself. He'd actually prefer it."

Melanie looked doubtful.

"It's just short term. If it becomes an issue, I'll deal with it. I promise."

"I can't babysit him."

"I know."

"All right," Melanie said. "If you think you're up for it, I am too. It will certainly make Jake happy. He hasn't stopped talking about your father since he came back from that visit. What did you guys do there?" She didn't expect an answer and didn't get one.

With the matter settled, they sat back in their chairs, sipped their beers, and pondered their decision.

4

Jack O'Hara walked out the door of Shady Acres, a place he hoped to leave behind forever, with a confidence he had not known in some time. He couldn't really comment on the four years he had spent there, but for the last week he had looked at Shady Acres as a prison. For the past few evenings, sleep had been scant and turbulent as he struggled with and dreamed of his escape.

He stood at the top of the stairs and took in the perfect Saturday morning. He couldn't remember a day, not a single one, as unspoiled and sublime. The sun shone brightly, the sky an ocean of blue, and there was a motivating crispness in the air. Jack raised the collar of his jacket and rubbed his hands together, generating some friction for heat as he looked out in wonder. He gazed upon the grounds of Shady Acres like Meriwether Lewis surveying the new world. It *was* a new world, fraught with excitement, adventure, and challenge, and it was all his.

Peter was on one arm, and Jake was on the other. Jack was all smiles; Jake was, too. They were almost giddy together. Jack stopped them at the top of the steps and held them back. He looked up toward the heavens, closed his eyes, and took a deep, exaggerated breath. He let it out with a loud, body-shaking *ahhhhhhhh*. He turned to look down at Jake, who looked up, closed his eyes, and took a similar deep breath. As a perfect mimic, he let his breath out with a loud and quivering *ahhhhhhhh*.

Peter looked at each of them and rolled his eyes.

With synchronized steps, they descended the stairway to the stone driveway where Peter's car was idling. They proceeded down the driveway, through the pillared archway, and out onto the street. Jack felt the urge to turn around and look back, for reasons he could not surmise, but he resisted. He wanted to leave the building, its confines, and its ghosts behind forever. He hoped and prayed that he would never return.

Jack asked if they could take the scenic route home. Having been away awhile, as he put it, he wondered how the neighborhood and the town might have changed. Peter happily obliged and extended the fifteen-minute ride to sixty. He circled the entire perimeter of the town, driving slowly and showing Jack the quiet residential streets that had been transformed through the latest housing boom. Fortunately, the town council went to great lengths to ensure the integrity of the historic architecture. Nearby towns weren't so lucky.

Peter worked his way inward, ending the tour with a slow cruise down Main Street. It was this particular street that had drawn Jack to the town so many years ago. Passing through on the way to meet his future wife, Jack was captivated by the small-town charm. After Jack and Jane married, there was no question about where they would go to live. The town really hadn't changed in more than fifty years, and Jack liked it that way. Peter did too, and when he married Melanie, they decided to stay. Driving through town now, they noticed that most of the small shops and restaurants hadn't opened yet, and only Jason's Café, the one restaurant in town that served breakfast, was open before lunch. The street was hushed and soothing.

"So, Pop, there have been a few small changes in town, but most things have stayed the same."

Jack looked out the front passenger window, taking it all in. "Good to hear," he said. Jake sat in the back seat, looking out as well. They were two kids looking around with wide-eyed wonder and fascination.

Peter looked over at his father and saw a man who was humbled but content. He could see that Jack was happy, that he was home. "The movie theater is still there. John's Marketplace, the antique mall, and Perry's Italian Restaurant are all the same way you saw them last. They're timeless. They'll all probably be around a hundred years from now."

"Sure as shit," Jack said.

"*Grandpa*," Jake said, scolding him from the back seat.

"Whoops—sorry about that, Jake," Jack said. "It's funny. I haven't said a word in four years, and that's what comes out?" He shrugged it off. "What about the cigar shop?"

"You don't smoke anymore," Peter said.

"I know, I know, but that doesn't mean I can't stop in to visit with the old gang. Speaking of which, are any of those old goats still around?"

"Well, Howard still opens up every morning at nine. Weather permitting, he's seated on that bench in front of the shop, having his first cigar of the day by nine-oh-five."

"Doesn't he know smoking is bad for him?" Jake asked.

"Oh, he knows all right," Jack replied. "He comes from a different time, though. A different world. He started smoking cigarettes when he was twelve. He's actually trying to prove that all the research about smoking and cancer is wrong. He thinks it's all just a big conspiracy, claims he's going to smoke at least five cigars a day for the rest of his life and live to be a hundred. He's only got twenty years to go."

"And there he is," Peter said.

Jack hurried to roll down his window as Peter slowed the car. In town, people liked to honk their horns as a means to say hello, and Peter obliged. Jack stuck his arm and head out of the window. "Hey, Howard!" he said as he waved.

Howard recognized Jack immediately. "Hey, Jack—welcome back," he shouted, smoke billowing from his mouth, yellow-corn teeth clenched on a cigar that seemed to be a foot long. That particular saying was Howard's own creation, and he used it every time he saw Jack, going on twenty years now. He was proud of it, and saying it made him smile like a kid.

Jack pulled his head back into the car as they passed. He said, "He must have said that to me a thousand times. *Hey, Jack—welcome back*. Every time I walked into the shop. I like that things don't change." He realized what he said and thought it ironic. "What about the rest of the gang?"

Peter said, "Last time I was there, I was with you, so I'm not as familiar with the regulars anymore. I know about Howard because I see him when I drive by. Mr. Jenkins and his son are still around. I see them around town quite often when we're here on the weekend. We'll have to stop in sometime and catch up with everybody."

"It's a deal. I'll buy," Jack said.

"No smoking, Dad," Jake insisted.

Peter said, "Just for a visit, Jake. Just for a visit."

They came to a stoplight at the end of the first block and sat waiting for the light to turn green. Jack leaned forward and strained to look down the next block. The light changed, and

Peter proceeded slowly, staying in the right lane to allow traffic to carry on around him.

"Jake, my boy, see this building coming up on the right here, with the light brick and the sign that says…" He strained to make out the script lettering on the neon sign above the doorway. "Chica's… Mexican… Restaurant? Where the heck did that come from?"

"That's been there a while," Peter said. "The food's pretty good too. It's your favorite: Mexican."

"I *hate* Mexican food," Jack said.

Peter grinned.

"You should try it, Grandpa."

Jack was shifting thoughts. "Yeah, Jake, maybe I will, *someday*." Then, with a sense of urgency, he said, "Say, pull over."

Peter pulled the car over to the curb in front of Chica's and stopped.

"Jake, that building there, that's where *I* used to work," Jack said, pointing to the light brick building with pride.

"You used to work at Chica's? Cool," Jake said.

"No, no, that's where my business used to be."

"Your business?" Jake said.

"Sure, sure. Your Dad didn't tell you?" He looked over to Peter. "Why not?"

Peter shrugged. "It just never came up."

"You couldn't *bring* it up?"

"I could have."

"But you didn't?"

"I don't know, Pop. I just never thought about it. Jake was always so young." Peter thought about it and seemed to question himself. "I was just waiting for him to get older, for the right time."

“I’m old enough now,” Jake said. “What kind of business, Grandpa?”

That’s all Jack needed. “The O’Hara Insurance Agency, specializing in life, health, property and casualty, disability, auto, marine. You name it, we had insurance for it.” He thought about what he said. “Come to think of it, we didn’t really specialize, did we? Anyway, your grandmother and I bought the building just after we were married. We borrowed from everyone and anyone to scrape up the down payment. She loved the brick and said we had to buy it. That’s what they call Chicago Common, the brick I mean. Anyway, she said it, and we bought it, the building that is. We moved in some rented furniture, hung out a shingle, and we were open for business.”

“You knew a lot about insurance?” Jake asked, quizzically. It was a good bet that he didn’t have a clue what insurance was.

“Not a thing, at first, but I learned, and I learned fast. I knew insurance was important, and there was no one providing it in town. It was what you call an opportunity. I went door to door at first while your grandmother watched the office and handled the books. She was the money wizard. I swear that early on she could spin money out of straw, ’cause we didn’t have a dime to our name, and somehow we always had enough to pay the mortgage and to eat. Anyway, after a while, word spread, and people started coming to me. I sold insurance to most everyone in town for almost forty years. People trusted me.” He sat up straight and stuck out his chest.

“I still have all of the agency Christmas cards,” Peter said.

Jack nodded. “Every year I hired Michael Murray, a local artist, to design a custom, full-color Christmas card. They were one of a kind, and every customer got one, personalized. After word got around, I think we got some new customers just because they wanted to receive one of our cards."

"They *were* beautiful," Peter said.

"You were an ON-trep-e-nooor," Jake said, happy he was able to use the word and sitting up close behind his grandfather.

"That I was, an entrepreneur and a pretty good one, if I do say so myself." The memories came flooding back. "Chica's, hmm," Jack said, shaking his head curiously. "Last I remember, after we sold it, the business and the building, the guy who bought it opened up a deli."

"Yeah, Archie's Deli," Peter said. "They had the best corned beef sandwich in town."

"Had the only corned beef sandwich in town," Jack added.

They sat a moment longer in silence.

"I like history," Jake said.

"It's ancient history," Jack said then motioned to Peter to move along. "Onward."

Peter pulled out into the street, and they continued on. At the end of the second block, Main Street ended. Peter turned right and headed up Elm Street where they lived.

Upon reaching the house, they pulled into the driveway to find a small welcoming party on the front steps, including Melanie, Jackie, Mike, and Murphy. They were all there, standing in a row like a portrait, still and smiling.

"What's all this?" Jack said.

"Welcome home," Peter replied.

Peter and Jake helped Jack out of the car, up the walkway, and up the stairs. Everyone gathered around Jack for a family hug, squeezing him tightly and expressing well-wishes. Even the dog joined in, giving Jack a playful hump on his right leg.

"What the?" Jack said, looking down.

Jake grabbed Murphy by the collar and pulled him off Jack's leg. "Murphy, leave Grandpa alone."

The dog barked.

Jack looked at the dog, stern but unemotional. The dog returned his gaze, tilting his head slightly for effect.

"He likes you, Grandpa," Jake said.

Jack wasn't convinced. The crowd circled closer, and that made him uncomfortable. He looked around for a break in the chain. He was not one for big displays of affection, never had been. He didn't like all the fuss, so he broke away and headed inside. Everyone followed closely behind and carried the festivities in through the front door.

Once inside the house, they all gathered together in the front hall. Jake had Jack by the hand in a death grip while he tried to keep Murphy at bay. His new pal was home, and he was not going to let him go any time soon. Peter was the last one through the door, carrying Jack's suitcase.

Jack looked up and all around and nodded his approval. "I like it. Looks like you've done a lot of work on the place."

Jake said, "Grandpa, your room is upstairs, right next to mine. Come on, let me show you."

"All right, Jake. Lead the way." He held on to Jake and to the stair railing, and they slowly ascended the staircase. Halfway up, Jack turned around and looked toward Melanie. "Melanie, thank you for welcoming me into your home. Thank you, all."

Melanie smiled. Peter came up from behind, put his arms around her, and squeezed her tight.

Jack looked up the stairway then turned back around to everyone. He smiled and nodded. "Yes-sir-ee, it's good to be home."

Jake whistled through his fingers, producing an exceptionally loud screech that startled Jack. "Murphy. Come on, boy. Let's go show Grandpa his room."

The dog bolted from the group at the bottom of the stairs and took the treads two at a time, brushing against Jack's leg on his way to the landing. Jack wobbled momentarily then steadied himself. He had an expression on his face of *what in the hell was that?*

"If you don't mind, I'm going to retire for a while, maybe take a nap. I've had enough excitement for today."

"Pop, it's only ten o'clock."

"Just the same." He turned and climbed the stairs, with caution now. Before he reached the landing, he turned around and again looked to Melanie. "Melanie, dear, don't wake me for lunch, okay? You can just leave a tray outside my room." He rubbed his chin with his right thumb and forefinger and pondered. "And I like my breakfast promptly at seven every morning. Scrambled eggs, bacon, wheat toast, and coffee will be fine." He turned and continued up the stairs.

Melanie looked at Peter, eyebrows raised. She didn't need to say a word.

"It'll be okay," Peter said.

Jackie nudged him gently. "Are you sure you want to go through with this?"

Peter didn't respond. Instead, he watched his father walk up the remaining stairs. At the top of the stairs, Jake turned around to look at his father, an enormous grin on his face. Peter said, "I'm sure." At the bottom of the stairs with the rest of the group, he stood and thought about what he had just said.

* * *

Days later, the family was gathered around the dinner table, enjoying a meal, laughing, and sharing stories of their day and of recent days past. Looking on, it was a scene plucked straight from a Norman Rockwell *Saturday Evening Post* cover. The setting was idyllic. Peter was at one end of the table, Jack at the other. Jake was next to his pal, down at the right corner of the table closest to Jack. The two had been inseparable since Jack came to live with them. Melanie sat on the opposite side, to the left of Peter. At Jack's suggestion, they started using the family china for dinner, and the place settings that were normally reserved only for Thanksgiving and Christmas now made a daily appearance. Jack took on the responsibility of setting the table. He insisted on using a formal tablecloth and the tarnished silver-plate candleholders and beeswax candles.

Halfway through their meal, Jack took the opportunity to work on one of his routines. It had been a while, but he'd been practicing. Jack was always a great storyteller and had the knack for remembering jokes. He had dozens of them stockpiled away for just about every situation. He started by sharing a joke, telling it in full animated motion, his bullhorn voice booming. You could say he was a *colorful* joke teller, often embellishing the punch line to the brink of decency. Even before he could finish the joke, he had everyone laughing, even himself, and he was a firm believer that a joke wasn't worth telling if it didn't make the joke-teller laugh out loud. Sometimes he even had trouble finishing a joke because he was in the hysterical throes of laughter. Even that helped improve the effectiveness of the joke, for his laughter was infectious. If he laughed, you laughed. It was as simple as that.

The laughing around the table subsided, and as Jack settled

down, his expression turned serious. He gave Jake an inquisitive look, peering at his ear. Jake wondered what was wrong. Without saying a word, but only, "Hmmm," Jack reached behind Jake's ear and miraculously pulled out a shiny new quarter.

Melanie was impressed. "Wow!" she said.

Jake was speechless, his mouth agape.

Peter smiled. He'd seen that trick a thousand times over the years as both a willing and unwilling participant. Once, when he was six years old, Peter had begged his mother to take him to the doctor because he was afraid that his head was full of quarters. Or maybe it was because he wanted money to go to the candy store in town, and he needed access to the vault. Either way, Jack's slight-of-hand trick had an effect on him. It was the first time for Jake, though, and he was mesmerized and awestruck.

"You're quite a magician, Pop," Peter said.

Jack raised his eyebrows, nodded, and smiled. "I still got it, and I'm just gettin' warmed up." He stretched out both arms, exposed each hand, and revealed that they were empty. He brushed a hand along each shirt sleeve, then reached behind Jake's other ear and with an exaggerated tug pulled out four tickets, which he fanned out to display for his audience.

Jake was amazed and started to clap. "That was awesome, Grandpa. What *are* those?

Jack said, "Can I interest anyone in box seat tickets to a ball game this weekend? Compliments of the gang at the cigar shop. It seems they missed me."

Jake beamed and looked at his mother and father, radiating admiration for his pal. "Can we be interested? Can we, please?" Jake said.

There was only one answer that his parents could give.

* * *

That Saturday, they made a pilgrimage to the ball park, a whole six miles away. The Westlake Snappers, a triple-A baseball club, trained and played there at Myers Field. Jack and Peter had always preferred the minor league games and had gone frequently when Peter was young. Peter had taken Jake to his first game when he was three years old, and from then on they went to see the Snappers several times every season. Going to a game was a time for father and son to hang out, to bond, and to just be boys.

This time Melanie came along, and you could tell that she was wondering why she hadn't come sooner. The park was spectacular and expansive. It had replaced the old park just three years ago. The new infrastructure was comfortable and more accessible, yet the playing field looked like it had been lost in time. The walls surrounding the field were made of a burnt-red brick that looked like it had been fired a century ago, and the ivy that covered the outfield walls appeared to have come from the time of Genesis.

They sat in the box seats just behind home plate, seven rows up. As they watched, Jack helped Jake score the game on his program and pointed out the intricacies of the action on the field.

Jake turned, looked down the row to his mother, and saw the expression of wonder on her face. "You like it, huh?"

With a delayed reaction, she said, "What?"

"You like the park," he said. It was a statement, not a question.

"I do. It's beautiful. It reminds me of when I used to go to games with my father and my brothers."

"You should come with us more often." Jake said.

She looked at Peter.

"It's fine with me," he said.

"Then it's settled. You'll come with us from now on, for every game," Jake said with authority.

"Okay, I guess I will."

"And what about me?" Jack asked.

"The four of us, every game," Jake replied.

"As long as you keep pulling tickets out of Jake's ear," Peter said, "you can take us to a game any time."

Everyone laughed. There was a crack of the bat, and the stadium came alive with a roar.

Sitting on the aisle, Jack leaned over toward Jake on his left. "Now, you see that guy, McMurray, who just got a hit? You mark that on your score card like this." He reached over and made a pencil mark on Jake's program. He made a similar mark on his own program. "You're eight now. You need to know how to score a game the right way."

Jake listened in rapt attention, wide-eyed and grinning.

Jack reached over Jake and pointed out a correction that needed to be made on Peter's program. "And you—you're getting sloppy in your old age."

Peter acknowledged the mistake, erased it, and made the correction.

A hot dog vendor came down the aisle, yelling through a red plastic bullhorn with an Oscar Mayer logo on the side. He was a young man, likely in college, and he descended the steps with a strut in his gait. "Red hots, get your red hots here!" he boomed, his voice like thunder.

The wind must have been blowing just right, because Jack caught a whiff of the hot dogs even before he heard the young man shout. He could even smell the sweet, steamed buns. His mouth watered.

There are times when a certain smell, sight, or sound immediately triggers a memory, and for a moment Jack was sixty years younger, watching a different game in a different time and place. He was sitting next to his own father, a hot dog that dripped ketchup and relish onto his blue jeans in one hand and a baseball mitt on the other hand, waiting for a souvenir to come his way. "You always have to be prepared," his father had told him, and Jack was always geared up like a member of the team. His red baseball cap fit snugly on his head and matched his red T-shirt, each sporting the home team logo. He looked up at his father, who was looking out at the field, and from there Jack glanced between his glove and his hot dog. Back to his father, to the glove, to the hot dog. He wished he could stay there forever, and he smiled.

Another roar from the crowd snapped Jack from his daydream. He shook the memory and turned around. He raised his arm and flashed four fingers. "Four dogs, please, with the works," he shouted.

The vendor made his way down to Jack and pulled four foil-wrapped hot dogs from the metal container strapped around his neck, and Jack reached to grab them. The hot dog vendor handed him the hot dogs and told him the price, as though he had stated that same price a thousand times just that day.

Jack reacted to the price, but he didn't say anything.

The vendor reached out and dropped a handful of small condiment packages on top of the hot dogs Jack held. "There you go, Sir. The works."

Jack looked at Jake, who shrugged. Jack shrugged back, and they both grinned as he set the hot dogs down on Jake's lap.

Peter reached back for his wallet. "Pop, let me get those."

"Get outta here. Your money's no good here," Jack said. He

pulled out some bills and paid the vendor, motioning for him to keep the change.

Surprised, the vendor said, "Thanks, Mister." He pocketed the bills and continued down the stairs to keep on selling.

Jack passed the hot dogs around and parceled out the condiment packages. "When did a hot dog get so expensive? I remember when . . ." He caught himself and stopped, turning to Jake. "Are you having a good time?"

Jake already had a mouthful of hot dog, but he talked anyway. "The best," he mumbled.

"You smell that hot dog?"

Jake looked at him, then at his hot dog. He raised it to his nose and drew in deep a breath. He turned back to his grandfather to make sure he had done it right.

"You smell that? That's the smell of baseball. There aren't many finer smells. From now on, any time you smell a hot dog, you'll remember this day, the field, the game. You'll remember us."

Jake bobbed his head, accepting what his grandfather said as fact and feeling pretty good about it.

Jack unwrapped his hot dog, added mustard and relish, and took a bite so large that half of the hot dog disappeared. He closed his eyes, chewed slowly, and savored the flavors and textures like it was his first or last meal on this earth. He thought for a moment about how much he loved food, loved to eat, and how he missed the enjoyment of such a simple thing.

"Wow," Jake said, giggling. "That's the biggest bite I ever seen."

Jack opened his eyes and tried to speak, but couldn't. He giggled a little himself. He chewed and chewed, and when the coast was clear he said, "You know, before coming to live with you and your parents, eating didn't matter. While I was Shady Acres, for four years, if you can believe it, I couldn't tell you a single thing I had to eat. I know I had three squares every day, but . . ."

"Three squares?" Jake said.

"Sorry, that's military talk. It means three good meals every day: breakfast, lunch, and dinner. I had more than fourteen hundred meals, and I can't remember a single one. They told me I had to have someone to help feed me every day. Can you imagine somebody having to feed you a hot dog?"

"Nope."

"Anyway, I can't remember a single meal. But this," he said as he waved the remaining half of his hot dog. "This, I'll remember."

"Me too."

Jack said, "If you like, maybe we could come sometime, just you and me."

Jake leaned back and turned to look at his father, who was busy watching the game. He turned back to Jack and nodded in confirmation, a big grin on his face.

"You know, Jake, I don't think there's any place I'd rather be." He looked out to the field and around the grandstands, contemplating his life.

Jake said nothing but nodded again in agreement.

"Yes, sir, Jake. This is our place."

There was a crack of the bat, followed by the cheering of the crowd. They were all up in an instant, as if ejected from their seats by springs, and they watched as the ball shot like a star on its course to the heavens. The crowd followed the arc of the ball across the ocean-blue sky and down toward the bleachers in left field. In a mass of flailing arms, a young boy not much older than Jake extended his gloved hand as far as he could and closed his eyes. There was a loud slap as the boy's glove folded around his new prize and held it firmly. The crowd roared as the batter circled the bases.

Jack and Jake were happier than ever, in a place they were meant to be, together.

* * *

The following day, the family took Jack to the cemetery to visit his wife's grave. Jack woke up thinking about making a trip to see it. He had dreamed about it throughout the night when his racing mind would allow him to sleep, and he mentioned it as soon as everyone came into the kitchen for breakfast. It was odd, but he hadn't thought much about his wife since he'd moved in with Peter and the family. But this morning, it was at the top of Jack's to-do list. It was the only thing on his to-do list. At the breakfast table, he asked Peter if he would take him, and Peter suggested that they all go. They finished their breakfast and were out the door by nine.

There's really no good day for a cemetery visit, but as days go, this one was good as any. Actually, it was a fine day. Summer was on the horizon, the morning air was warm and comforting, and the sun lit up the dew on the grass like a million sparkling lights. The air was still, and the birds sang like it was the day of creation. As the family walked through the grass, their shoes became wet from the dew, but they didn't notice and didn't care.

At the grave site, Peter stood by Jack's side with his arm around him, comforting him. Jake and Melanie stood in the background, held hands, and watched.

Jack looked down at the headstone:

JANE O'HARA
Loving Wife and Mother

It was a somber moment for Jack. He was never really an emotional man, but this day was different. It seemed to him that *everything* was different since he had "woken up." That's how he thought of it because he had no plausible explanation for his lost years or how that time away had miraculously come to an end. How or why this had happened to him wasn't important now; it was in the past. He hoped to leave his pain and regrets in the past along with it. But no matter how hard he tried to fight it, being in this place and looking at the cold granite slab that now represented the love of his life made him feel sick and rotten. There was a knot in his stomach the size of a grapefruit and a corresponding uneasiness in his chest that he couldn't explain.

He was sad that his wife was gone, but that's not what bothered him. Instead, he thought about what she must have gone through, alone, without him by her side to help her. That's what chewed at his stomach lining. He felt as though he had let her down, again. After a lifetime together, taking care of each other, the game had changed at the end. He wasn't there for her, and why? Why was it that he was away, at Shady Acres, while his wife was alone and suffering? Why wasn't he there for the end? He didn't have answers for those questions, but he hoped that someday he might make sense of it all.

They both stood quietly looking down at the headstone. Jack held on to Peter's arm, knelt down, and laid a single rose across the glossy surface. He ran his finger across the letters of her first name, outlining each letter and feeling the deeply carved grooves. While on the "E," he caught an unexpectedly sharp edge, and his finger jumped. He turned it over and watched as a drop of blood formed. Jack tipped his finger, and the drop broke loose and spilled off the edge and into the groove of the letter. He put the finger into his mouth and tasted only salty bitterness.

"Pop, what happened? Are you all right?" Peter asked. He handed Jack a handkerchief.

"I'm fine," he said as he wiped off the headstone and smiled. He stood back up, stiff, and his knees creaked as his legs straightened. He shifted on each leg to ensure his footing, then folded his hands and bowed his head. His lips mouthed silent and secret words.

Peter watched. He folded his hands and took the opportunity to think through his own words.

"I should have been there for her," Jack said. "I've felt regret for a lot of things in my life, but none so much as for not being there for her. She deserved better."

Peter remained silent.

"She was a good woman, your mother. How she put up with me all those years, I'll never know." He choked up a bit and raised a fist to his mouth to stifle the emotion. He cleared his throat and took a deep breath.

Peter noticed. "You two were good together. You were made for each other."

"That we were." He turned to look at Peter. "You're who *you* are because of her. We're *all* who we are because of her."

Peter acknowledged the undisputed fact with a nod. He had no argument.

They turned to leave. Peter rubbed Jack on his back, and they both smiled, ever so faintly.

"You okay, Pop?"

"I'll be all right," Jack said.

They walked a few steps, and Jack extended his arms out to Jake, who ran to him, grabbed him around the waist, and hugged him tight. They embraced and held each other for a long while.

"You're a good boy," Jack said.

"You're a good grandpa," Jake replied.

Jack kissed Jake on the top of the head, and when he looked up, Jack rubbed him there gently, sufficiently messing up his hair. Jake didn't care, and Jack hugged him tightly once again. Then he grabbed Peter and Jake each by an arm and led the way toward Melanie, who looked on. She hooked on to the trio, and they all walked back to the car in solemn silence.

* * *

The three men of the O'Hara clan sat in a motorized rowboat sharing a quiet summer afternoon fishing at Whitewater Lake, their favorite place to go wet a line. Actually, it was the only lake they ever fished. Though it was small, the lake was close, and it was theirs. That's the beauty of any lake; it's owned by the people on it at any particular point in time. On this day, few owners were present.

Peter sat in the rear of the boat. Jack was in the middle, and Jake was up front. They did not consciously notice the gentle rocking motion as the wake from a passing fishing boat approached them and lightly splashed their hull. However, their bodies recognized the motion that relaxed their muscles and dissipated any worries they had brought along with them.

Peter had last gone fishing with his father when he was seventeen, but he remembered it like it was yesterday. He cherished the times that he spent fishing with his father, and it was unfortunate that life and circumstance had prevented any such get-togethers for so many years. Peter always looked forward to their trips with eager anticipation, often finding it difficult to sleep much, if at all, the night before, and he would usually be dressed and ready to leave when Jack's alarm went off in the morning. This trip was no exception. He couldn't wait to get to the lake, sit in the boat with his father and son, and waste the day away together.

If you asked Jack when he last went fishing, he'd say he didn't remember. He did, but it was easier to just let it go as forgotten, as that approach usually eliminated the possibility of any further discussion. He enjoyed the time out on the water as well, but for his own selfish reasons. Mostly, he had enjoyed going fishing to get away from work, from the people, the problems, and the challenges that seemed to always be present. On the lake, there was none of that nonsense, and it was all replaced with unspoiled solitude. The lake was peaceful, soothing, and never judgmental. For Jack, the lake was his remedy for anything troubling his mind, and he was always regenerated after a day of fishing.

He sat in the boat on this fragrant day like it was his first time fishing, adventurous and with no limitations. He felt fortunate to have the opportunity again. "The lake smells great today," Jack said. "I've got a good feeling." He took a deep breath and savored the moist and scented air. He smacked his lips a couple of times and tried to taste the air, and he could swear there were pine trees nearby. "You smell that, Jake?

The broken silence caught Jake off guard. He was leaning over the side of the boat and studying the minnows that were lurking in the water just below the surface, dancing around his submerged line. "Huh?"

Jack said, "Yes, sir, it's gonna be quite a day."

It was good to be outside, and although the temperature had already reached the high seventies, Jack soaked in the warmth and hoped it would never leave. For a long time, longer than he cared to remember, he had been cold and numb, and the chill had lived in him for years. But, today, the chill was gone.

If you asked Jake, he would tell you the precise date of his last fishing trip: May sixth of the previous year, the day after his seventh birthday. The memory was still fresh in his mind, the seed just recently planted. It was the one and only time his father had taken him fishing. That May sixth was a great day, one he would always remember. He had a good feeling about this day as well.

The three of them huddled in the boat with every bit of fishing tackle they could amass. They fished for crappie, stripers, and any other species that might be willing to dangle off the end of their lines. They fished with aggressive abandon, but their first two hours produced only talk. That didn't seem to bother them, mostly because the talk was sparse, as it is supposed to be while fishing. They didn't need to talk. They were together, the three of them, and nothing more needed to be said. Also, Jack tended to insist on silence, dead silence, so as not to scare the fish.

Later that morning, with light reflecting off the glass surface of the lake, Jack finally caught the first fish of the day. Without a second thought, he traded poles with Jake and helped him to reel in the fish. It was a smaller fish, but Jake fought it like a marlin, pulling back hard on the pole and reeling frantically as if it was the biggest fish in the world.

"Easy, boy. We don't want to lose him," Jack said.

To make it interesting, Jack reached over and loosened the drag of the reel so the fish could pull out some line as it fought. After a few minutes, though, the fish tired, rose to the surface, and surrendered. Jack netted the fish and pulled it into the boat. He was on it quickly and removed the hook with care. He held it out for Jake. "That's one fine fish."

Jake grabbed hold of the fish, struggling briefly with the slippery scales, and held up the fish for all to see, his smile radiating across the boat. It was a ten-inch crappie, and it was silver, brilliant, and perfect. For many, the joy of fishing is in the act, in the solitude. For kids, the joy is in *catching* a fish, and this catch had just made Jake's day. He moved over and sat next to his grandpa so his father could take a picture to preserve the memory for a lifetime.

At the day's end, they tied up the boat at the small marina and packed up their gear slowly, not wanting the day to end.

Jake was out of the boat quickly, a stringer of a half dozen fish in one hand as he hurried down the dock. "I'll run to the car and put these into the cooler."

Peter and Jack unloaded the boat and, once up on the dock themselves, they looked with surprise at the gear strewn about.

"Where did this all this stuff come from?" Peter said. "I think we have more than we started with."

"Maybe Jake can bring the car over," Jack joked.

"Nope, we're on our own. Just you and me."

They loaded up their arms with everything they could possibly grab, looking like a couple of mad shoppers at the mall, and they headed for the car.

"I really appreciate you taking me in," Jack said.

Peter smiled.

"I mean it. I was lost when I came to; even more so when I found out about your mother. I'd be finished without you and Jake and Melanie."

"No problem, Pop."

"I know we've had our issues in the past, but . . ."

"Pop, forget about it. That's all in the past. What do you say we leave it there?"

"Fine."

They walked on, and as they got to the car Jack said, "You sure?"

"I'm sure. I'm glad you're around," Peter said.

"That's good to hear. I'm glad to be around too."

Jake popped his head out from the trunk. "I'm glad you're around too."

"Well, then, that's all I need to know," Jack said.

For each of them, the day was complete, only to be improved upon by the thoughts of what they might do together in the days, weeks, and months to come.

* * *

The way the O'Hara family spent their weekends had changed drastically over the last couple of weeks. From Jack's perspective, it was quite simple: activity was up, way up, and that was all that mattered to him. He'd been a mummy for too long. For Peter, Melanie, and Jake, the days were just as active as always, but now the days had a different focus and a greater feeling of significance, even if they weren't always aware of it.

Before Jack had come to live with them, they spent their Saturdays and Sundays taking Jake to one of his baseball games or to some other kid-focused activity. It was good for them, as they were both really kids at heart. It didn't matter what they did with the days as long as they were together. They were always together. With Jack as part of the equation now, they approached the weekends with a heightened sense of urgency, like each one might be the last. They packed the days full. For Peter and Melanie, they did their best to put any work they had, house, career or whatever, on the back burner and let it simmer for another day. The work would always be there when they got to it, that much was certain. Weekends were for family, especially now that Jack was with them.

The process of integrating Jack into domestic life wasn't a difficult one for the O'Hara family. Having Jack around felt quite natural, like it was supposed to be that way. They each lived their lives as a part of the whole, striving to be together and enjoying their time together in whatever they did. Things had changed, that much was true, but in a good way. If you asked any one of them, they would tell you that it was right and good and that they wouldn't change a thing.

Deep down, each of them wished this new life they had would continue on forever. Deep down, each of them wondered if it would.

5

He didn't force it, but Jack was deliberate in his effort to make himself part of the home, the family, and the routine. He hadn't participated much in taking care of his own home when his wife, Jane, was alive, but now it was different. He could just as easily have kept to himself in his room, but he felt he had a purpose now. He didn't believe in second chances. It was the first one that he was worried about, that he might end it on the wrong note, with regret. His first act wasn't over, and he'd be damned if he would let it slip away now. So he approached each new day with a mission and vigor to ensure that his efforts mattered.

Jack would often walk into the living room, and instead of heading directly for a chair—which was the instinctual course of action for him—he would stop to look around. He'd notice a painting on the wall and wonder about the artist's love and passion that brought the scene to life. He would pick up a book from the coffee table, open it to a random spot, and begin reading. His goal was to get a message, any message, from the author. And sometimes, as he did on this day, he would see a speck on the carpet that prompted him to walk over to the hall closet to get the vacuum cleaner.

Jack moved the vacuum through the living room with ease, the stiffness in his legs a distant memory. He whistled to himself with a newfound vitality, and the melody of "As Time Goes By" sailed through the air. Once done, he turned off the vacuum and stepped back to assess his work. He realized for the first time that there was a noticeable smell to vacuuming, as all the scents of the days and weeks were sucked from the carpet fibers. With a single whiff, you could re-live a moment. Jack liked the smell and breathed in deeply. He nodded to himself, acknowledging a job well done. He straightened the pillows on the sofa, stacked up some magazines on the coffee table, and left the room to put the vacuum away.

He heard the clanging of pots and the sound of jangling silverware coming from the kitchen. As he entered the room, he saw Melanie walking toward the stove, having just filled a big pot with water. He watched her set it down and turn on the burner. There was a frying pan sizzling and steaming that caught his attention. Melanie was unaware as Jack came up behind her.

"Can I help?" he said.

Startled, Melanie turned her head quickly. "Oh, hi. I didn't hear you come in."

"Let me help? I used to fancy myself quite a wizard in the kitchen."

"Really?" She looked at him curiously. "Are you pulling my leg?"

"Don't act so surprised," he said. "My wife was a great cook, but I was on my own for some time before we were married. I persuaded her to marry me through her stomach." He was pleased with his wit, and he smiled as he looked over his eyeglasses at the sizzling pan. "It looks good. Let me take over."

She raised her eyebrows, surprised at the unusual request. She was sautéing some vegetables, swirling them around with a wooden spoon, not sure of her next move.

"C'mon, let me do it. Why don't you go back to your writing, and I'll finish up dinner."

"Well, I . . ."

"Go on, go back to work, I know it's important."

"Okay. Here you go," she said as she took a step back from the stove.

Jack took the spoon. "Thank you," he said. He stepped forward with confidence. He reached into a drawer to the left of the stove and, with his free hand, pulled out a white apron with strawberries on it. He didn't notice the pattern but looped the apron over his head, tied it in the back, and got to work. Melanie thought he looked cute.

He attended to the vegetables, nudging them along like he were coaxing them to some better place. He breathed deeply, as he often did now, his brain instantly recognizing the red and green peppers, onion, garlic, and olive oil. Jack worked at the vegetables with chef-like care and attention; for him the significance of the task could not be underestimated.

Melanie turned to leave the room.

"Say, what are you working on, anyway? I never wanted to pry, but I'm interested."

"It's a novel," she said and left it at that. She never liked to talk about her work until it was finished; for until it was finished, she was never really sure *exactly* what it was she was working on.

"I read your first book. Hope you don't mind, but there was a copy on the bookshelf in the living room. I liked it."

"Oh, no, I don't mind, and thank you."

"What's the next one like?"

She tried to hold back.

"C'mon, really, I'm interested."

"It's the second book in the series: same characters, different predicament, and hopefully the same or better level of suspense."

"Is there money in it?"

"Sorry?"

"Money, you know, a paycheck? Can you make a living from writing?"

"Yeah, it's okay, but I do it more because I feel I have something to say, and . . ."

"What?"

"I don't know, maybe this sounds crazy, but I want to leave something behind."

Jack chewed his bottom lip. "I can understand that. Well, go get to it."

She turned away again, and just as she was about to walk down the hallway, Jack called her back.

"Say, Melanie, can I ask you something?"

"Sure."

"Do you ever feel like going out into the backyard for a cigarette?"

"Excuse me?"

"I can't tell you how I remember, but I seem to recall Peter telling me something about how you two met. You used to smoke, right? Don't you ever get the urge?"

"That was a long time ago."

"I know. It's just that back in my previous life I used to enjoy a good smoke every once in a while. I've been fighting this urge to head into town and get me the biggest cigar I can find."

Any prior good feelings had dissipated and were replaced with concern. Melanie said, "I don't think that's a good idea. We don't smoke in this house, and the last thing we want to do is be a negative influence on Jake."

Jack moved the spoon around in the pan.

"Jack?"

"Yeah, yeah, I understand. It was just a thought, and you're right. We don't want to influence Jake. Forget I ever brought it up."

Melanie watched him for a minute, his back turned to her, and she wondered what he was thinking. She turned and left the room, and this time Jack didn't stop her.

* * *

Baseball carried over into the O'Hara home with little effort. It seemed they couldn't get away from it. Ever since their ball game outing, the topic of baseball arose frequently, like a cute puppy on the street looking for attention, and they always responded. They couldn't deny it; it was a part of them now. Baseball was everywhere: at the breakfast table with the sports section circulating around, in the kitchen as the evening news reported the afternoon sports scores, and even in the evening as Jack flipped back to the sports-only channel in between commercials.

Even when baseball was in the background, it became the single, unifying theme which wove the threads of the O'Hara family together. On certain days, however, baseball was in the foreground.

Weeks earlier, Jake had suggested a family Wiffle Ball game and urged his father to take him to the sporting goods store to get the plastic goods. He had the money, he assured his father, having saved some of his allowance money over the past few weeks. He justified the trip and the expense as a game in which the whole family could participate. It took two weeks of gentle pestering on

Jake's part, but they made the trip after dinner.

Upon their return, Jake bolted from the car in the driveway and hurried up to the house. "We're back," he shouted through the front screen door. He peered into the foyer for any sign of life. "Mom, Grandpa, come on. It's game time." He saw no movement but heard footsteps approaching from the kitchen.

"We're coming," his mother said.

Melanie and Jack were at the front door seconds later. Jake stood aside and opened the door for them, using an exaggerated sweep of his hand to direct them down the stairs. "Sir, Madam." He giggled.

Jack stepped out first, saw Jake's face, and said, "Nice nose."

Jake scrunched up his nose, squinted, and looked cross-eyed down at its tip. He didn't understand, but there was a black checkerboard pattern on his nose from when he had leaned against the screen. "Huh?"

As his mom stepped out, she saw the confusion on his face.

"What's wrong with my nose?" he asked.

She stopped, licked her thumb, and wiped the dirt from his nose without providing an explanation about his nose or her cleaning method. Mothers and fathers alike had been washing their children's faces with their own saliva for years and would no doubt continue to do so for generations to come.

"Mom," Jake pleaded as he pulled back. "That's gross."

"I love you too," she said as she reached to put her arm around him. "Come on, let's go play some baseball."

So they gathered for what would become a fairly regular family event: Wiffle Ball on the front lawn. Sometimes the game would last an hour, sometimes just fifteen minutes. The length didn't matter. It only mattered that they played. After twenty minutes of this, their first night game, they had made it through the batting order four times, and the game was already winding down. Peter was pitching to Jake; Melanie and Jack were playing the outfield.

Jack waved to Jake and yelled to him through cupped hands, "All right, Jake. Hit 'er to me."

Jake swung twice but missed, close on both attempts.

"You're swingin' wild, kid. Slow it down," Jack yelled.

On the next swing, Jake connected solidly with the ball, and it whistled through the air.

The sailing ball sent Jack backward a few steps toward the street. He moved for the ball pretty well, considering his age and lack of exercise. He managed to get under it, but he juggled the ball, which fell to the ground. Jake sped around the bases of Frisbees and wood scraps, going for all the glory. Jack picked up the ball and hobbled to home plate.

Peter was already there, motioning for Jack to throw the ball. "C'mon, Pop, throw it."

After a few more strides, Jack threw the ball to Peter while stumbling forward. Meeting at home plate, Jake slid, Peter missed the tag, and Jack toppled into the pileup. Melanie ran over and carefully added herself to the pile. Everyone laughed as they rolled off each other and leaned up on elbows to catch their breath.

* * *

Later that evening, Melanie and Peter stood at the door of Jake's bedroom and looked in. Jake was in bed, and Jack was sitting on the edge, tucking him in. It was a scene that Peter could easily place himself in several decades ago, and yet it was a sight that neither he nor Melanie ever expected to see. They were entranced, stuck in the door frame as they watched and listened.

"I'll be right next door if you need anything," Jack said. "Now, come here and give me a big hug and a kiss."

Jake sat up and they embraced. When Jack loosened his grip, Jake reclined quickly, half his head disappearing as his head hit the pillow.

"What about the old smack-er-oo?" Jack said, pointing to his lips.

Jake laid there, uncomfortable and not sure what to do.

"What?" Jack said. "You're too old to kiss your grandfather? You kiss your Dad goodnight, don't you?"

"I'm eight, Grandpa," Jake said, a little embarrassed and a lot reluctant. His hands were folded on his chest, and he looked at them, not wanting to make eye contact. "My friends at school started to make fun of me when Mom or Dad, especially Dad, would kiss me when they picked me up from school, so we kinda stopped that."

"I guess I could understand how that might be a problem." Jack paused. "You know how many times I kissed my father?"

"I bet it was a lot," Jake said.

"Funny thing is, I can't remember a single time."

"Not once?"

"I guess it was different when I was growing up. I never thought about it much until years later when my father was sick. It was near the end, and I remember being in his hospital room, looking down at him. He was so thin and white and tired, I almost didn't recognize him. He was like a ghost. He didn't know I was there, and I wanted to kiss him. I didn't know if I should or not. While I was deciding, he died. After he was gone, I wished I had kissed him a million times."

Jake thought about it, then said, "You miss him?"

"Sure do. I think about him a lot more the older I get. I know it probably sounds silly, but I wish I could go back, kiss him just once, and tell him that I love him."

They both were quiet and lost in their thoughts.

"Jake, your family is all you've got. Love 'em while they're around, and remember that you're never too old to give your grandpa a kiss."

Jake thought about it for a moment, then sat up and kissed Jack on the cheek. It all happened in a blur, and Jake was back down on the bed, smiling.

"That'll do," Jack said, and he tucked the covers in around Jake. He pulled the big blanket up under Jake's chin and tickled his neck, which made him squirm and giggle. "I'll see you in the morning, Pal."

Jake replied, "See you in the morning, Pal."

"Are we best friends?"

"Best friends."

Jack reached forward, tousled Jake's hair, and made one final adjustment to the blankets. He got up and walked to the doorway.

"Good night, Grandpa," Jake said.

"Good night, Jake." Jack switched off the light, stepped out of the room, and gently closed the door as Peter and Melanie stepped back into the hallway where they congregated together.

Peter reached over and pinched Jack's cheek, something he learned to do from all the older relatives in the family who felt it necessary to torture him when he was a young boy. It was payback time. He said, "If you'd like, I can tuck *you* in, young man."

Jack waved him off and started toward his room. "Aw, get outta here. If you had any brains, you'd be pinching and paying attention to someone else." Jack nodded toward Melanie.

Peter put his arm around Melanie, and they both smiled as they turned to go to their room. Peter turned back. "Good night, Pop."

Melanie added, "Good night, Jack."

Jack stood at the doorway to his room. His eyes were bright, almost radiant, and the corners of his mouth edged up. He turned, entered his room, and closed the door behind him.

* * *

Peter and Melanie were at the kitchen table, a place they often found themselves at the start of the day. It was their Command Central for life. Like their parents and their parents' parents, the kitchen's two main purposes were for addressing family matters—priority number one—and cooking. The kitchen was the first stop for an O'Hara coming in from the garage, the backyard, or down for breakfast in the morning. Peter often commented that they really didn't need a three thousand square-foot home when all of life's most important needs could be met in a twelve-by-twelve room with a refrigerator, a table, and chairs. Nearly every personal crisis Peter had encountered was addressed at the kitchen table, usually with his mother. In fact, most of his memories of family gatherings revolved around that thin slab of oak.

The room was dark and quiet, as it usually was at six-thirty in the morning. All across town, beds were starting to empty, and bodies were moving in a slow and silent fog to begin their daily rituals. A few dogs barked, and the birds and squirrels were getting a jump on the day with their chirping and chattering. Aside from that, if you listened very closely, you might hear the mist rise as the morning sun burned the dew off the grass.

Peter and Melanie sat drinking coffee and reading the newspaper under the light fixture that hung over the table. Peter was dressed in a dark business suit, the color indiscernible in the dim light of the morning. Melanie was wrapped snugly in her white terry cloth robe.

Peter looked up from the newspaper, reflective. "It's been quite a month."

Melanie took a moment to process the words. Most mornings they didn't talk much since they both needed time for the fog to clear, for the caffeine to take effect, and for the stories in the newspaper to sink in.

"It sure has," she said. She could sense that Peter had something on his mind. "Jack seems to be adjusting pretty well," she said. "And I don't think I've ever seen Jake happier."

She sipped her coffee and returned to the national news. She tried to read the words, but their meaning was elusive. After reading the same paragraph three times, she set down the paper and looked at Peter. "You know, you and Jake have always had a great relationship. He adores you. But he's never really had a grandfather around before. Jack's the only one, and Jake was so young when your father got sick. I think the last month has been great for Jake, and for Jack."

Peter nodded. "Is it just me, or do you see Jake coming out of his shell a little?"

Melanie nodded.

"He's become more talkative and excited about everything. And he's been walking around with more . . . I guess I want to call it confidence, but it's more of a bravado."

Melanie nodded.

Peter added, "It seems they're talking all the time, about God knows what, but whatever it is, Jake's interested. I'd like to think he listened that well at school. And you know my father, he likes to talk, but with Jake he actually turns the table, making sure it's a two-way discussion. The more Jake talks, the more comfortable and confident he becomes."

"It's been kind of nice having your father around," Melanie said.

"Mel, I never would have thought it was possible. In such a short time, life around here has changed pretty drastically, all because of one person, one person who I never expected to set foot in this house again." He shook his head. "I still can't believe I asked you if he could stay here. I can't believe we went ahead with it." He set the newspaper down and got serious. "I know that I suggested this would just be a temporary situation until we found someplace for him to go." He paused to check Melanie's reaction before continuing on. Hers was a face of stone, but he continued anyway. "How would you feel about keeping him around for a while?"

Melanie had known it was coming. It was just a matter of time, but she pretended to give the question serious thought. She raised an index finger to her chin and furrowed her eyebrows as if she was thinking about the question for a long time. She smiled. "Sure."

"Really?" Peter had hoped for but didn't expect that response, at least not without a little more selling.

"Was that the wrong answer?"

"No, no, that's a good one."

"But don't stop looking for a more permanent place," she said before Peter could get too excited. "He really *needs* a more permanent place."

The last sentence didn't register. He smiled and nodded. "You know, you're the best." He could never tell her that enough.

"I know."

They both went back to reading the newspaper and drinking their coffee. The coffee part was easy; concentrating on the newspaper again was a challenge.

"Peter?"

"Yeah?"

"I'm still worried about him."

"Jake?"

"Your father." She set the newspaper aside for good and folded her hands in front of her. "Everything's been great. I don't want to jinx it, but he's relapsed before."

"I know, but maybe this time is different."

"Maybe it's not."

"I think he'll be fine. Either way, it's best that he's here with us so we can keep an eye on him."

She knew there was no point arguing any further.

For Peter, the weight of the world had lifted some, but for Melanie, not as much. She was more practical and realistic, and deep down she felt that things might not continue to go so well.

* * *

Peter's love of architecture, his passion for designing and building things, was a fire lit and fed from a young age. It was a seemingly uncontrollable passion that consumed him. It excited and propelled him through his early years. It was unusual for a boy so young to have a passion of that intensity. Unfortunately, in his teen years the fire was extinguished, but by the time he was in college, the fire re-ignited into a raging inferno. True passion can be derailed, but it never goes away.

Every Sunday morning when Peter was a young boy, he would sit on the floor next to his father, who sat in his La-Z-Boy, deeply engaged in the thick wad that was the Sunday paper. Most kids begged for the funnies, but Peter wanted the real estate section. Funny thing was, Jack had a routine for reading the paper, and it was a routine Peter seldom interfered with, for his own sake. To do so would create newspaper havoc and delay him in getting what he wanted. As he sat next to Jack and watched the process unfold, Peter would wonder: *Will he ever get through the whole paper? How much longer will I have to wait?* Patience was not Peter's virtue.

Jack went through the paper section by section, and only when he finished reading a section would it be available for someone else. The order and process could not be compromised. The real estate section was usually the fifth section in, and Peter would wait as patiently as he could, like a dog waiting for a treat. Eventually, the treat would come, and he would scurry off to the other side of the living room to spread the pages out before him. In those pages were the lines, the angles, and the ideas that made his neurons fire and sparked his creativity. Peter especially loved the home renderings and the diagrams of floor plans. He would trace his favorite designs and tape them into a scrapbook that his mother had given him. She saw the fire in his eyes. His father didn't notice, but that didn't mean he didn't care.

As a senior in high school, Peter told his guidance counselor, Mr. Engle, that he wanted to study architecture in college. There was an introductory architecture class offered at the high school, and he hoped Mr. Engle would provide the necessary recommendation for him to take the class.

Instead, Mr. Engle warned Peter about the competitive nature of the field of architecture and urged him to consider studying something else. "It's for your own good. Believe me. Say, maybe you could learn a different trade," Mr. Engle had said, like a robot programmed to say that to a hundred other kids that same day. Unfortunately, Peter was still impressionable. He took Mr. Engle's advice to heart and decided to pass on the architecture class. He started college with an undecided major. Like a real life Smokey Bear, Mr. Engle had squelched the wildfire in Peter's belly before it could get out of control.

There's really no place for fire fighters in high school.

Peter's mother had been furious. How could a nearly complete stranger so drastically change the course of a young person's life in a single day? She had seriously considered going to the school to wring the man's neck in person, but Jack said she would do no such thing. He said that Peter would work it out on his own, that no one could really tell *that* kid what to do. She let that day pass but insisted that Peter continue with his original plan to go to the university. Fortunately, Peter had never considered changing *those* plans.

Once at the university, it didn't take long for Peter to get back on track. His new roommate, Dylan Stalls, introduced Peter to a friend of his in the engineering program, Frank Cox, who in turn introduced him to his "Design and Perspectives" instructor, Greg Grosset. Grosset connected Peter with the department head, Dr. Frederick Selig. It seemed to be fate. Like Peter's mother, Dr. Selig saw the fire. It was only smoldering at the time, but it wasn't long before he had stoked Peter's passion once again and made it possible for Peter to enter the architecture program the following semester. Peter's mother wept with joy when she heard the news.

From that point on, Peter's career as an architect flourished. He graduated in the top ten percent of his class and received the Award of Distinction from the School of Engineering. In his final year at the university, he received an internship at Jackson, Parker & Finch, one of only two firms offering such an opportunity. His new boss Tim, having graduated from the university just four years earlier than Peter, was in charge of college recruiting, and he easily picked Peter out of the crowd. Tim reported back to the partners that the choice was an easy one, for the new recruit was a "beacon in a mass of mediocrity." Peter's year-long work program was more like a full-time job, and it prepared him for the position of associate of the firm, which he was offered after his graduation. Again, Peter's mother wept with joy when she heard the news.

It was an easy decision for Peter to take a job with the firm. He had envisioned this day and this particular job for years. He imagined having to wear a suit and tie every day and looked forward to the commute downtown to where he was certain that "everything happened." His friends thought he was nuts. He had his ideas, his preconceived notions, and a clear plan as to how he would showcase his skills and advance his career with the firm. His father had told him, preached and insisted actually, that success was dependent on one thing and one thing only: hard and *effective* work. Jack stressed the word *effective*, making the point that you not only had to work harder than everyone else, but you also had to be more effective. It was what he called the "career double threat," and he was adamant in his conviction that it would ensure success. Peter listened to what his father preached. He listened to what other people said too, filtering through it all to find his own mantra.

Prior to applying for the internship, Peter had extensively

researched the firm: its background and history, current customers and prospects, and the personal details of each and every partner. Most importantly, he reviewed and studied the firm's portfolio of projects. He studied the buildings, the designs, and the genius that found its way from imagination to reality. The award-winning buildings were impressive and mirrored Peter's vision for the future. He also knew about Tim Parker.

Tim lived on the other side of town, where the cars, the yards, and the houses were a little bigger. He seemed nearly a generation older than Peter because of their age difference, but Peter remembered Tim's athletic achievements at the high school. Then, in college Dr. Selig mentioned to Peter that someone from his old neighborhood had just completed the program. Peter had always looked up to Tim, and knowing he was an architect drew him in even more. Everything about the firm had met Peter's expectations, and he knew early on that he would take an aggressive path to becoming a partner. *He* had selected the firm of Jackson, Parker & Finch before the firm ever knew he existed.

* * *

Peter was center stage in a meeting with Tim Parker and Victor Gattling, the firm's most important client. It had been a little over a month since Peter received the news about Jack and bolted out of the office, missing the opportunity to meet with Mr. Gattling. This particular meeting had been scheduled weeks ago, and there was no way Peter was going to miss it. Tim and Gattling were seated at one end of the large conference room table, the wood glossy like an ice rink. Peter stood before them, ready to commence with his presentation. On the table was a scale model of the Gattling Building, the firm's newest and most technologically sophisticated design–Peter's design. Behind Peter were several video monitors showing renderings of the building from different perspectives.

Victor Gattling had a commanding presence. He was impeccably dressed in a light gray suit and perfectly starched white shirt. His satin blue tie matched his pocket square. Even though he was only in his late forties, his full head of gray hair made him seem much older. He wore his hair long in the back, and not a single strand was out of place. A neat goatee accentuated his chiseled jaw. Gattling was rich and confident, professional yet surprisingly personable.

Tim sat before Peter with an air of pompousness that was neither warranted nor appropriate. "So, Peter, why don't we get started."

"In a moment," Gattling said.

Tim wasn't used to being told what to do. He always felt he was smarter, more clever, and more astute than everyone else. But Victor Gattling was a client, so he went along.

"Peter, how's your father?" Gattling asked.

Tim's immediate expression was one of concern, maybe even contempt.

Peter was taken aback. "Umm . . . He's doing just great. Thank you for asking. And I do apologize for missing the—"

Gattling stopped him, raising a hand. "Please. There's no need to apologize. I understand. A few years back, I had to take care of *my* father. Ended up, I had to put him in a home. Thinking back, it's one of the few things in my life I truly regret." With his index finger and thumb he smoothed the edges of his goatee into a "V." "You do what's necessary to take care of your father for as long as he's around. When he's gone, you can't help him."

Tim appeared bored with the discussion.

“I will, thank you,” Peter said, and a connection was made, simple as that. Prior to this meeting, he had certainly respected Victor Gattling, but it was different now. Gattling understood what Peter was going through and, with that, Gattling took on the role of a mentor for Peter, whether he knew it or not.

Gattling turned back into a hard-edged businessman. Time management escalated in importance and priority. Tim was interested once again.

“So, what have you got for me today?” Gattling asked.

Peter began. “Our last task before beginning construction was to finalize all of the utility specifications. We’re going to be sure you realize your dream of having the most technologically advanced and energy-efficient building available today.”

Peter turned and directed Gattling to one of the display panels behind him. A video presentation began, a series of images, one fading into the next, with a soundtrack of soothing music playing in the background. Peter narrated. “Mr. Gattling, what was most challenging for us, and what will be most beneficial to you, is the solar energy system we have planned for the building. Using the latest solar technology and what we feel is a revolutionary method for integrating that technology into the building’s structure, you will get the best of both worlds: the most effective energy production, approximately 700 percent greater than a conventional solar panel installation. And you won’t even realize the panels are there.”

On the display, a sleek, full-color rendering of the Gattling Building appeared. The building was elegantly modern with sharp lines, effortless simplicity, and a unique and striking silver color not unlike Gattling’s hair.

Tim looked at Gattling, curious.

Peter looked at Gattling for a reaction and thought, *we've got him.*

Peter continued, "Mr. Gattling, obviously you've seen your building before, but let me show you how we've integrated the solar technology. It's a revolutionary, flexible film that we'll use to cover and seal the steel posts and beams. We've been able to work with our steel fabricator to perfect a seamless adhesion, while still facilitating ease of maintenance. And it's a hundred and fifty percent more cost effective than any window glass technology available on the market today."

On the video display panel, the solar film was superimposed over the steel structure to show what Peter had described.

Gattling smiled. "That's fantastic—a wonderful job. Get all of the final engineering specs over to my office, and let's move forward." He started to rise from his chair.

Tim took the opportunity to grandstand. "You're really going to be impressed with how we've incorporated the solar technology. It's a process we've patented here at the firm. You're going to have the most environmentally responsible building on the planet."

Gattling straightened, smoothed the lapels of his suit jacket, and tightened the knot of his tie. "Tim, I'm already sold. If there's nothing else, I'll see you both at the groundbreaking." He reached over to shake hands with Peter, then with Tim. He walked out, leaving Peter and Tim to enjoy the moment.

Tim walked up to Peter and shook his hand. "Nice job, Peter."

"Thanks."

"Peter, I've been talking with the other partners about you. We're considering adding another full partner to the firm, and I suggested that you be evaluated as a candidate. I know you were just recently promoted to associate partner, but what the hell? I moved up quickly, and maybe you can as well."

"Wow, that's great. I appreciate your confidence in me."

"Unfortunately, it's not a slam dunk. Marc is also being considered."

Peter deflated a bit.

"I think you know how I feel about him," Tim said. "But as the nephew of the senior partner . . ." Tim paused to shake his head, disgusted. "I don't know what more to say about him. I want our decision about the next partner to be based solely on the candidate's ability to deliver for the firm. That's how it was when I got promoted. It should be about the work and nothing else. A *full-time* commitment to making the Gattling Building the firm's crowning achievement will make the difference. If we do that, the decision should take care of itself."

Peter was excited again. For Peter, it was all about the delivery, the end product, the final building. That was the point of it all, and he knew that Tim and the other partners felt that way too. At the same time, he couldn't help feeling that Tim was making a statement, possibly about his current issue with his father by emphasizing the "full-time" nature of the work. He shook off the thought. "Of course, I agree. I'll do whatever is necessary to make sure this project is a success."

"Good. I know you will."

Peter asked, "Anything else?"

"No, that's it." Tim picked up his leather portfolio, looked at Peter, and smirked. He turned and walked out of the room.

Peter stood at the end of the conference room and contemplated what had just transpired.

* * *

Later that day, as he arrived home from work, Peter pulled into the driveway. Out of the corner of his eye, he saw his father, who was on his knees planting some flowers in front of the house. Instead of continuing on to the garage, Peter stopped at the brick-paved path that led up to the front steps. He got out of the car and walked toward the front of the house. Jack didn't notice him approaching.

"Hey, Pop!"

Jack looked up. It took a few seconds until he put the face with the voice. "Peter. Just the man I want to see." With some difficulty and a few cracking joints, Jack rose to his feet and walked over to Peter, moving slowly to stretch his muscles. He exaggerated his gait, which looked more like a hobble. "You're home early."

"Nope, it's the regular time—six o'clock."

Jack looked at his watch, perplexed and deep in thought. "That can't be right."

"What?"

"Naw, that's crazy," Jack said to himself.

"What?" Peter asked again.

Jack tapped on the face of his watch. He raised the watch up to his ear and listened. *Tick, tick, tick*. He shrugged, as everything appeared to be normal. "It seems I've been out here for three hours." He took a handkerchief from his pocket and wiped his brow. He studied the handkerchief, and after seeing nothing unusual, he put it back into his pocket.

"How much did you plant?" Peter asked.

"Oh, I don't know." Jack turned, and waved a hand toward a row of annuals between the existing bushes and the brick of the raised bed in front of them. He looked at what he had done, again perplexed.

"It looks nice," Peter said.

"I hope you don't mind. I had a few spare minutes today, so I walked over to the nursery. It was six blocks. It seemed closer the last time I went. That had to be, what, eight years ago?" He thought about it. "Anyway, I thought the house could use a little more color. And look . . ." Jack raised his arms up to the sky as if making an offering. "Can't be inside on a day like this."

Peter said, "I like it. How much do I owe you for your services?"

Jack waved him off. "Get outta here." He looked at his flowers, his hands now resting on his hips, and you could tell he liked what he saw. He turned back to Peter. "Are we going to look at some places today? How about that condo you were telling me about? I've been here a while now, and I don't want to overstay my welcome."

"There's no hurry. You can stay here as long as you like. How about we take our time to find the perfect place?"

"If you're sure it's all right," Jack said. He grabbed his pants at the belt and pulled them up high. He looked down and noticed a good four inches of white sock showing, so he pushed the waist back down some. "You know, I do like spending time with Jake."

"And here I thought it was Melanie you were after."

Still looking down, Jack chuckled. He turned quiet and appeared wistful. He looked up to Peter. "Say, when's your mother coming home?"

Peter was speechless. An obvious look of surprise showed on his face.

Jack noticed and thought about what he had said. Nervously, he grabbed his belt with both hands and pulled his pants up again. He leaned forward and slapped Peter on the arm. "I meant Jake.

When's Jake going to be home from school? I've got a surprise for him."

At that exact moment, Jake appeared at the front door. "Oh, hi, Dad. It's time for dinner."

Jack said, "And there he is. That was quick." He grabbed Peter by the arm and directed him toward the steps. "Perfect timing. C'mon, I'm starving."

Peter was concerned, not sure what to make of what his father had said. Maybe it was just a slip. It was probably nothing. He walked with Jack up the steps, and before walking through the screen door, he turned to look back at the flowerbed. He chewed his bottom lip, turned, and followed Jack into the house.

6

Days later, the sun rose in the east above the lake, distant, emerging from behind a wall of office buildings and skyscrapers up into the morning sky. It was a cloudless, bright day, and glints of sunlight bounced harshly off the glass of the buildings, warming the Chicago sidewalks below. Heat waves rose from the concrete. People walked the busy rush-hour streets like ants under a magnifying glass.

Peter sat behind his desk, with his chair swiveled around, and he gazed out the window through partially opened blinds. The office was quiet, lit only by the sunlight seeping in. He squinted to see through the slats, but he decided to be content with the limited view since he could not muster the energy to get up and raise the blinds. His body was relaxed and his pulse was slow and steady. He was again relishing the start of a new day while it was still new.

A knock at the open doorway interrupted his solitude.

"Peter, good news! It looks like we're going to be partners."

Peter snapped out of his trance. The words made his body tense and his heart jump. His first thought was that it was too early in the day for such a rude interruption. It was too early in the day for any kind of interruption. He turned his chair around to find Marc standing in the doorway, much too happy and grinning like a fool. His right arm was up and resting at head level on the door frame. His right leg was crossed over his left with one foot resting on the toe of his shoe. Peter thought if only he could move the doorway, the goof would tip right over. "What? What are you talking about?"

"Partners. I met with Tim and my uncle this morning, and they asked me to get involved in the Gattling Project." He nodded and smiled and nodded again, seeking approval.

"Really," was all Peter could come up with. The idea of this happening was so improbable that it wouldn't compute.

Marc said, "Yes, sir, you and me, partners in crime. Butch Cassidy and the Sundance Kid, the Lone Ranger and Tonto, Bonnie and Cly . . ." He stopped and his face twisted, realizing he had gone too far.

Peter sighed and shook his head.

Marc said, "Anyway, maybe we could get together this afternoon to talk about strategy."

"Strategy?"

"Yeah, you know, how we're going to work together to make this project a success."

Peter raised an eyebrow.

Marc said, "Goals, deliverables, process, maximizing our available resources."

"Maximizing our available resources? What are you talking about?" Peter said, annoyed. "And the project is already a success."

"I didn't mean . . ."

Peter cut him off. "I know what you meant." He shook his head and looked at his calendar, realizing he had just one way to get rid of his unwanted visitor. "Our staff meeting is tomorrow morning at eleven, if you'd care to attend."

"Perfect. Location?"

Peter glared at him.

"Never mind; I'm resourceful." He opened his leather portfolio and scribbled some notes. He thought for a moment then scribbled some more.

Peter couldn't imagine what he might be writing. "Marc?"

"All right, then. I'll see you tomorrow at eleven o'clock." He turned and left.

Peter stared at the open doorway, thought about Marc and what his involvement might mean, and became angry. He got up from his desk and bolted out of the office. He turned left and walked down the corridor past two conference rooms on his left and a group of eight cubicles on the right. The people in the cubicles only noticed a flash in their peripheral vision; by the time they turned to look, nothing was there.

Just beyond the second conference room was an open reception area fronting Tim's corner office. There was a single desk, flanked on one side by a low, rectangular glass table. Behind that was a sleek, black leather sofa. On the other side were three rows of waist-high filing cabinets. Vivian Gardner, Tim's assistant, sat at the desk. Her dark hair was pulled back tightly, accentuating her cheekbones and the small designer glasses resting on her nose. She was professional and experienced, but she made Peter think of Ruth Buzzi.

Peter walked up to the desk, and with impatience and a curt demeanor said, "Good morning, Vivian. Is Tim in?"

Vivian looked at her phone console. "He's on the phone. Would you like to have a seat and wait?" She gestured toward the sofa.

He looked over to the sofa and thought it looked like no one had ever sat on it. He wasn't going to be the first, so he remained standing and stared at the door to Tim's office.

She sensed that something was awry but said nothing.

Peter continued to gaze at the closed door, anxious. Vivian looked at him with concern, and an uncomfortable silence passed.

She looked at her console again and said, "He's off the phone now. I'll let him know you're here."

"That isn't necessary," Peter said. He walked around the desk and opened the door forcefully, walking in. Peter closed the door hard behind him, shutting Vivian out.

Tim was at his desk, scribbling something on a note pad. In his free hand was a bottle of Pepto-Bismol. He looked up to see Peter walking toward him at a fast clip and set the Pepto-Bismol down in the open drawer of his desk. He dropped his pen, raising both hands with palms out, as if trying to hold Peter back.

Peter kept coming.

"Now, take it easy," Tim said. There was a thin Pepto mustache on his upper lip, which he licked away. He grimaced.

Peter stopped at the desk and leaned down with both hands on the front edge. "Are you kidding me? Marc? Like I don't have enough to do without having to babysit that son of a bitch."

"Take it easy," Tim said, trying to diffuse the situation and quiet Peter down. He wiped his mouth and looked at his hand.

In a firm voice, Peter said, "Does Gattling know? What kind of nonsense is this, Tim? Do you have a problem with how I'm managing the project? Jesus Christ!"

"Peter, relax, have a seat."

Peter settled down a notch but remained standing in front of Tim's desk. Uncomfortable seconds passed.

Tim said, "It's nothing to worry about."

"Really," Peter said with sarcasm.

Tim said, "I met with the other partners today. I suggested that our decision to select the next partner should be based on delivery for the firm, as we discussed. Phillip liked the idea. Unfortunately, he also realizes that the Gattling Project is critically important for the firm, so he thought it would be a good idea to get Marc involved. He feels it would be good experience for him."

"That's just great," Peter said.

"Nothing's changed. You're still in charge, but now you have an extra resource. Everyone's always complaining about having to do more with less. Now you get to do more with more." Tim seemed pretty proud of himself.

Peter's expression said, *Are you kidding me?*

Tim didn't want to argue. "I'll make sure it's clear to Marc what his role is."

"Which is what?"

"His role is to assist you in managing the project and to be a support resource for the team. *You're* in charge." Tim said it with a fair dose of conviction.

But Peter wasn't convinced. He folded his arms across his chest, and the muscles in his jaw bulged as his teeth ground together. He struggled for the right words.

Tim said, "Given all you've got going on, I thought you would appreciate some help on the project."

"Oh, thanks for your support," Peter said. He turned and walked toward the door, shaking his head. He seemed to be doing that a lot today, and the feelings of disgust and loss only grew stronger with each passing minute. With his hand on the doorknob, he turned back around. "I can manage the project just fine on my own, and our team is working very well together. Don't *you* let Marc screw this up."

Tim acknowledged what Peter said but appeared unfazed. He didn't reply. Then his eyes grew concerned as he leaned back in his chair and rested his folded hands on his stomach, his eyes narrowing further as his eyebrows edged downward. He licked his lips again, searching and hoping for more Pepto.

Peter walked out and headed back to his office, the day all but ruined.

* * *

Later that same day, the O'Hara family gathered around the dining room table for their evening meal. Food was passed around, and silverware clinked against dishes. There was no other sound, save the chewing and breathing.

Peter had a mouth full of food and stared down at his plate, deep in thought as he moved things around with a fork and made unlikely pairings. He swallowed hard. "Can you believe Tim? He actually had the nerve to put Marc on my team. That's the last thing I need right now." He set his fork down and shook his head.

"Did he give a reason?" Melanie asked.

"You ought to just leave," Jack blurted out.

Peter looked at his father with surprise. "What?" He turned to Melanie. "What?"

"I assume he had a reason," she said.

"Yeah, he said that Phillip suggested it, that he wanted to get Marc more experience. I don't buy it. For some reason, I also think he was trying to make a statement about my work and commitment to the job."

"Who's Phillip?" Jack asked.

Peter said, "The senior partner at the firm *and* Marc's uncle. Why?"

Melanie said, “Putting Marc on your team doesn’t change the fact that you’re the lead manager on the project, does it?”

Jack looked down at his plate and chewed. “You ought to just leave,” he said as he spoke under his breath.

“Pop, what are you talking about?”

“Just leave.”

“My job?”

“Sure.”

“I can’t just quit my job.”

“Sure you can.”

Now Peter was upset. He’d brought up the topic just to vent a little and maybe get some words of encouragement, but even those weren’t necessary. It was the venting he needed, and the vent was getting clogged. He rested both his elbows on the table in front of him, hands folded. He took a deep breath. “I’ve spent my entire career at that firm, working my ass off.” He turned to his son. “Sorry, Jake.” Turning back to Jack, he said, “Working to make partner, and I’m just about there. I’m too close to throw it away now.”

“They’re not going to promote you,” Jack said.

“They’re not?”

“Nope.”

“And you know this how?”

“It looks to me like they’re setting up this Marc fella to take the job.”

“Well, thanks for your professional opinion, Pop, but I don’t believe that’s the case.”

“Either way, you should still leave. If you’re at the top of your game—and it sounds like you are—then now’s the time. You’re a great architect. You should be on your own, with your own firm.

Playing second fiddle doesn't suit you."

"Second fiddle?" Peter wondered where it all was coming from.

Jack said, "It's a—what do you call it?—a metaphor."

"I know what it is," Peter said. He didn't want to argue, so he said nothing further.

Jack shrugged it off as he mixed the corn and mashed potatoes together on his plate. He lifted a forkful of the mixture then stopped. He said softly, "You're too good for them."

Silence engulfed the table as everyone attempted to get back to their own plates and thoughts.

Jake was uncomfortable with the silence. He set his fork down and took a gulp of milk. "Hey, Grandpa, tell everyone the story you told me this afternoon, 'bout how you took on the Japs in World War II."

Peter looked up from his plate and toward Jake with a stern expression. "Excuse me? We don't talk like that in this family." He turned to Jack with a scolding look.

Jack shrugged, unconcerned. "It was just a figure of speech."

"And since when were you in World War II?" Peter asked.

Jack didn't respond.

"Pop?"

Jack looked confused. "Don't mess with me. You know what I'm talking about. I must have told you that story a hundred times before. When you were Jake's age you wouldn't stop pestering me. 'Pop, Pop, tell me about the time on the ship, tell me more, tell me more.' Damn, you were hard to please. You were relentless."

Peter could see that thoughts were racing all around the table. Jake turned quiet, likely feeling he had gotten his grandfather into trouble. Jack looked irritated. Melanie looked on with growing concern, and it was obvious she couldn't make sense of it all. Peter himself was dumbfounded.

"And what exactly did you tell me?" Peter asked.

Jack took a moment for himself and settled in to tell the story he had shared with Jake earlier. He did so with excitement and enthusiasm. "It was early dawn on a cold and blustery day, October 2, 1944. The crew of the LST-148 had awoken early that morning in preparation . . ."

Everyone listened with rapt attention, curious and intrigued.

Jack finished the story minutes later to a stunned and quiet audience. He had worked himself up quite well, his face flushed from the adrenaline coursing through his veins. He paused and collected himself. "And there you have it."

"That was great, Grandpa. Even better than the first time," Jake said.

Peter sat frozen. He broke free and looked at Melanie, who set her fork down and folded her hands, unsure of what to say.

Jack picked up his fork and started for his plate, but he stopped and set it down, thinking.

Jake looked at Jack, then to his father for confirmation. "It was a good story, right, Dad?"

"Pop, you've never told me that story before."

Jack looked up from his plate. "What?"

"I've never heard that story."

"Sure you have."

"Sorry, no."

Jack was perplexed. He said, "What are you talking about?"

"Pop, you've never told me that story."

Now Jack was irritated and abrupt. "Say, I don't need to listen to this crap." He reached for his fork, grabbed it, then stopped and set it down. "Are you calling me a liar?"

Peter sat quietly and stared at him.

Jack tried one last time, picking up his fork and going for his plate, but he stopped short, unsuccessful, and said, "Why do you always have to ruin everything? Do you always have to be such a stick in the mud? Jesus, Pete!" He set his fork down for the last time and got up from the table, pushing his chair back hard and nearly toppling it over. He threw his napkin onto his plate and walked toward the living room. He was noticeably agitated and upset, and no one dared to say a word, not wanting to make the situation any worse. After a few steps, he stopped and turned around. To Peter he said, "You need to learn to show some respect," and with that, he walked out of the room.

Jake sat still, uncomfortable, and didn't say anything. He looked down at his plate and picked at his food. He looked up at his father apologetically.

Peter sat back in his chair and sighed. He turned to look at Melanie, who was at a loss for words.

* * *

As the day came to a close, Peter was in his home office, sitting behind his desk, meatloaf turning cartwheels in his stomach. The room was lit by a small, brass desk lamp that illuminated only the phone on his desk. He looked out the window into the backyard as dusk loomed, and he tried to make out the large apple tree that had blended into the twilight. He knew it was there but could not see it clearly.

He had the telephone handset to his ear. "Hello, Dr. Halper. It's Peter O'Hara."

"Peter, how are you?" Dr. Halper said.

"I'm fine, thank you. I'm sorry to trouble you so late, but you said to call if anything came up."

"What is it?"

"There have been a couple of circumstances where, where my father just doesn't seem right. I don't want to make a big deal out of nothing, but a couple of days ago he asked me when his wife would be home, and this evening he told us a story about his time serving in World War II."

"I didn't think he served in the war," Dr. Halper said.

"Right. He never had the opportunity to enlist. He tried, but they wouldn't take him. At least that's what our entire family understands and believes. I don't want to overreact, but I'm concerned."

Dr. Halper said, "That's understandable, and I don't think you're overreacting. Why don't you bring him in to see me? I'd like to talk to him. How's tomorrow morning, say ten o'clock?"

Peter scanned the next day's work schedule in his mind, not able to find an opening. "Tomorrow? Well, sure, we can make that."

"Good. I'll see you both at ten."

"All right, we'll see you then. Thanks." Peter hung up the phone, crossed his arms, and continued to stare out the window, wondering if he had made the right decision by calling Dr. Halper.

* * *

The following morning, Peter and Jack left the house at nine-thirty. Their drive across town would take about twenty minutes, even with the worst of traffic and an accident or two, which was unlikely in their small town. In the car, they both were silent and gazed with blank stares at life on the street. Peter, dressed for work in another of his dark suits, this one gray, seemed to be in a hurry.

He fidgeted and looked at his watch often.

Jack was wearing a flannel shirt buttoned to the neck with a corduroy jacket. A tweed hat covered his head, and he looked inconvenienced. "I don't know what you're making such a big deal about," he said. "So what if I never told you about the war before. It was *war*. I didn't exactly enjoy it, and I never had the desire to talk about it until Jake made me think about it yesterday."

"Jake?"

"Yeah, he was playing with one of those cast metal airplanes he has, and for some reason it just made me remember. It popped into my head, like it happened just last week. Actually, I'm kind of surprised I remembered at all."

"But why now?" Peter said.

"I don't know. Why not? I'm an old man, and all I've got left now are my memories. Up until a month ago, I didn't even have those. Listen, if you don't want me to talk about it, I won't ever bring it up again."

They both gazed out the front window of the car, not wanting to look at each other.

Jack said, "Don't you have to be at work?"

Peter had his mind on something else.

"Peter?"

"Oh, yeah. Don't worry. I'll go to the office when we're done." He got restless, sped up, and passed the car in front of him. He checked his watch again.

"You don't want to piss off the first fiddle," Jack said.

"Pop, please."

"What? What did I say?"

"Humor me, okay? Let's just go meet with Dr. Halper and make sure you're all right."

"I'm not going back there, you know," Jack said defiantly.

"Where?"

"To Shady Acres."

"Pop, I wouldn't think of it. It's just a check-up. We'll be in and out, and I'll have you back home in time for Oprah."

"Very funny."

Peter checked his watch once more, and they drove on in silence.

* * *

The doctor's office was bright and sterile, with stark white walls, stock artwork hanging in a strict pattern, and a limited amount of furniture. The décor was much too sterile to be comforting. Dr. Halper shared the space with three other doctors, who each provided care in a different specialty related to geriatrics. It was obvious that not one of them had taken an interest in decorating. The building looked relatively new, but the furnishings made it seem old and lived in. It didn't work.

Peter sat by himself in a surprisingly comfortable faux-leather chair and leafed through the latest issue of *Golf Digest*. He didn't play golf, but it was that, an *AARP* magazine, or a pamphlet on controlling and managing incontinence, so the choice was an easy one.

An elderly woman sat across from him. She was fragile, like a little porcelain doll with brittle, gray hair. She looked up from her magazine sheepishly and glanced in his direction. She looked down and up again at him several times.

Peter noticed her looking at him. The next time their eyes met he said, "Hi!"

The woman immediately looked down, uncomfortable at being noticed. She reached into a large bag that was jammed down into the seat next to her and pulled out a cat-sized ball of ivory yarn and two knitting needles. She moved the needles as if they were an extension of her hands; they crissed and crossed in a flurry of movement as she quickly got to work on her project.

Peter's phone rang. He pulled it from his breast pocket, checked the caller-ID, and answered it. "Hi, April, what's up?"

"Are you on your way?" she asked.

"Not really. I'm running a little late."

"Your staff meeting starts in less than an hour, and Marc is already hanging around."

"Damn. I forgot about that. Can you cover for me until I get there? Make something up. Be resourceful, and just don't let Marc get out of control."

"How long will you be?"

"It'll likely be at least another hour. I'm with my father, seeing his doctor."

"Is everything all right?"

"Yeah, he's fine, and nobody needs to know."

"Not a word."

"All right, thanks. I'll get there as soon as I can."

"Peter?"

"Yeah?"

"I realize today's not good, but could we re-schedule our lunch?"

Peter had forgotten about that too. April had been suggesting they get together for lunch for weeks, and today was the day.

"I'm sorry."

"It's not a problem. We've waited this long. Maybe next week?"

"Sure." An uncomfortable silence followed. "I'll see you later."

Peter hung up the phone and put it away. He shook his head,

frustrated and now, stressed. He looked up and saw the elderly woman staring at him. This time she did not look away.

Peter's facial expression suggested *can I help you?*

"You in trouble?" the elderly woman asked feebly.

"Me? No."

"Sure sounds like you're in trouble." She sounded like a sweet and caring grandmother.

"Nope, just forgot about something I had to do this morning."

"That's all?"

"A lunch appointment, too."

"Sure is nice of you to come here with your father. My name is Clara."

"Peter."

"That's a nice name. *My* son lives in San Francisco." *Knit one, pearl two, knit one, pearl two.* She looked up again. "This nice young fella from the church, Francis, brings me here every month. I don't know what I'd do without him. He's such a nice boy." Her needles stopped moving, and she picked at her dress. She lifted a piece of lint and flicked it to the floor, then smoothed the fabric across her lap. The knitting resumed, and the discussion was over.

Peter thought about the staff meeting, about how adding Marc to the mix would shift the chemistry. The thought made his left eye twitch and his head hurt. But he quickly moved on to the lunch meeting with April, the now re-scheduled lunch meeting. He thought that lunch with her would be nice, a way to get away from the office for a couple of hours and not think of the daily toil—no problems or issues to deal with and no unnecessary phone calls.

He recalled the day two weeks ago when she walked into his office early, when no one was around, and the glint in her eyes when she asked if they could get together for lunch. *No business*, she suggested. His mind trailed off. *No business*. He pictured her face and the creamy complexion of her skin. Her coloring seemed to be the perfect complement to the auburn locks that framed her face. He thought of how her slender neck led down to her collar bone, a slight and sculpted ridge visible on the canvas of fine skin above the plunging neckline of her dress. The color of the silk dress was not unlike a ripened peach, and the neckline seemed to be in constant motion, as his eyes trailed . . .

Dr. Halper and Jack came through a door at the far end of the room and crossed the reception area. Dr. Halper approached Peter, Jack trailing with his hat in his hand. "Peter?"

Peter broke free and rose from his chair. He glanced over at the woman who sat across from him. Her head was down. She was concentrating on her project and didn't know that Peter existed.

Dr. Halper said, "We had a nice talk. I ran a few tests, and everything came back fine."

"Still no answers?"

"Excuse me?"

Peter waved him off. "Sorry. Forget it."

Dr. Halper said, "For now, I don't see that there is anything to be concerned about. I would like to see him a little more frequently for a while, maybe every other week." He turned to Jack. "Jack, are you okay with seeing me a little more often?"

Jack pointed to Peter. "Sure, as long as my ride is okay with it."

Dr. Halper turned to Peter. "He told me he was having trouble sleeping. Here's a prescription for a mild sedative in case he needs it." He handed the script to Peter.

"Well, I'm glad the tests went well." Peter took the small sheet of paper and looked at it. The hieroglyphics were indecipherable, so he just slipped the paper into his pocket. "I wasn't aware that he was having trouble sleeping." He gave Jack a scolding look.

Jack held his hat in front of him and looked down at his shoes. He was being coy and smirking. "Sorry, Papa. I didn't want to trouble you or make you mad."

Peter looked to Dr. Halper, hooking a thumb toward Jack. "See what I'm up against? Always joking. A real comedian I have to put up with."

Dr. Halper looked to Jack, who shrugged.

"I'll keep an eye on his sleeping. Maybe I'll send him to bed early tonight." Peter said to Jack, "Maybe without dinner."

Dr. Halper said, "All right. Amy here can schedule your next couple of appointments." He stepped forward to Jack and shook his hand. "Jack, you take care." He shook hands with Peter.

Peter held on and pulled Dr. Halper aside. Very softly he asked, "What about . . . what we discussed on the phone?"

Jack blurted, "You know, I'm right here! I'm a big boy. You can talk in front of me."

Dr. Halper turned so he could address both Jack and Peter simultaneously. "Given what Jack has been through, I'm not surprised to hear that he has had a couple of episodes."

"Episodes?" Peter said.

"Peter, your father was on quite a regimen of medications for an extended period of time. We've had him on nothing at all since he left Shady Acres, and I'd like to keep it that way. Actually, I'm a little surprised it's been this uneventful. Together, let's just keep a close eye on him over the next few weeks. I think he'll be fine."

As usual, Peter was not convinced. A knot tightened in his stomach as he said, "All right, thanks."

Dr. Halper walked back across the reception area and through the door.

Jack motioned toward the exit. “Shall we?”

Jack could not get out of the waiting room quickly enough. As they passed the elderly woman, Jack noticed her staring at him but kept walking. Peter was looking at his watch and didn’t notice.

“Good-bye, Mister,” the elderly woman said, in a loud voice that was meant to be heard.

“Oh, good-bye. Very nice to meet you,” Peter said.

“You too,” she said with a nod. She smiled and returned her attention to her knitting. The needles went back to work, weaving the yarn into what looked like a baby’s mitten.

As they left the reception area, Jack said, “She’s a little old for you, don’t you think?” He chuckled.

“She said she was interested in the distinguished lad I was with,” Peter said.

They both smiled. Jack took Peter’s arm, and they walked down the hallway and out of the building.

* * *

On the way home from the doctor’s office, Jack and Peter were talkative, which was unusual. When Peter was young, Jack often professed the virtue of silence. He often told Peter that sometimes what a person didn’t say was just as important as what he did. Jack preferred what people didn’t say and thought that people talked too much just because they liked the sound of their own voices. They didn’t say anything of interest or real value. As a young boy, Peter was stumped by this revelation, and he asked his father how people were supposed to communicate if they didn’t speak. Jack’s reply was quick and direct. Communicating was one thing; just talking or babbling was another. He told Peter that if he had something *important* to say—and he would emphasize the word *important*—then that was just fine. Otherwise, he should keep his thoughts to himself.

At first, this made Peter question himself every time he attempted to speak to his father, but he learned quickly. In retrospect, Peter felt that Jack's advice was good advice. God knows Peter wished more people in his office would follow that advice. Jack's other regular piece of advice was "if you don't have anything nice to say, don't say anything at all." That one stuck with Peter even more, and he found himself sharing it with his son. Peter was amazed at how he blurted out these Jack-isms when he was talking to Jake or Melanie or others. But, then again, he was glad that he was able to pass them along, especially to his boy.

During their short drive, they discussed a variety of topics, all of which were initiated by Jack—again, unusual. Jack was very interested in Peter's family, now *his* family, but the discussion veered quickly to the most important topic: Jake. Jack wanted to know everything about Jake: his likes and dislikes, his favorite subject at school, his hobbies and interests, friends, sports, and the like. Jack asked a question, Peter answered, and Jack was right back at him with a follow-up question in the waiting.

"What's gotten into you?" Peter asked.

"What?" Jack replied. Peter saw Rodney Dangerfield in Jack's expression.

"What do you mean, 'what?' You're awfully talkative, and you've got a lot of questions for so early in the morning. I think we've talked more in the past half hour than we have in the last ten years."

"That's not true. Four of those years, I couldn't talk. I had an involuntary speech impediment. Those don't count." Jack chuckled.

Peter smiled. "You know what I mean."

"I'm just curious. That's all. Can't I be interested in my grandson?"

"Of course you can be interested. Ask away."

"Listen, I think I just have a different perspective on things these days. You don't know what's it's like to have lost four years of your life. You also don't know what it's like to be an old man. Both those things together gave me a good slap of reality upside my head. I don't know how long I've got, but what I've got left has got to be *right*. *Right* is our family." Jack looked down at the hat in his lap. He said, "I need to be a better father."

"You were fine," Peter said. "You *are* fine."

"Well, then I need to be better than fine. More importantly, I need to be a great grandfather for Jake. I'm the only one he's got, his only link to the past, to the family."

"What about me?" Peter said.

"Quit gettin' sensitive. I've got stories, history. Plus, we're pals, Jake and I. It's my right and duty as a grandfather to teach him. I probably still have a few things to pass along to you if you'll let me."

Peter came to a stop at a red light and turned to Jack. "All right, but just be careful with him. He's young, influential. I don't want him running around telling all your bad jokes."

"Me? What bad?"

"You know what I mean. Keep it clean, and keep it appropriate."

"You've gotten stiff," Jack said.

"No, I just want you to be careful."

"You need to lighten up a little. Don't worry so much. I'm his grandfather, not a schoolyard pal. Trust me."

"Yeah, trust you."

"What do you mean by *that*?"

"Nothing. *You* quit getting sensitive."

Peter pulled into the driveway and up to the house. Jack opened his door, got out, and started up the walkway. Peter leaned over, and through the open passenger window, he yelled, "Hey, Pop?"

Jack turned around. "What?"

Peter thought for a moment.

"What is it?"

Peter said, "Never mind. Listen, I'll see you at dinner."

Jack shook his head. "Okay, thanks for that." He turned and walked up the steps to the front door.

Peter leaned back and looked up the driveway. He wanted to tell Jack that he was glad to have him around. But then analysis kicked in, and it made him hold back. Peter hoped that Jack knew. Peter hoped he'd have another chance to tell him.

7

After he dropped Jack back at home, Peter drove to the office, his foot heavy on the gas pedal. He was surprised that with the exception of the call from April, he really hadn't thought about work for a good hour and a half. Through the morning he was somehow able to turn it off, much like he did when he had something scheduled with Jake. However, no matter how good he was at turning off his work, it always came back, and now he was late. The pressure was back on.

At the building, Peter hurried down the hallway toward his office. The workers in the cubicles bordering the walkway felt the air move. Some looked up, and some could not have cared less.

He stopped at April's desk, just outside his office and said, "Hi, April. What did I miss?"

"Oh, good morning," she said. "You missed quite a bit, actually."

Did he detect an edge in her voice? It was probably his imagination. "Forget it. I don't want to know," he said, impatient. "You can fill me in later. I need to wrap up a few details for the partner's meeting. Can you get the team together in the small conference room?"

"Marc's in there with them now," she said. She waited, looking for a reaction.

Peter tensed. His heart quickened, his blood pressure rose,

and the stomach acid began to flow. His light breakfast earlier in the morning wouldn't help to ease the oncoming irritation to his stomach lining. He felt a heat wave come over him that made his face flush and his hair follicles tingle. Frustrated, he said, "That's just great. For how long?" He found it difficult to look at her when he spoke.

"For about the last hour," she said. She could see he wasn't happy and watched him unconsciously rub his stomach.

"Just great," he said. He stepped into his office, grabbed a leather portfolio and a thick three-ring binder from his desk, stepped out, and headed down the hall.

April watched his back as he hurried down the hallway and disappeared into the conference room. She wondered if she should have handled the morning another way.

* * *

Peter entered the conference room without missing a stride. He was able to push down on the lever and open the door in one smooth motion, but the lever escaped his grip and the door slammed hard against the doorstop behind it. It was enough to startle everyone in the room, all of whom seemed to have been expecting him. They were already up from their chairs, and their heads were twisted toward the door. It wasn't Peter's planned entrance, but it would do.

He checked his frustration and flashed a smile. "Hello, everyone. No need to get up on my account," he said as he walked toward the head of the table. "I'm sorry I'm late. Where are we?"

His team continued standing. They were gathering up their things. Most of them found it difficult to make eye contact with him.

Before what was happening could register with Peter, Marc welcomed him and said, "Our fearless leader." He gestured to the group with both arms open wide, like a priest. The team sensed the sarcasm; they likely all felt it in their stomachs. Everyone looked at Marc, then to Peter, then back to Marc. The discomfort hung in the air, thick and unsettling.

Marc said, "Peter, we were just wrapping up. I looked at the final plans this morning and saw your notes regarding the open items. I got the team together, and I think we've addressed everything. There were a few issues I had as well. I hope you don't mind." To the team he said, "Thanks you guys, and gals; good effort. Couldn't have done it without you. Remember, there's no "I" in "TEAM." He rattled the statements off quickly and without taking a breath, like he knew he might get interrupted.

The team members filed out of the conference room, each with a different expression, but all along the lines of *I'm glad that meeting is over*. No one said a word.

Peter waved to the team, deflated and apologetic. "Thanks, everybody. I'll catch up with you after the meeting this afternoon."

"*We'll* catch up with you," Marc said.

Peter had enough. "Listen, Marc . . ."

"No need to thank me, Peter. It's the least I could do."

"I wasn't going to thank you."

"Ungrateful, are we?" Marc played sad, keeping the situation light.

"No, no. I do appreciate you covering for me." Peter set his portfolio and binder down on the table. "Let me see what you came up with."

Marc handed a document to Peter.

Peter read it and nodded his head in approval. "Not bad," he said. “Listen, I’ve got to run. I’m meeting with Tim and Phillip in twenty minutes. Ask April to type up these notes and get them distributed to the team.”

“*We’re* meeting with them in twenty minutes,” Marc said.

“What?”

“What?” Marc said, mocking Peter.

In a raised voice, Peter said, “What did you say?”

Marc cowered at the tone of Peter’s voice. He raised both hands, surrendering. “Hey, take it easy. Tim asked me to sit in. Don’t shoot the messenger.”

Peter didn’t like the idea at all. “Tim asked you?”

“Yeah, *and* Phillip.”

“All right, but it’s my meeting. I’ll take the lead.”

Marc saluted and smiled. “Yes, sir, Captain.”

Peter shook his head, wondering why he had to put up with this guy. “Don’t ever do that again.” He turned and walked out of the room. Marc followed, trailing him close.

* * *

That afternoon, Peter and Marc sat in on the weekly partner meeting. The meeting of the firm partners was usually a closed-door affair that the rest of the people in the office only talked about at the water cooler, and *talk* they did. There had been two rumors floating around for weeks: one, that the partners had made some unsound investments which were putting the firm in a pinch, and two, that the firm was considering adding a new partner, hoping for a sorely-needed cash infusion. Neither rumor was true, as far as anyone but the senior partner could attest, but it made for good gossip.

The partners decided to allow additional participation

periodically, mostly as an opportunity to get a first-hand update and account of an important project. The Gattling Project was the number one revenue generator for the firm for the current fiscal year and likely the next one too, so it was the one and only item on the agenda.

They met in the executive conference room, a lavishly appointed room used only for the partner meetings and for meetings with clients. The room looked clean enough to eat off of the carpet. The room exuded success, from the framed awards adorning the walls to the crystal trophies displayed on the side tables. The room was decorated with the finest wood furniture, and the artwork on the walls was worth millions. Not too many companies had the financial fortitude to hang an original Dali in their conference room. The purpose of the room was simple: to communicate the firm's success to every person who entered. If you wanted to have a great building designed and built, that's what you looked for: proof of past accomplishments and confidence for future success.

Phillip Jackson, the senior partner, sat at the head of the conference table, ready to hold court. He drank imported spring water from a glass shaped like a chalice. Phillip was in his late fifties, balding and portly but still quite distinguished. He was the type of man who got what he wanted without having to ask for it. You could see it in his face: the confidence, success, and just a glint of arrogance to round out the personality he projected. He had put in his time, and now it was others who did the asking. People came to him for one thing: to have their dreams realized. Most would pay handsomely just to have Phillip and his firm in the driver's seat.

The only other partner in attendance was Tim. While

Randolph Finch's name was on the company letterhead, he always seemed to have more pressing interests, like real estate, fishing, and younger women. Frank Magill and Adlai Sorensen were older and mostly silent as far as partners go, and it was mutually understood that their attendance was optional. More often than not, they opted out, and that was fine with Phillip and Tim. The fewer decision-makers in attendance, the better. While Tim was the most active partner, he was certainly second in line to Phillip and, as such, was quite submissive to him. Tim sat to Phillip's left on one side of the table. Peter and Marc sat on the other side, Marc closest to Phillip.

"Gentlemen, why don't we update Phillip on the status of the Gattling Project," Tim said.

Peter spoke first. "Phillip—" It was the only word he could get out before he was interrupted.

Marc leaned forward on the table, elbows spread wide. He turned toward Phillip, effectively taking Peter out of the picture. "Uncle Phillip, I just met with the team, and we've addressed all of the outstanding issues that have been identified. I'd like to go through each of them one by one."

Peter looked at the back of Marc's head with contempt. He grabbed Marc by the arm and pulled him back in his chair gently but with force. "Excuse me."

Marc reacted like he didn't have a clue. "What?"

Phillip took control. "Marc, Peter's the lead on this project. Why don't we give him a chance to speak?"

Peter leaned forward himself, resting his folded hands on the table in front of him. "Thank you, Phillip. There were six outstanding issues we needed to address for Mr. Gattling. We have solutions to each that I'm confident he will be comfortable with."

There was another interruption: a knock on the conference room door. Phillip spoke with a booming voice, "Come in!"

The door opened wide, and Phillip's assistant stepped in.

"Yes, Marci, what is it?"

"I'm very sorry to interrupt, but I have a Jack O'Hara on the line, asking to speak with Peter. It sounds like an emergency."

Peter turned to Phillip, ill at ease.

"Well, you better take that," Phillip said.

Peter rose from his chair. "If you'll excuse me." He grabbed his portfolio and hurried to the door. He stepped sideways past Marci in the doorway and disappeared. She turned and closed the door behind her. Tim seemed embarrassed and felt the need to explain. Marc had a devilish grin on his face.

"I'm sure it's nothing," Tim said. "He should be right back."

Phillip turned to his nephew. "Marc, why don't you continue? Given your preemptive move earlier, I assume you're prepared to walk us through the status until Peter gets back?"

Marc smiled a confirmation and again sat forward in his chair. "I am. Regarding the first issue, the technical specifications for the . . ." Marc proceeded to give the status report in excruciating detail.

Tim periodically looked to the door and could only wonder where Peter had gone and when, or if, he would return. God help him, and Marc, if he didn't return soon.

* * *

Marci had caught up with Peter as he reached her desk. She hurried around and picked up the phone. "You can just take it here," she said, extending the handset to Peter. "If you'll excuse me, I need to run down the hall." She handed the phone to Peter, compassion in her expression, and walked away.

Peter didn't like that look. He spoke into the phone. "Hello, Pop? What's the matter?"

"You know damn well what's the matter."

"Listen, I'm in the middle of a meeting."

"What—now that you've got the cleaning crew lined up, you can just go back to work like nothing happened?"

"What are you talking about?" Peter was lost.

"Don't bullshit me. The car to take me back to Shady Acres will probably be here for me any minute."

"There's no car coming," Peter said, trying to reassure him.

"I heard you talking to Dr. Halper this morning. I heard it all. All you want is to dump me back into that hell-hole." Jack was furious.

"Pop, that was—is not my intention. Just calm down."

"You calm down. I told you before that I'm not going back there."

"Listen, Pop, I can't talk about this right now."

"Oh, no?"

"Is Melanie there?" Peter asked.

"Who? There's no one else here." Jack was unconvincing.

Peter was losing his patience. "Pop, I'll be home later, and we can talk about it then."

"You're trying to take Jake away from me!" Jack yelled.

"That's not true, and I really can't talk about this right now." Peter realized he'd raised his voice, and he looked around to see if anyone was within earshot. He was safe, and that was good, because his expression was a mix of concern, frustration, and agitation that likely would have drawn stares. "Pop, I need to go.

We'll talk about this later."

"But you can't—"

"I said we'll talk later. And don't call me here again." Now Peter was angry, and his temples pulsed. He set the phone down firmly and looked around again. He took a moment to compose himself, and, confident that no one had seen or heard what just transpired, he adjusted his tie and returned to the conference room.

As he walked back into the room, the meeting was breaking up. *How long was I gone*? he wondered. He couldn't believe it. Marc and Tim were standing, and Phillip was walking toward him.

"It seems I have a crisis of my own to attend to," Phillip said to Peter as he approached him. "Marc briefly summarized the status for us. I think Mr. Gattling will be quite happy. Tell your team that I appreciate all of their hard work." As he walked by, Phillip patted him on the arm. "Peter."

"Good-bye, Phillip," Peter said.

As Phillip walked away he spoke to the approaching doorway. "Tim, are we still on for drinks later?"

Tim walked toward the door, passing Peter and almost ignoring the fact that he was standing there. He said to Phillip's back, "Five-thirty, at Tony's down the street. I'll see you then."

Phillip and Tim walked out of the conference room and down the hallway.

Marc approached Peter. "Me, covering for you, it's getting to be a regular thing." He patted Peter on the arm exactly as Phillip had, and he left the room.

Peter was left standing alone in the conference room, and he wondered how the day had taken such a drastic turn.

* * *

Peter's drive home late that afternoon was mostly silent, yet the conversation with his father played and re-played in his mind. He analyzed the words and meanings they implied, but it proved fruitless. Peter couldn't make sense of the conversation, and, while frustrated, he accepted the fact that an answer would not likely be forthcoming in the near future.

An unexpected afternoon storm erupted on his way home. Peter wasn't used to *unexpected*, yet *unexpected* was becoming more the rule than the exception. The sky was dark, and the driving rain created a fog-mist in the air, cutting visibility to a dangerous level. The raindrops were the size of dimes, and the wipers on his car had a tough time keeping up. What was worse, he found the sound of the pounding raindrops to be intolerable and distracting, impairing his thought process and often taking his mind off the road in front of him. Juggling the replay of the earlier call with his father and keeping his eyes on the road proved difficult for him.

The scales tipped when Peter received a call from Tim, inquiring about why Marc had distributed the formal status report at the end of the day, a document that was laced with mistakes. *Marc, that son of a bitch.* The call, too, was unexpected, and the tone of discontent in Tim's voice, coupled with Peter's rising rage against Marc, was enough to cloud his vision. He didn't see the raccoon crossing the highway until the last minute.

The animal got caught up and tumbled around in the car's wheel-well. The rumbling and death screeches caused Peter to swerve hard from the right lane, and he ended up in a slight depression of grass and crushed stone at the side of the road. He was unhurt, physically at least, and after taking a few minutes to compose and collect himself, he navigated the car back onto the road. Fortunately, the earth held firm under his spinning wheels. Unfortunately, his mind continued spinning for the rest of the ride home.

Peter pulled into the driveway and stopped by the front door. He turned off the car engine and sat for a moment, wondering if he should wait out the storm. But that wasn't really an option; he was much too impatient to resolve the issue with his father. He got out, draped his suit jacket over one arm, covered his head with his briefcase, and ran for the house. He made it to the front door in record time, but the rain still won.

He opened the front door and hurried in, trying to keep the rain at bay. He closed the door and stood in the foyer, the briefcase still resting on his head. He glanced at himself in the hall mirror. He quickly realized how bad he looked, soaked to the bone. His hair was disheveled and flattened, and water dripped down his face. He wiped his face with his suit jacket and hung it up on the coat tree. He wiped his feet on the hall rug and ran a hand through his hair. As he wiped his hand off on his pant leg, he wondered why he had done that. He sighed with exasperation and shook his head. "What a day," he said to no one.

Melanie had heard the front door open and close, and she came into the front hall. She was wiping her hands on a small dish towel. "Peter, what happened to you?"

He didn't say anything, feeling it was fairly obvious.

She extended the dish towel toward him. "Here," she said. He took it, held it up to observe its tininess, and used it to dab his soaked body. It was like trying to dry off with a square of toilet paper; it was useless.

She stepped up close and kissed him, not worried at all about getting a little wet. "Welcome home."

"Where's Pop?" he asked. He had no intention of mentioning the drive home.

"I don't even get a 'hello'?"

"Sorry." He put his arms around her and held her tightly. He looked into her eyes and kissed her.

"That's better," she said. She swept a hand across his forehead, clearing away his soaked bangs. "He's up in his room. I was just up there to tell him dinner was ready, and he said he wasn't hungry. He's just sitting in his room, looking out the window."

"I need to go talk to him," Peter said.

"What's the matter?"

"I don't know." He released his grip, handed her the dish towel, and walked away. He headed up the stairs to the second floor.

Melanie watched. She said, "Jake's on his way home from the Petersens' house. Margie is dropping him off." There was no response. "Dinner is in ten minutes." She realized that Peter did not hear her, so she said a little louder, "Dinner in ten?"

He was halfway up the stairs when it registered. He turned around, distracted, while continuing up the stairs. "Yeah, sure, ten minutes." He made it to the top of the stairs then turned and disappeared down the hallway.

* * *

Melanie remained for a moment, looking at the empty stairway with concern. She knew her husband well, and something definitely was not right. At first, she couldn't put her finger on it, but she knew that her husband's recent expression was one she had seen in the past. Peter had a repertoire of standard expressions. She guessed most people did. He had a certain loving expression that was easy to pinpoint: a slightly upturned corner of his mouth on the left side, a certain sparkle in his eye. He had a truly comedic expression whenever he had a funny story to tell or was horsing around with Jake: a big grin, raised eyebrows, and bulging eyes. His face was serious when he was engaged in any activity related to his work and he furrowed his brow so intensely that over the years it developed several permanent creases. He even had a mean expression, one that Melanie last saw ten years ago when one of Jackie's boyfriends had physically abused her. Though it was all in the past now, that expression and what happened along with it still sparked fear in Melanie. She was thankful she had not seen that look on Peter's face in the years since Jake was born.

Melanie thought about it more and struggled to remember the last time she had seen Peter upset the way he was tonight. Was it the depth of his stare, if that was possible to measure? Was it his noticeable anxiety? Was it the fact that he was obviously holding something in and not wanting to discuss it, even with her? She played back the last minutes from the point when Peter walked in the door. Then, it came to her.

As her mind replayed the events, she saw herself stepping up close to him, and just as she was about to kiss him, she saw it: the ever-so-slight twitch of his left eye. She kissed him, and she saw it again, that same twitch. The last time she saw that twitch was when they got the news that his mother was near the end of her life. She had seen it too just after Jake was born prematurely and was holding on by a wish. She thought that Peter's twitch seemed to be correlated with a certain look of dread, a particular expression saved for times where he was confronted with a dilemma he just did not want to deal with. The reasons didn't matter; that's just how it was.

Melanie could only imagine what was on Peter's mind.

* * *

Jack was in his room, sitting in a straight-backed chair by the window, looking out on the gloomy afternoon. The rain was pelting the glass, rapping on it hard and wanting to get in. The room was dark. Only the last remnants of clouded daylight lingered.

There was an aggressive knock at the door. Jack flinched faintly.

"Hey, Pop, can I come in?"

Jack didn't answer. He didn't move a hair.

The door opened, and Peter stepped in. "Pop? Are you in here?" He reached in and felt for the wall switch. He found it and flipped it to turn the light on. A lamp on one of the nightstands came on and illuminated the room with an eerie glow. He saw Jack sitting by the window. "Pop, what are you doing sitting here in the dark?"

Again, there was no answer.

Peter walked around the bed and sat down, facing the windows. Jack was in the chair to his right. He reached over and touched his father on the shoulder.

Jack said, "I'm sorry for calling you at work. I just didn't know what else to do."

"What the hell was that all about? You were talking like a crazy person."

Jack turned and sneered at him with piercing eyes. He turned back to look out the window.

"I'm sorry. I didn't mean that. What's going on, Pop?"

Jack shook his head. "I just don't know anymore. Maybe

you're right. Maybe I should go back to Shady Acres."

"Pop, I never said that."

"You don't know what it's been like. I've tried to carry on, to be positive, but it's not working. I can't get over the lost time. I can't get past the regret I feel for what I did to your mother. I guess I can understand you not wanting me around anymore."

"Pop, that couldn't be further from the truth. I want you here. *We* want you here."

"I heard the way you talked to Dr. Halper. I see how you act when I'm around. I can see it in your eyes. You don't trust me." He thought for a moment. "I don't trust myself. I shouldn't even be here. I'm a washed-up old codger who doesn't know when to leave. Guys like me, we need to get kicked in the head to realize that our time's up, that it's time to make some room for the next guy. I've overstayed my welcome and I should be moving on."

Peter wasn't sure how to react. He said, "Don't be silly. You're not going anywhere."

Jack's gaze remained fixed on the window, and he glared out. "Don't you argue with me! I'm no good here, no good to you or Melanie and certainly no good to Jake. How much does he know? God damn it, what have you told him? I bet, deep down, he's scared to death of me." Jack turned his head and looked at Peter with contempt.

It was a look that Peter hadn't seen in a long, long time. He said nothing and waited for the mood to calm.

Jack said, "You still resent me."

"Sorry?"

"It was a long time ago, and I can't do anything about it now. I would if I could, believe me. I was stupid, disillusioned, an idiot. Okay? Is that what you want me to say?"

"I don't want you to say anything. I've let it go."

"How many times do I have to apologize? It was one time. It meant nothing. It tore me up inside when I saw what it did to your mother. It took years, but she eventually forgave me. Why can't you?"

"Pop, really, it's in the past, and it's not worth dwelling on."

"You shouldn't be so judgmental."

"I'm not."

"You know, you're not all that different from me. Actually, I'd bet you're just like me. Given your position and your office and your secretary and your expense account and your business dinners and all the schmoozing—yeah, I'd bet you're exactly like me."

There was deafening silence, and a brooding tension blanketed them. They sat, quiet and unmoving.

The silence was broken by quick footsteps coming up the stairway, and seconds later Jake appeared. He tried to catch his breath before talking but couldn't wait. "Grandpa, Dad, time for dinner."

Peter and Jack were still looking at each other. Jack turned away to look out the window. Peter turned to Jake but did not get up.

Jake said, "Come on! Dinner's gonna get cold."

"Hey, Jake, what have you got planned for Grandpa tonight?"

Jake took a few deep breaths and raised a finger to his chin to ponder the question. "Well, my homework's all finished, so we're starting with a clean slate." He thought about it for a few seconds more. He added, "Well, I need to do some work on my science project—Mars Exploration, remember? Grandpa said he could help with building the Mars landscape we talked about. So we can do that, and then there is that new magic trick he showed us. I'd really like to show my friends at school tomorrow. And then there's always the story about *the old days* before I go to bed." Jake nodded, pleased with his agenda for the evening. "Yep, I think that'll do."

Peter turned to Jack. "Pop? How does that sound? Think you could spend some time with Jake this evening? He sure could use your help on that project. I don't know the first thing about building a Mars landscape." He waited for a response. "And I'm too darn young and foolish to know anything about *the old days*."

Jack turned to Peter and flashed a faint smile.

"What do you say, Pop? We'll go downstairs for a nice dinner, and then you can hang out with your grandson."

Excited, Jake said, "Would that be okay, Grandpa?"

"I guess," Jack said.

Peter stood and helped Jack get up from his chair. Jack brushed him away. "Jake, be a good boy and walk with Grandpa downstairs."

Jake hurried over and hooked his arm around Jack's. Together, they walked out of the room.

Peter watched for a moment and thought about what his father had said. He wondered if he really was like his father and what that might mean.

8

A large crowd attended the groundbreaking ceremony for the Gattling Building. Everyone at the firm was required to attend, and they were surrounded by city officials, special guests, and four buses filled to capacity with Victor Gattling's closest friends, associates, and supporters, all two hundred of them. For Gattling and the firm of Jackson, Parker & Finch, this was the single most important event of the last ten years.

The press had been notified weeks earlier, and there were cameras and crew from every major network in attendance. Even Marie Langora from the NBC national office was there, making it a newsworthy item for the country. Victor Gattling had invited her personally, which made it all the more special for her, but she would have come anyway. The Gattling Building's creation had all the major trappings of a rags-to-riches story: Self-made millionaire, EPA clean-up, energy-efficiency, radical design, and the latest technology. Victor Gattling also had a certain influence with people, and if you were privileged to be invited to one of his events, you attended.

All cameras and eyes were focused on a ceremonial plot of dirt and the people standing behind it. They lined up in a row behind the plot: Marc, Peter, Gattling in the middle, Phillip, and Tim. The group was flanked by the mayor, the governor, and EPA Director

Kathryn Tate. All were dressed in business suits and wore yellow construction hats, which made them look a little silly. They held their shovels out in front of them, all pointing to the ceremonial rectangular patch of dirt that was prepared for the occasion.

Behind the group was an open land site, weeds shooting up from the ground in all directions. Behind the site was the downtown landscape, the early morning sun reflecting off the glass and steel, making it difficult to look at. The buildings in the distance provided a stark contrast to the desolation surrounding the area where everyone was gathered. The site was an old steel mill operation, left abandoned years earlier. If you were familiar with the site, you could almost see the last of the structures looming like dinosaur ghosts. Gattling had championed the effort, working with the EPA and state and local governments to clean up the site to allow for future development. It took five years and four million dollars from Gattling's own coffers, but the site was finally cleared for development, and now there was nothing to stop Gattling from realizing his dream.

The camera crew focused in on the shovel-bearing group then panned out to include the wasteland and the downtown area in the distance. The evening broadcast would go further by superimposing a rendering of the Gattling Building on the image, then speculating about the development that might ensue as a result. The project had "environmentally friendly" and "economic growth" stamped all over it, and the news reporters were eating it up.

The cameras zoomed in on Victor Gattling as he stepped up to a microphone to address the crowd. The crowd grew silent.

"Ladies and gentlemen, it is my honor to be here today for the groundbreaking of what will be a prominent architectural addition to our fine city: The Gattling Building." There was applause and a roar from the crowd with an enthusiasm that made Peter wonder if they were being paid to cheer. "I would like to thank Mayor Stevens and his staff, EPA Director Kathryn Tate and her team, and Governor Malcom for their undying commitment to this project and to the future of our city. Today not only marks the beginning of a new wave of economic growth and development for the city but also the start of a program for how our city will lead the country as we embrace a future of environmentally friendly and energy-efficient construction." More applause followed.

Gattling took a step back and turned to look at his fellow diggers. He paused for just a moment then stepped back up to the microphone. "Ladies and gentlemen, I would like to make one more introduction, if I could. I've had the fortunate opportunity to work with one of the finest architectural firms in the world, Jackson, Parker & Finch, and they were wise enough to assign this project to one of the leading talents in the industry." Phillip stood tall. Tim adjusted his suit jacket, assuring himself that it was buttoned, and inched forward. "Ladies and gentlemen, the person responsible for helping me to realize my dream is none other than Peter O'Hara." There was another round of applause as Phillip smiled and Tim caught himself, standing as still as possible.

Marc leaned over and whispered into Peter's ear, "Nice, teacher's pet."

Peter was more surprised than anyone, and he simply smiled and acknowledged the crowd with a gentle wave.

Gattling stepped back in line and led the group. With one synchronized motion, they pushed their shovels into the dirt, stepped on the blades, and turned them over. The crowd responded with another round of applause and more cheering.

The event aired on every local station at six and ten and made the national news at nine. Gattling and the firm had made the most of their PR expenditure, and Peter was an unplanned beneficiary. The project was a win-win for everyone involved, with plenty of financial, political, and public relations benefits to go around.

* * *

The last bus was pulling away as Peter made his way to the car. He was hoping to get back to the office before the rush, but Tim stopped him just as the ceremony concluded. It seemed that Tim wanted to make sure Peter understood who the *real* team leader was, and it became perfectly clear in just a few short seconds that Tim wasn't at all thrilled that Gattling had mentioned Peter specifically in his remarks. Peter didn't think it was a big deal, but the last thing he needed right now was for his boss to feel threatened. That would likely result in some negative implication further down the road. Peter knew Tim, and he knew that nothing good could come from Gattling's transgression, no matter how good it might make Peter feel.

Peter reached for the car door, but someone stopped him again.

"Peter!"

"Yeah," he said irritably, without looking to see who it was. He swung his head around and checked his tone. "Mr. Gattling, hello. What can I do for you?"

"Peter, I wanted to catch you before you left." He stood before Peter like a gilded statue of a country's great leader.

"Sure. Listen, Mr. Gattling, I'm sorry if I sounded short just then. I'm just trying to get back for a meeting with the team."

"I didn't notice."

"Mr. Gattling—"

"Please, call me Victor."

"Victor, thank you for your kind words earlier. I really appreciate it."

"That's what I want to talk to you about. I didn't think you would mind, but it was a last-minute decision on my part. For these types of events we work from a script, and my comment on the fly likely caught some people off guard."

"Yeah."

"How is Tim?"

"It seems he's not too pleased. He has a big ego."

"Don't worry about Tim. He'll be fine as long as I keep paying the bills. And I'll make it up to him."

Peter still didn't think it all was such a big deal.

"Peter, I like you. The work you've done on my building has been phenomenal. The design, the engineering—it's all perfect. I think you're the only person at the firm who really understands exactly what I want."

"Well, thank you, I'm glad to be part of the team."

"Peter, you've got great potential. I see in you a lot of myself when I was your age."

Peter wasn't used to all the flattery, and he couldn't think of anything to say in response.

"Complete this project for me as your firm has proposed, and you'll have the world in the palm of your hand."

Peter must have given Gattling a skeptical glance.

"Believe it," Gattling said.

"Oh, I do, and I will."

"And failure is not an option Peter. I need you to do whatever you have to in order to keep this project on schedule."

And there it was: the statement, the expectation, the demand.

"Mr. Gattling—"

"Victor."

"Victor, you have nothing to worry about. I'll make sure we meet all of your expectations—on schedule and within budget. Your building is going to be the envy of the world." The words he spoke were from some deeply ingrained and subconscious playbook, and for just a second Peter questioned whether he believed them.

Gattling smiled. "I know."

"I'll talk to you soon," Peter said.

"Peter? One other thing: how's your father?"

Peter wasn't sure how much to share or if he could spin it positively enough. "He's doing well, thanks for asking."

"He's living with you?"

Peter wondered how Gattling could possibly know that. "Yes, he is."

"That's good to hear. It's not too much for you, for your family?"

"It's been an adjustment for everyone, but it's been good having him around." He forced a smile. He could tell that Gattling knew more that he was letting on.

"Good. Take care of him."

"I will."

"Remember, when he's gone, you can't help him." He turned and walked away toward the black Lincoln Town Car that had just pulled up. Before getting into the back seat, he turned back and waved.

Peter waved back and watched the car pull away. He tried to

picture Gattling behind the car's darkened windows as the car disappeared into a cloud of dust.

* * *

Peter went to the Gattling building site weeks later to check on the progress of the excavation. The site looked substantially different than it had the day of the groundbreaking. The people and cardboard figures had been replaced by bulldozers and dump trucks in all directions. The once flat and weedy site was now a deep hole surrounded by mounds of dirt. It seemed like a perfect place for an Apollo lander. As Peter surveyed the site, he wished he still had the motocross bike he had bought from his friend, Jeff, when he was fifteen. He could have had some fun with it at the site.

Marc stood next to Peter as they both watched the activity. They were grateful to be out at the site and not stuck in the office. It's every young boy's dream, to be able to play in the dirt. Marc said, "You're putting in quite an effort on this project." It was like he was talking to himself. "It has *got* to be impacting your family life."

Peter watched a bulldozer descend into the crater and tried to ignore Marc, but unfortunately the last words sunk in and he became annoyed.

Marc said, "Me, I can put in a full day, then have the rest of the evening to myself. It's nice, not being tied down." He pondered his revelation. "I think I'll keep it that way for a while."

"That shouldn't be a problem," Peter said and smiled.

"What do you mean by *that*?"

"What?" Peter played dumb.

Marc looked hurt. "What did you *mean* by that?"

Peter said, "Nothing. Relax. Listen, I asked you to follow up with the surveyor regarding the east elevation. What did you find out?" He wanted to change the subject.

"So, now you're glad that I'm part of the team, available to help out?"

Peter didn't have time for Marc's nonsense. "What did you find out?" Each word escalated in volume, and the last one echoed.

Startled, Marc said, "Hey, take it easy."

"I'm not in the mood to deal with your incompetence today, Marc. Either you resolve that issue by the end of the day, or I'll get somebody on it who will." Peter turned and walked away to the parking area, leaving Marc alone and pouting. Halfway there, his phone rang. He wondered if he could go back and accidentally drop his phone into the crater. He looked at the caller-ID and answered the call immediately. His frustration with Marc lingered.

"Hi, honey," he said.

"Peter, there's been a fire at the house!" Melanie was frantic.

Peter said, "What? What happened? Is everyone all right?"

"Yes. Everyone is fine. We couldn't find Murphy for the longest time, but the firefighters found him hiding under Jake's bed."

"And Jake and Pop?"

"We're all standing by the street in front of the house. The fire is out, but there's smoke everywhere. There's been quite a lot of damage."

"How did it start?"

There was silence at the other end of the line.

"Mel? Are you there?"

"Yeah, I'm here." There was a calmness now in her voice.

Peter asked again, "How did it start?"

There were a few more seconds of silence then Melanie said,

"Peter, your father started it."

"What?" He couldn't believe what he heard. "What do you mean, Pop started it?"

She said, "I don't know. The firefighters were asking questions, talking to Jack, and he told them he started it. Right now, I don't know what to believe. Peter, the kitchen is destroyed. We could have lost the whole house."

"Listen, I'm at the Gattling site. I'll leave right now. I'll be there in twenty minutes."

"Peter?"

"Yeah?"

Melanie lowered her voice. "We have to do something, about . . ."

Peter didn't need her to finish the sentence. "I know." He hung up the phone, put it in his pocket, and continued on to the parking lot, the activity of the building site a distant memory.

Marc yelled at him from a distance. "Hey! Peter! Where are you going? Are you coming back?" He paused then said, "Sorry, I didn't mean it!"

Peter didn't hear a word as he got into his car and sped away, tires spitting rocks and leaving a trail of thick dust in his wake.

Marc pulled out his phone, dialed a number, and watched cunningly as Peter drove away. "Hello, Uncle Phillip?"

* * *

Peter made it from the Gattling site to his house in eighteen minutes flat and was lucky he wasn't pulled over. As he made his way down the street and approached his house, he was greeted with fire trucks, flashing lights, and commotion. There were three trucks parked in front of the house, and an ambulance was in the driveway. The area around his house was blocked off with yellow tape, and most of the neighborhood was out in the street and on the neighboring lawns. They watched, gossiped, and stretched limited facts into fabulous stories. He evaded the crowds by parking down the street, then he got out of his car and ran a block to the house.

Melanie was in the street, talking with a group of neighbors but alone in her own thoughts. One of the neighbors, Maggie Dresden from next door, was commenting on how lucky they were that they got out alive while at the same time remarking about how cute one of the firemen was. Melanie was gazing down the driveway and tuning out the comments. She saw Peter approaching and ran to him. They embraced and held each other tightly.

"Mel, are you okay?" he said.

"I'm fine. I was just scared."

Peter looked at the house. It wasn't the house he remembered. "How's Jake?"

"He's fine too. I sent him over to the Petersens' to play with Patrick. They invited him to stay for dinner, so he'll be there for a while. The Dugans said they would take care of Murphy for the night."

"And Pop?"

"He's in the garage," she said.

Peter turned and looked down the driveway. Between the firemen, equipment, and hoses strewn around, he saw Jack sitting in the garage.

Melanie tugged on him. "We need to do something, Peter. He needs help."

"Yeah, I know," he said, distracted by the garage.

She could tell his mind was elsewhere. "Peter?"

"What? I know!" He looked at her, realized he had raised his voice and had startled her. He thought of Marc. "I'm sorry. It's just . . ."

"He could have killed us today!"

The tables turned, now Peter was startled. "Let's not overreact."

"Overreact? He almost burned the house down!"

He let go of her and walked down the driveway.

"Peter!" she shouted.

Without turning around, he said in a loud voice, "I'll take care of it," and he continued down the driveway toward the garage.

Jack was sitting by himself in the garage, a third of the way in, slouched on a rickety wooden chair like a discarded rag doll. The shadows were heavy, and Peter saw him come into full view as he crossed the threshold. Jack was silent, still, and sagging, staring down at his hands which were folded in his lap. He did not notice Peter approaching.

Peter said, "Pop?" Jack didn't react. He walked closer and put a hand on Jack's shoulder. "Pop? Are you okay?"

It took a moment, but Jack processed the words and recognized Peter's voice. He looked up slowly. His eyes were glassy and confused, and he looked like he was ready to be scolded. He averted his gaze and looked back down to his lap. In a childlike whisper he said, "I'm sorry."

"What happened?"

Jack could not look back up. To his lap he said, "I don't know. I, I, I can't remember."

Peter raised his voice and said, "You *have* to remember. I want to know what the hell happened."

Jack flinched and retreated within himself.

"You almost burned down my house! What the hell happened? Say something. Anything. Pop, I want to know!"

Already slouched and somber, Jack collapsed further and began to sob slowly. His crying grew more intense as the seconds passed.

The sound of the weeping made Peter sick to his stomach. Oddly, Peter thought about Marc again. He stood there, not sure what to do and unable to console his father. Melanie walked up from behind and stood beside him. She saw and heard Jack sobbing and turned from angry to compassionate to concerned, her motherly instincts taking over. She looked at Peter, who mirrored her concern in his own expression. He shook his head, unsure what to do.

The sobbing subsided, and Jack looked up at Peter. Then he looked to Melanie. His expression changed from sadness and despair to contempt and rage in an instant. Pointing toward Melanie he said, "She's the one! She's the one who started the fire. It *had* to be her."

Peter and Melanie were surprised beyond words.

"Stop it," Peter said.

"Who else could it have been? Jake wouldn't do something like that." He was continuing to point at Melanie, jabbing at the air. "It had to be her. It had to be!"

"I said stop it!" A vein in Peter's forehead pulsed. His neck stiffened.

The contempt and rage disappeared as quickly as it had arrived, and a blank stare crossed Jack's face. Then his expression changed again to that of a man in despair. He looked back down to his lap, quiet and sullen.

Peter had nothing more to say. What could he say? He turned

to Melanie, who was speechless as well. He put his arm around her and led her out of the garage. "Let's go take a look inside."

With the interrogation over, they walked away, leaving Jack to himself and the shadows.

* * *

As Peter and Melanie approached the rear entrance of the house, they noticed that the screen door had been removed. It now rested against the large oak tree that loomed in the middle of their yard. The smell of smoke lingered in the air, pungent and sharp. Charred kitchen cabinets lay on the lawn, dismantled and doused as if part of a strange bonfire that had recently been extinguished. They walked past the debris, up the stairs, and into the rear foyer.

As they stepped into the kitchen, they braced themselves. They looked around, inspected the damage, and felt overcome with anguish. Half the cabinets had been ripped from the wall surrounding the stove; the stove itself looked like it had been incinerated, a block of charred steel. Where the cabinets once hung was now a blackened wall with the studs exposed. The walls and ceiling above the stove were charred, and white foam from the fire extinguishers was everywhere. The air was heavy. It stung Peter's eyes and made Melanie choke.

The fire captain came through the doorway from the dining room to find them both standing there, looking in astonishment at what once had been their kitchen. "Mr. and Mrs. O'Hara?"

Peter and Melanie unfroze and in unison said, "Yes?"

"I think we're all done here."

Done indeed, Peter thought.

"Mrs. O'Hara, it was a good thing you had those fire

extinguishers available. If not, you could have lost the whole house. We've checked all the walls in this section of the home, both on this level and upstairs, and we're confident that you caught the fire before it had a chance to spread beyond this room.

Peter and Melanie were somewhat relieved.

The fire captain said, "It could have been worse. A lot worse."

They both nodded but had difficulty letting go of what *had* happened.

"Thank you so much, for everything," Melanie said.

"Do you know how it started?" Peter asked.

"Our best guess is that it was a grease fire on the stove. We noticed the curtain rod and the path the flames took, and it seems like the curtains on the window next to the stove caught fire." He reached into his jacket pocket, and a curious expression replaced the very serious one. "And we found *this* down in the gap between the stove and the base cabinet." He held in the palm of his hand an indiscernible brown object that resembled cooled molten lava.

"What is that?" Peter asked.

"It looks like the remains of a brown plastic ashtray, melted, of course."

"An ashtray?"

"Does anyone in the house smoke?" the fire captain asked.

"No," Melanie said quickly. "I keep an ashtray in the cabinet above the stove, for guests. It's been in there for years."

The fire captain didn't say anything. He handed the melted mass to Melanie. "Grease fires, they happen quite often, unfortunately. Again, lucky you had the fire extinguishers." He nodded and turned to leave. After a step, he turned back around. "How's the old man?"

Peter and Melanie paused, unsure of what to say. Finally, Peter said, “I think he’ll be all right.”

“Your father?”

“Yeah.”

“Keep an eye on him,” the fire captain said, and he turned and left the room.

Peter put his arm around Melanie. They looked around, and while they knew they needed to start cleaning up, they were unsure where to start. More significantly, they couldn’t get past the *how* and the *why* and the *now what?*

* * *

Later that evening while on his way to bed, Jake stopped at the closed door of his grandfather’s room. He had sensed that something wasn’t right with his grandfather even before the fire, but he couldn’t put his finger on what it was. Now there was no question in his mind. His Grandpa was in trouble, and he was afraid for him. Jake knocked on the door with trepidation and waited but heard nothing. He cautiously opened the door, and he stuck his head into the dark room.

“Grandpa?” Jake searched the darkened room and still heard nothing. “Grandpa, are you in here?” He opened the door wider. Enough light from the hallway crept into the room to allow him to see Jack sitting in his chair by the window. He reached for the switch and turned on the light.

“Who’s there?” Jack shouted.

Jake leaned back into the door frame. “Grandpa, it’s me, Jake.” He didn’t move. Neither did Jack.

Confused, Jack said, “Jake? Jake, is that you?”

“I just wanted to say good night.”

Jack remained in his chair, hushed and unmoving. Jake left

the comfort of the door frame and walked closer. It looked to him like his grandfather was frozen solid, as he stared blankly at the opposite wall. With caution, Jake said, “Grandpa?”

Jack thawed some. Stern and with authority, he said, “Who’s there? What do you want?”

“Grandpa, look. It’s me, Jake.” He could tell that Jack had heard him and was thinking about it, processing it.

“I don’t know any Jake.”

“C’mon, Grandpa, stop kidding.”

“Grandpa, I’ll give you Grandpa. Are you that punk kid from next door? Are you the one that took my watch? Get out of here, you little son of a bitch. Get out of here before I call the cops!”

Jake’s shoes turned to cement. His bottom lip quivered as he tried to remain brave. “But . . .”

Jack yelled, “Thief! Get out of here before I give you a good one upside your head!”

Confused and scared, Jake turned and ran from the room, leaving the door wide open. He turned a hard left and bolted down the hallway, ran into his room, and slammed the door behind him.

Jack’s room became quiet once again as he calmed and gradually adjusted his gaze from the blank wall to the darkened view of the coming night beyond the glass of the window. He refroze, thoughtful and yet lost.

* * *

Ten minutes later Melanie came up the stairs to tuck Jake in for the night. The door to Jack’s room was open, and she walked by without giving it a second thought. She didn’t want to face him again for the rest of the day. She continued on to Jake’s room where the door was closed, which she thought was unusual.

Inside the room Jake was on his bed, face down and crying. He didn't notice the approaching footsteps and was startled at the knock on the door. He moved quickly and got underneath the covers. "Come in," he said, the words muffled some from talking through the blankets.

Melanie opened the door and walked in. The nightstand lamp was on, and she saw Jake in bed, an elongated lump under the covers, facing away from her. "Hi, honey. I just came to tuck you in." She walked over to the bed and adjusted the blankets. As she did, Jake rolled over to look at her, his wet eyes red and swollen.

She sat down on the bed. "Jake, honey, what's the matter?"

"It's Grandpa."

"What about him?"

He took a deep breath. "I went into his room to say good night. He didn't know who I was." He took three breaths in rapid succession, emotion kicking in. "He started yelling at me, calling me a thief and saying he was going to call the cops. He wasn't making any sense. I got real scared and ran out." He ground a fist into one of his eyes and sniffed hard.

Melanie leaned forward, put her arms around him, and hugged him. "Oh, honey."

"Is Grandpa going to be all right?" he asked.

She thought for a moment. "I don't know, Jake. I don't know."

"He's family, and family's all we got," he said.

"Yeah, I know."

They held each other tightly, each looking off into the distance and wondering.

"I'll say a prayer for him," he said. "Will you say one too?"

"I will Jake. I will."

* * *

It took a good twenty minutes, but Melanie was able to calm Jake down. He eventually fell asleep in her arms. She smiled faintly as she looked at his restful, angelic face and remembered what it was like way back when he didn't have a worry in the world. She laid his head down on the pillow and pulled the covers up snugly under his chin. She eased herself off the bed so as not to wake him. She tip-toed to the doorway and flicked off the nightstand light. She could see his face in the hallway light, and he did indeed look like an angel. Melanie wished for happiness but had a tough time summoning it. All she felt was a growing concern.

She went back downstairs and into the kitchen to find Peter at the table, looking out into the backyard. He was noticeably distracted and distraught. She walked into the room, pulled up a chair, and sat next to him. She said nothing. She simply stared at him.

He wouldn't look at her. "I know. You don't have to say anything," he said. "I'll talk to his doctor. We probably just need his medication adjusted." She didn't say anything and he turned to look at her for some form of acknowledgment, consolation, or comfort. He really didn't expect any and wasn't surprised when none came.

The room was silent except for the vibrating hum of the refrigerator.

Melanie huffed and gave Peter a *look* of surprise, maybe even bewilderment.

"What?" he said.

"Do you realize what happened today?"

Peter turned away and gazed out the window again.

She couldn't imagine what he might possibly be looking at.

"Peter?"

"I realize," he said.

"Peter, this is not just an issue about his medication. He needs help, the kind of help we can't give him."

"What are you suggesting?" he asked.

"Peter, he started a fire in the house today. He could have killed himself. He could have killed *us*."

Peter thought about Jack's confession, about the garage scene, the fire captain, the melted ashtray.

"Peter, you can see he's not well. Can't you?"

"So you're a doctor now?" As soon as the words escaped his lips he realized he shouldn't have said them. Melanie paused and stopped herself from saying something she would regret. He turned to her. "I didn't mean that."

She leaned in toward him, her arms resting on the table. "Jake went to say good night to him earlier. Jack didn't recognize him. He called your son a thief and said he was going to call the police. He scared Jake to death. He's upstairs crying himself to sleep right now." She stretched the truth but felt it necessary to make her point.

He turned away but knew he couldn't turn away, not from her or from Jake.

"Peter?"

"What do you want me to say?"

"Say you're going to do something, anything."

He was stuck. No answer came to him.

Melanie said, "I'm not going to live in this house being scared all the time."

That got his attention. "What are you saying?"

She was insistent and firm. "Peter, find a place for your father where he can get the help he needs. If not, Jake and I are leaving."

"You're not serious."

"I am. Find somewhere for him to go, *tomorrow*, or Jake and I are leaving."

Peter couldn't believe she had just dropped that kind of ultimatum on him. His chest tightened as the blood shot to his head, and a feeling of rage that he had not known for some time grew quickly within him. He turned and looked at her with contempt for just a second then turned away one final time.

"That's it? I have to choose?" he grunted.

"Tomorrow, Peter."

The discussion was over. She rose from her chair, stepped away from the table, and left the room.

* * *

Peter sat alone at the table for a long while, staring out the window. He sat motionless, as still and quiet as the night. He breathed with purpose and concentrated, all of his effort focused on trying to put out the fire in his chest. His left eye twitched. He felt trapped, lost in his own world that no one could possibly understand. For most of his life, he was a master of the game of control, but now the rules were suddenly changing right before his eyes. He knew he didn't like how the new game was to be played.

He tried in desperation, time and again, to lose himself in some other thought, but nothing came. His only option at the moment was to retreat into himself and leave his problems behind. He gazed at the shadows lurking beyond the single pane of glass that protected him from the outside world. It felt to him as though his eardrums had turned to stone, and silence engulfed him. All he felt was a pulsing heartbeat in his temples. His mind was filled with a thick and overwhelming fog.

He was startled when a branch from the nearby pear tree slammed against the kitchen window. The wind howled outside, and it whistled through an invisible crack somewhere. Peter sat upright, tensed, and immediately noticed how damp and cold his shirt was. He felt his forehead and wiped the perspiration that had collected on his brow. He looked at his watch, and his heart rate quickened. It was three o'clock in the morning.

9

That morning, Peter awoke at six, groggy and unrested. He felt like he did on those infrequent mornings when he woke up on the couch with the television still on, his mind having been badgered and subconsciously manipulated by an endless stream of infomercials and late-night westerns. His mind was racing, but his thoughts seemed clearer than they had been the night before. He passed on taking a shower and dressed in a hurry, his body moving on autopilot as he picked out a suit, shirt, and tie to wear. He stopped at the kitchen on the way to his office and didn't notice that half of the room was missing. On the counter, in the half that still resembled a kitchen, was the coffeemaker, and there he found coffee still in the carafe from the day before. He poured a cup and sipped it cold. It tasted like wet smoke. But, somehow, it was sufficient, and he continued on to his office, which was just down the short hallway on the other side of the house.

The darkness of night still lurked, and only the walls were listening.

Once in his office, he sat behind his desk and turned on the lamp. He took another sip of coffee and almost choked. The taste made him twist up his face, and he wondered why the hell he was drinking the sludge. He set the cup down at the far end of the desk so that it was sufficiently out of sight and picked up the phone. He dialed a number and stood, looking out into the backyard as he waited for an answer.

"Hello, Dr. Halper. It's Peter O'Hara. I'm sorry to be calling so early, but I'm very concerned about my father."

"What's going on?"

"It's not good. Doctor, my father started a fire at our home yesterday."

"My God, is everyone all right?

"Yes, yes, everyone's fine, everyone except my father."

Jack stood just outside Peter's office door, a fly on the wall. He had woken earlier when he heard Peter rustling around in the bathroom and had heard the footsteps as Peter passed his doorway and walked down the stairs. At the time, Jack looked at the alarm clock on his nightstand and thought it was a bit early for Peter to be up. It made him wonder. He had grabbed his robe, put on his slippers, and sauntered downstairs, unbeknownst to anyone. Now, with his back up against the wall and out of sight, he listened to Peter's phone conversation.

Peter said, "I thought we could make it work here, I really did, but things are just getting worse, out of control. *He's* been getting worse. It seems his memory is slipping, and he's confused more often. Sometimes he doesn't even know who we are."

Dr. Halper tried to be calm and reassuring. "He may just need time. He's been through a lot, and his new living arrangements are quite a drastic change from anything he's dealt with recently."

"It's not that," Peter said, losing his patience.

"Otherwise, I can see him more frequently if you'd like."

It sounded to Peter like Dr. Halper would just as soon not have to deal with the situation. He said, "I think we need to do more than that; a lot more. You need to help me. This is a *medical condition* again, and you need to take him back at Shady Acres."

"Peter, I'm not sure I can do that."

"You have to," Peter demanded. "It's gotten to the point where my wife and son are scared to live in the house with him." He wasn't sure that he really believed that, but it was necessary that Dr. Halper believed it. "Either my father goes, or they're going to leave, and that's not an option. I don't like it, but there's really no other choice. You have to take him back."

"Peter, I'd like to see him right away. Bring him to my office at Shady Acres. I'll evaluate his condition and we'll discuss where we go from there. Can you be at my office at one o'clock this afternoon?"

Peter had no calendar to consult, but it didn't matter because nothing was of a higher priority. "One o'clock will be fine. We'll see you then." He hung up the phone and sat back down behind his desk, wondering how he was going to get Jack back to Shady Acres.

Jack understood what Peter wanted to do with him. His face showed a progression of expressions as his emotions took hold: sadness, then despair, then fear. A thought came to him, and he straightened. His expression turned stolid. Careful not to be noticed, his slippered feet shuffled quietly, and he hurried away, determined.

* * *

After speaking with Dr. Halper and checking his messages, Peter had a distinctly different perspective, a brighter outlook. His burden seemed to have lifted some. He realized that he looked and felt terrible, and though his feelings were improving, he knew the only way to get back on track was to head upstairs and start over. He went up to his room, undressed, and took a long, hot shower that melted away the headache that was forming behind his eyes. Sometimes he did his best thinking in the shower, and today he had a lot to think about. As the hot water hit the back of his neck like the tiniest massaging fingers, he lost track of time and, without realizing it, fixed his gaze on a single shower tile while his mind worked things through. Afterward, he toweled off and walked into the bedroom. He looked at the clothes he had picked earlier, now strewn across the bed in the order in which he had taken them off. He looked quizzically at his suit-tie pairing in particular and shook his head, not knowing where it came from. He picked up the clothes, went into the walk-in closet to drop them into a hamper, and started over.

He had a quick breakfast of cereal and fresh coffee, cream and sugar included this time, while he read the morning newspaper. Again, he really didn't notice that his kitchen was no longer a kitchen, nor did he notice the pungent smell of smoke that still hung in the air. At the time, it didn't seem to matter. His usual departure time came and went, and he decided to hang around to have breakfast with his family. He wanted to see Jake off to school, as he couldn't remember the last time he had been home to do it.

Melanie and Jake joined him a little after seven and were surprised to see he was still home. Melanie kept to herself as she opened all of the windows in the kitchen as well as the sliding door to the back deck in the hopes of replacing the burnt air that lingered.

They moved to the dining room, and the conversation over breakfast was spirited, as Peter wanted to know all about Jake's time spent at the Petersens'. Jake was more than happy to oblige and provided all the details of their fancy spaghetti and meatballs dinner and the popcorn and soda they had during their post-dinner movie. Peter was glad to see that the frightening episode of the previous day had had no noticeable impact on him. Jake was bright eyed and happy and appeared to be looking forward to going to school.

Right now, that was all Peter could hope for.

After breakfast, Jake finished getting ready for school, and, as Peter was finishing his third cup of coffee, Jake came back into the kitchen to say good-bye. Melanie had already run out to the garage to start the car.

"Bye, Dad," Jake said.

Peter looked up from the newspaper. "Oh, good-bye. You have a great day, and I'll see you back here for dinner."

"It's a deal," Jake said, smiling. He walked over to Peter, put his arms around him, and gave him a big hug.

Peter swiveled on his seat to get a better hold. "I love you, buddy."

"I love you too, Dad." Jake held on and pulled his head back so he could look directly at his father. He stared.

"What?" Peter asked.

Jake smiled. "Kiss?"

Peter smiled, kissed him, and pulled him close to hug him tightly once more.

"Okay, Dad, I got to go."

Peter released his grip, and Jake bolted.

"See you for dinner," Jake said as he opened the door.

As the door was closing, Peter yelled, "Fill up that head!"

Jake heard that a lot, and it always made him chuckle. He bounced down the stairs and jumped into the car.

The house was silent again. Peter looked around at what

had been his kitchen and didn't seem to be bothered by the forthcoming inconveniences. He was grateful that the fire had only caused some physical damage to things that were replaceable. He would have to make some calls to get the remodeling process started, but those calls would have to wait. He looked up toward the ceiling and listened for any sign of life, wondering if his father was up yet. He knew that Jack was sometimes a late sleeper, but not always. It all depended on the day. Peter guessed he would be sleeping late, given the circumstances.

* * *

Peter walked into the front hall with his briefcase in one hand and his suit jacket in the other. He stopped at the round antique mirror that hung beside the coat tree and set down his briefcase. He put on his jacket and looked over his appearance. He adjusted the knot in his tie and smoothed his hands down the lapels of his jacket, and after doing so, realized he had made a good decision with the clothes. He was back in control. He picked up his briefcase and went for the front door.

Peter stopped and turned back, looking up toward the second-floor landing. "Hey, Pop! Are you up?"

Not a creature was stirring.

He shouted louder, "'Hey! Pop!" He heard footsteps, waited, and saw Jack appear at the second-floor railing.

"What's all the ruckus about?" Jack said. He was dressed and ready for the day and seemed inconvenienced.

Peter was surprised to see him dressed and sporting his usual tough-guy exterior. "Oh, there you are. Listen, I need to run to the office for a couple of hours. Melanie took Jake to school and should be back any minute. What do you say you and I have lunch today?"

"Sure," Jack said indifferently.

"You'll be all right by yourself until Melanie gets back?"

Jack smiled. In a reassuring tone he said, "Go on and get outta here. Don't worry; I won't burn the house down. I promise. When she gets back, I'll help her straighten up."

Peter assessed the situation and felt as comfortable as he could, considering. "Okay."

Jack said, "Actually, I'll have lunch with you on one condition."

"And what's that?"

"That we talk about how I'm going to pay to have the kitchen remodeled."

"Pop, that's not necessary."

"Otherwise, you can have lunch by yourself."

Peter chewed his bottom lip. "All right, we'll talk about it. I'll be home at eleven-thirty. We'll go into town to that restaurant you like, McNally's."

"Wow, big spender." Jack was trying to give Peter a bit of a hard time. McNally's really was his favorite restaurant.

"All right, I've got to go. I've got an important meeting with Tim at the office." Peter turned, opened the front door, and walked out, closing the door behind him.

Jack yelled to Peter through the closed door. "Give 'em hell!"

With his hand still on the doorknob, Peter thought about that for a moment then walked down the front steps, got into his car, and drove away. *Yeah, give 'em hell*, he thought.

* * *

Back in the house, Jack stood at the railing, both hands gripping it tightly as he watched Peter pull out of the driveway and disappear down the street. He went to his room and returned a moment later carrying an old leather suitcase. He walked down the stairs carefully. This was no time to fall and break a hip. When he got to the coat tree, Jack grabbed his jacket and hat and set the suitcase down to put them on. Then, he picked up the suitcase, opened the door, and stepped out onto the front stoop. He closed the door behind him, pulling it firmly and twisting the knob a few times to make sure it was locked. He stood there for a moment, scared, as he looked out at the quiet and desolate street. If you happened to be walking by and saw him, you would think he was lost. You would want to walk up and ask him if he needed help. But there was no one around and no one there to help. He looked left, then right, and somehow it all made sense to him. He straightened with a look of confidence and determination and started down the front steps. Jack continued down the walkway. At the sidewalk, he turned left and walked down the street, a man on a mission.

* * *

Peter stepped into the doorway of Tim's office and waited for Tim to notice him.

Tim sat at his desk, talking on the phone, listening without much interest. He looked like he often did: much too serious and mad at the world.

Peter often wondered how a man could be so successful yet so miserable at the same time. He had vowed early in his career that he would take a different path. It seemed to Peter that Tim was stuck in a rut he could not get out of. Without knowing it, Peter was stuck too.

When Tim didn't notice him, Peter cleared his throat. Tim

looked up and motioned for Peter to come in and sit down. Peter felt like he was interrupting. Tim always made him feel that way. He walked over and sat down opposite Tim, then shifted his weight in the chair, frustrated in his quest to get comfortable. Peter could never get used to those damn chairs.

"That sounds good. Have it to me by end of business, today. Thanks." Tim hung up the phone and busied himself with some unnecessary paper shuffling, then stopped, as if he'd had a brain freeze. He folded his hands in front of him as he leaned forward on the desk, peering at Peter. "So, Peter, how are you?"

The question wasn't genuine. Peter looked around, curious. "Where is everyone?"

Tim leaned forward further, his elbows on the desk. He had a peculiar look in his eyes and, given his expression, Peter was glad they had the desk between them.

Is he trying to be sensitive? Peter wondered.

Tim said, "It's just you and me today. I hope you don't mind. I thought it was time for a talk."

"O-kay." Peter was more curious now.

"That really was a nice introduction you received at the groundbreaking."

Peter felt it was a loaded comment. "It was, and quite unexpected."

Tim stared at Peter. Peter stared back.

"Listen, Peter, I know you've been working your ass off the last few weeks to keep the Gattling Project on schedule, and I appreciate that, I do." He paused and looked down at his desk.

The seconds lingered too long, and Peter wasn't sure if Tim would continue or where he might be going with the discussion. "But?" Peter said. There was always a "but" with Tim.

"It's just that I also know that you've been distracted." He stared straight at Peter and pressed for a reaction.

"Tim, the project is on schedule, and Gattling is happy. Everything's fine. And you know that I'll do whatever I have to in order to keep it that way." Peter tried to lean back in his chair, hoping to extend the distance between them, but the hard chair back resisted.

Tim thought for a moment and pursed his lips. It was a standard expression, and Peter could tell he was uneasy.

"What is it?" Peter said.

"Peter, there's no easy way for me to say this."

"That doesn't sound good," Peter joked. "Nothing positive ever came from a start like that." He was trying desperately to lighten the mood, and he waved Tim off and smiled as he said it.

It didn't work. Tim was a statue, intent on saying what he needed to say. "I came out of a meeting late yesterday with Phillip. Let's just say *he's* uncomfortable."

"Really. And why would that be? Gattling is happy." Peter edged forward in his seat.

"This isn't about Gattling. Unfortunately, Phillip listens to Marc, God knows why. And Marc seems to think that your personal matters are jeopardizing your responsibilities to the firm, that you're jeopardizing the project."

Peter said, "Are those his words or yours?"

Tim was insulted. "Peter, c'mon."

"And where are you on all of this, Tim? After everything I've done for you and this firm, you couldn't back me up?"

"I did."

"It sounds like it."

Tim shook his head. "I told Phillip I would talk with you. I assured him that you would keep your personal matters personal and would increase your effort on the project."

An involuntary burst of air escaped from Peter's lungs and shot out of his throat in a show of exasperation. "Increase my effort? Are you kidding me?"

"I'm sorry. That's how it needs to be. Otherwise, Marc becomes our new partner." He looked around his desk for a distraction.

"So that's it—an ultimatum?" Peter's face flushed. He clenched his jaw tightly and held the words back. Oh, how he wished he had the nerve to say what was on his mind. His jaw muscle pulsed and twitched, and he could hear his teeth grinding.

"Peter, get some help. I can appreciate what you're doing for your father, but the job comes first."

Peter took in a deep breath through his nose, held it for a second, then let it out slowly. It helped only a little. "I hear you. Perfectly clear. I'll do what I need to." With surprising calm, he got up and walked out. He did not look back or say good-bye.

* * *

Peter was driving back home from his meeting with Tim, feeling better now that a little time had passed. He was looking forward to having lunch with his father. He needed the break, time to *not* think of work. Peter planned to talk with his father, then go visit with Dr. Halper. Somehow, a miracle solution would present itself and make all his challenges go away. Jack would go back to Shady Acres, Peter's home life would go back to normal, and he could get to work on managing the negative perception of his work and of his career. Peter was an eternal optimist, but he knew this was only wishful thinking.

Peter had grown to loathe his cell phone, no matter who was

calling, so his manners were short when he received the call.

* * *

Melanie ran into the kitchen, frantic. She skirted the island and headed for the counter next to the refrigerator. She picked up the phone, dialed a number, listening while her heart raced. He finally picked up on the third ring.

"Peter? It's me."

"Hey," Peter said.

"Peter, it's your father. He's gone."

"What?"

"Your father—he's gone."

"Gone? What are you talking about? I just saw him a couple of hours ago." There was an edge to his voice. He thought he detected an edge in hers.

"I came home from dropping off Jake, and I just assumed he was up in his room. I just went up to check on him, and he wasn't there."

"Well, he has to be around somewhere."

"Peter, I've looked everywhere. I don't know where he is."

"Maybe he took a walk down to the nursery to pick up some more flowers for the house." It was all Peter could think of, and the thought was plausible.

"Peter, his closet is cleaned out, and his suitcase is gone."

That's not good, Peter thought. "Listen, I'm on my way home, about fifteen minutes away. I'll see you soon."

"All right, bye." Melanie hung up the phone, chewed a fingernail, and worried.

He pocketed his phone and gradually pressed his foot down on the accelerator.

* * *

Peter wove his way through the highway crowd and took his normal exit. Back on two lanes, Peter eased up on the gas a bit as the obstacles were fewer and farther between. With a clear road ahead of him, he took out his phone and made a call.

"Dr. Halper, it's Peter. I can't believe I'm going to say this, but it seems my father has run away from home."

"Run away from home?" Dr. Halper said in disbelief.

"Yes, this morning. He packed his suitcase and left. There's no sign of him."

"But why?"

Peter *had* to find his father a new doctor. "I don't know why, and I don't know where he might have gone. Listen, I need your help. You've got to have some contacts or some pull with the local authorities. Call it in, and see if you can get the police out looking for him."

"I know Sergeant White," he said. "We worked together on a case not too long ago. You may remember reading about it in the newspaper about a year back. They had a young man in custody, apparently homeless and troubled, who they were trying to get some information from regarding a recent burglary. Sergeant White thought I could help with—"

"Doctor, please."

"Right. Sorry. I'll call him as soon as we hang up. I'll give him whatever he needs to get the process started right away."

Maybe the new doctor search could wait. "That would be great. I appreciate it. Thanks." Peter terminated the call and quickly dialed another. He got the messaging system. "Mel, it's me. I spoke with Dr. Halper. He's going to talk with the police to see if they can get out and start looking for him now. I'm going to drive around a while, see if I can find him. I'll keep you posted. Love you." He set the phone down on the center console. As he entered town, he slowed and began his search.

It would be a nearly futile search, but Peter didn't know it and didn't believe it. He couldn't believe it. If you were in a helicopter with a good aerial view of Peter's car driving into town, however, you would have a much different perspective. You would see his car moving down a crowded street, just a speck in a sprawling suburban town, arteries branching off in every direction, cars mixed with houses mixed with commercial and retail establishments. The O'Hara family lived in a small town, but it wasn't *that* small. From above it would be easy to see the scope and challenge of Peter's search.

* * *

Jack looked at his watch and tapped the face with his finger. He lifted it to his ear to see if it was still working. *Tick, tick, tick.* It was, but he still couldn't quite believe what the hands on the watch were telling him. It was eleven-thirty, and he had been walking for a just a little over two hours. That was his watch's opinion. He felt it was more like six, and the muscles in his thighs were throbbing.

He was in town, walking thoughtfully down the street and trying to manage his exertion. Jack was tired, that was for sure, and it was becoming quite obvious by the way he was shuffling his feet along the sidewalk. He came to a stop at an intersection and stood still and cautious. He listened, scanning the streets and stoplights, his head jerking back and forth in time with the passing traffic, and he found himself unsure of what to do next. Eventually the streets cleared, yet Jack's feet were stuck to the curb. The crossing light turned from red to green then to red again. He noticed the blinking WALK sign and looked down at his feet. Nothing. A man he did not know walked up beside him and stopped at the curb. He paid no attention to Jack and instead looked both ways, stepped off the curb, and hurried to cross the street. Jack watched the man, hesitated for just a second, then jumped forward and followed the man across the street. At the opposite curb the man turned left, and Jack watched him as his own feet kept him on a straight path. He continued walking down the next block, looking all around and searching for something he recognized.

10

It was later that afternoon when Jake came home from school and walked in the front door. It was just after four o'clock, and he was in good spirits as he hung his coat and kicked off his gym shoes. He'd had a pretty good day at school. Gym class had been cancelled, thereby eliminating the dread he typically felt at the prospect of changing in front of his friends in the boy's locker room. In the cafeteria they had served chicken pot pie—his favorite—, and he really enjoyed his reading class. They were reading and discussing the book *Dandelion Wine* by his favorite author, Ray Bradbury. He'd gotten an 'A' on his math test, and nobody had messed with him on the way home. All in all, it had been a pretty good day.

"I'm home," he shouted as he stood in the middle of the foyer, his backpack on with the weight making him stand up straight. He had both hands in the front pockets of his jeans, his balled-up fists locking them in there tight. There was no response. "Anybody home?" he tried again. He looked up and around and strained to listen. He heard nothing but a car passing by in the street. He shrugged, hung up his baseball cap, and walked through the doorway toward the kitchen. He marched in and, with all his strength, lobbed his backpack up and onto the island counter, relieving the massive weight. He slouched, stood up straight, and slouched again, working the sore muscles in his back.

His mother came in the back door, hurried and short of breath. “Oh, hi. Did you just get home?”

“Yeah.” He was rubbing his stomach and thinking about what he was going to do next.

She walked over and gave him a kiss on the forehead. She usually insisted he kiss her on the lips. *Otherwise, what’s the point?* she would say. She gave him a quick half-hug then turned to the counter behind her.

“Are you okay?” he asked.

“Yeah, I’m fine. I just had to run an errand, and I wanted to be sure to get home before you did.” She wasn’t going to tell him that she was out looking for his grandfather, who it appeared had run away from home. How could she possibly explain that to him? She hoped that maybe Peter would find him soon and have him back home without Jake being the wiser. She took a deep breath. “I left a snack for you in the refrigerator. Why don’t you take it up to your room and get started on your homework?”

Jake thought nothing more of it, and he went to the fridge and took out a small plate. He searched the shelves for a juice box and stuck one in his pocket. He closed the refrigerator and pulled his backpack down from the counter.

“You know where to find me,” he said as he left the room.

Melanie quietly watched him leave and listened as he took the stairs two at a time up to the second floor. Her bottom lip was raw from chewing it for the last few hours.

Jake walked into his bedroom. He threw his backpack on the bed and watched it bounce up and down on the mattress. Then he walked over to his desk, setting down the plate and turning on the desk lamp. Ripping the attached straw from the side of the juice box, he jammed it into the small foil hole. Jake would tell you that the juice box was one of the greatest inventions *ever,* and he thought about that as he sucked down half the contents and set it down next to the plate. He turned back toward the bed so he could unpack his backpack and noticed an envelope with his name on it lying up on the pillow. He picked it up, looked at it curiously, and pulled out a single sheet of paper, which he read.

Dear Jake,

We're pals, right? So I can tell you anything?

Sometimes things happen that I don't have any control over. It's hard to explain, but sometimes I say and do things that aren't right. I know it's not right, and I just want you to know that's not the real "me." When I know what I'm doing and saying, I'm fine. You remember all the good times we've had, right? That's the real "me."

I woke up this morning, and I didn't feel too good. That's why I had to leave. I just had to leave before things got worse. I hope you understand.

I'm sorry I didn't say good-bye to you in person, but because we're pals, I'm hoping you'll forgive me. Don't worry about me. I'll be all right.

Your Pal,
Grandpa

Jake tried to fight back the tears streaming down his face, his lower lip quivering as he sucked in short gasps of air. He wasn't really a crier, but under the circumstances it was out of his control. A stream of thoughts raced through his mind with a blur. *Did Grandpa really leave? Is he okay? Where could he have gone?*

Was it because of what happened last night? Was it my fault? The questions kept coming, one after another in rapid succession, but no answers followed. The tears continued to flow. Then, out of nowhere, came a question, and he said it aloud as it came to him. "*What should I do?*" He thought for just a moment. Fortunately for him, an answer followed. He stopped crying and wiped his eyes with his sleeve as he hitched up his pants. He dropped the letter on the bed and ran from the room. He plodded down the stairs, now three at a time, and ran out of the house, slamming the door hard behind him.

Melanie heard the front door slam, and it jostled her from her thoughts. "Jake, is that you?" She didn't hear anything, so she hurried out of the kitchen toward the front door. Once there, she stepped up and looked out the window to see Jake on his bike, pedaling fast down the walkway, nearly out of control. She watched as he turned and sped down the sidewalk with a look of unbridled determination.

She opened the door and shouted, "Jake! Where are you going?" He kept pedaling, now harder and faster, and he didn't turn around. She could see, could sense, that something was wrong, and she began to worry again. But this worry was different. It was a worry she could feel in her stomach and in her chest. Maybe it was a mother's intuition or simply that she knew her son well enough to know when something was wrong. "Jake," she said, this time quietly and only to herself. She folded her arms and held herself tightly. She could only wonder where he might be going. She was overcome with a wave of nausea.

Melanie watched him for a brief time, and when he was finally out of sight, she stepped back into the hallway, closed the door, and ran up the stairs. She quick-stepped on each tread, her feet making the sound of machine gun fire. She rushed into Jake's bedroom and looked around, panicked. Spotting the letter on his bed, she picked it up and read it. The nausea she was feeling was replaced with fear and despair.

* * *

Peter scoured the streets for hours. When his gas tank was empty, he stopped at the Shell station in town to refill. While there, he talked with the clerk. As Peter described his father, the young lady popped her gum and looked past him, seeming more interested in the Slim Jim rack than anything else. She hadn't seen Jack, but Peter left her with his phone number to reach him in case she did. It was the fifteenth such inquiry he had made so far that afternoon.

As he walked back to the car, Peter received a call, and he dutifully ignored it. He had only been out of touch with the office for a short time, but the tether was intact. The attempts to get in touch with him had increased with each passing hour. Each attempt garnered his attention for a second and annoyed him for a few seconds more before he disregarded it. He couldn't turn his phone off in case Melanie called with some news, so he had no choice but to keep the line open to all. He had received no fewer than five calls from Tim, four from Marc, and a few from April. It was likely that Tim and Marc both were badgering April to get in touch with him, given their own failed attempts. While Peter didn't normally ignore April's calls, he couldn't make an exception. When he left the office, he had decided to officially take himself off the clock. He wanted to spend some quality time with his father over lunch before their meeting with Dr. Halper. He had vowed to refuse all interruptions; now that circumstance had changed so drastically, he had absolutely no time to deal with the office. Nothing could be *that* important.

Peter replaced the pump nozzle and screwed on the gas cap. As he looked around, he realized he was on the far side of town, and he couldn't remember exactly how he had gotten there. He sat in the car for a moment to plan his next steps, wearied and concerned. *Where could he be?* he wondered. He started up the car and pulled out of the gas station driveway, momentarily looking left then catching something out of the corner of his eye. He looked back, but the car continued to move forward. He held his gaze a second too long and did not see the young girl walking her bike across the street just a few feet in front of him. At the last possible moment, he slammed on the brakes and startled them both. He breathed a sigh of relief as he motioned to the young girl to cross. She gave him a stern look. Peter knew he deserved it, but it was a little too severe and unsympathetic, coming from a girl so young. He guessed she was six years old at the most, and her expression hurt him. He acknowledged the expression nonetheless and yelled to her out the window, "Sorry!" She kept walking and lifted her bike up onto the curb at the opposite side of the street. He wondered where her mother or father was. The person in the car behind him leaned hard on the horn, and Peter's hand shot up in a wave. He refrained from making any other gesture.

Before he could get going again, his phone rang. He pulled back into the gas station so he could answer the call without killing anyone.

"Hello, Peter?"

"Hey, Mel." Peter suddenly felt better when he heard the sound of his wife's voice.

"Where are you?" she asked.

"I'm over on the north side. I've crisscrossed town several times, and there's still no sign of him.

"Can you come home? The police are here." She sounded unsettled.

"The police? What happened?"

"No, uh, nothing. Dr. Halper called them. They're going to go out and look for Jack, but they wanted to speak with you first."

"Okay, I'll be home in ten or fifteen minutes."

He pulled out of the gas station again, this time trying to be more careful. He made a sharp right at the next street and sped home. He hoped the police had a plan that would prove more effective than his.

* * *

After she hung up with Peter, Melanie let her guests know that he would be home shortly. They reacted with indifference. She offered to get them drinks and excused herself to the kitchen. She returned after a few minutes with a tray and set it down on the coffee table in front of them.

She sat in a chair, and the two police officers, Sergeant White and Officer Markley from the first district station, sat on the sofa next to her. Everyone was quiet, almost as if one person was waiting for the other to speak. She poured each of them a cup of coffee, and they reached forward to the tray to satisfy their individual cream and sugar needs. Melanie took hold of an ashtray hidden behind the coffee carafe and set it before her. She pulled a cigarette from somewhere and lit it. She had her own needs to attend to. She sucked hard on the cigarette and exhaled slowly with her head reclined, launching a cloud of smoke toward the ceiling. She stared at the cloud and then looked down at the cigarette like it was a long-lost friend. It seemed to calm her nerves some.

She looked at the police officers and said, "I don't usually smoke. It's just that . . ."

Sergeant White spoke up, not letting her finish her thought. "No need to explain, Ma'am."

Melanie took another long drag, exhaled another billow of smoke, and looked at the cigarette once more. The friend had left, leaving only a trespasser, and she felt betrayed as she tasted the burnt tobacco in her mouth. She leaned over and snuffed out the cigarette in the ashtray. *What I am doing?* she wondered. She sat back and instantly realized she wasn't sure what to do with her hands, so she folded them tightly in her lap and held them there while she watched the officers drink their coffee in silence.

The front door opened, then it closed. Peter rushed into the living room.

Melanie was up first. The police officers set down their cups.

"Peter! I'm so glad you're home." She hugged him. He returned the hug while looking over her shoulder at the police officers, who stood up at the same time. He smelled the lingering smoke and made an inquisitive expression that Melanie didn't see.

"Mr. O'Hara, I'm Sergeant White. This is Officer Markley." He motioned with his head toward his partner. Sergeant White reached across the coffee table, extended his arm, and shook hands with Peter.

"Sir," Officer Markley said.

Sergeant White said, "We spoke with Dr. Halper earlier today, and he briefed us on the situation with your father. The doctor has done a lot of work with the department, so we're more than happy to help. As you're probably aware, there's a required twenty-four-hour waiting period for a missing person's case, but we went ahead and filed a report anyway. Our entire shift is aware of your father's disappearance, and we'll do our best to find him."

"Thank you. I appreciate that." Peter's mind shifted gears. He looked around then turned to Melanie. "Where's Jake?"

Melanie took a moment too long to respond.

"Mel?"

"He's not home yet."

"No? Where is he?"

She still held to him tightly. "Peter, your father left Jake a letter in his room this morning." Melanie bent down and lifted a folded piece of paper from the coffee table. She handed it to Peter, and while he read it, she said, "I found it on Jake's bed, just after he ran out of the house without saying good-bye. He took off on his bike down the street toward town."

Peter looked at her.

"I thought about going after him, but I was hoping he was just blowing off some steam. I wanted to be here in case your father came back." She paused and thought about what she wanted to say. "I think he went to look for Jack."

Peter finished reading the letter then lowered it. He wasn't sure what to say, and a new wave of despair overwhelmed him. He sighed.

Sergeant White said, "Mr. O'Hara, there's a good chance he'll be coming home any minute. It's dinnertime, and it'll be getting dark soon. When we leave here, Officer Markley and I will look around the neighborhood—the school, the playground, the candy shop in town—, and we'll see if we can find him. Your wife gave us a picture." Sergeant White held up Jake's recent school picture, showing a happy young boy without a care in the world. "In the meantime, call all your friends and family in the area, as well as the parents of all of his friends and classmates. Maybe someone has seen him."

Sergeant White and Officer Markley walked toward the front hall while putting on their hats. Sergeant White said, "Make sure someone is home at all times in case your boy or your father return and also so we have a way to reach you immediately. You have my mobile number in case you need to contact me."

Everyone shook hands, and the police officers walked out the front door.

Peter turned to Melanie. "I have to keep looking. If I stay here, I'll go crazy."

"Go ahead. I'll call if there's any update."

They kissed, and Peter hurried out the front door and followed the police officers to the driveway. As he waited for the squad car to pull out, he sat in his car and plotted his next move. Unfortunately, clear thought was eluding him, and a plan never took hold.

* * *

Dusk was settling in fast as Jack wandered through a less desirable part of town, but he was no more lost than he had been earlier. He clearly was not the same man who had left the comfort of his son's home almost twelve hours earlier. His hat rested loosely on his head as though the day's exercise had trimmed the weight of his skull. He walked with a limp, not unlike the way he had when Peter saw him for the first time in the Gathering Hall at Shady Acres, the day he got his new lease on life. Now it seemed like the lease had expired. Jack had last eaten at one-thirty, having stopped in a small shop for coffee and a donut. That small source of energy had been depleted hours earlier, and his strength was gone. He moved on animal instinct alone. He shuffled down the street, wearing away at the soles of his shoes with each step.

At the next corner Jack came upon a homeless man who was sitting on the ground with his back to the building and rattling an old Folgers coffee can for spare change. Jack looked at the man, strangely interested, then looked down and squinted at the red can with white lettering.

"You lost, mister?" said the homeless man, with a rattle of his can.

"Huh?" Now Jack stared at the man's mostly toothless open mouth.

The homeless man tried again. "You lost?"

"No," Jack said, abruptly. "I don't think so."

"You sure look lost," said the homeless man. "I can tell that *look*. I've worn it some myself." He licked his dry and cracked lips and grinned widely, revealing a sea of red and swollen gums and two bottom teeth.

Jack just stood there, still inquisitive, looking at the man and trying to make the pieces fit. The homeless man looked back and gave Jack the once-over, up and down. They studied each other through a long ritual masked with uncomfortable silence. Eventually, Jack turned and looked around at everything and nothing at all. He tried desperately to find anything he recognized, but nothing registered, and he frowned.

The homeless man rattled his can again, this time louder and more deliberately, and he motioned to Jack to add to his take for the day. "Ante up, and I can help you find your way." The coins in the can rattled.

"What?" Jack said.

"I'm from around here." *Rattle, rattle.*

"Where?"

"Here." *Rattle, rattle, rattle.*

Again with indifference, Jack dug into a pocket and pulled out a wad of crumbled bills. He flicked away some lint and separated some of the bills. He bent down and put them into the homeless man's can, then looked around again as if nothing had happened, still searching. He watched a few of the cars pass by in the street then looked up at the sky, wondering where the sun had gone. He leaned forward and whispered something to the homeless man, words the man seemed to recognize and understand immediately. The homeless man pointed to his left and then stretched to point further left while he mumbled a stream of words to Jack, which also seemed to register. Jack adjusted his brim, nodded to the homeless man, and shuffled on his way. His limp seemed to go away, and he continued down the street, invigorated, into the cool and darkening night.

* * *

Jake pedaled slowly down the sidewalk, his eyes wide and searching. Storefronts were dark, and shopkeepers were deep inside somewhere finishing up their days. Only a few people were walking down the sidewalk. He maneuvered his bike with keen agility to stay out of their way, navigating the streets with expert care and determination.

He didn't realize the time and hadn't called home, which was very unlike him. Actually, calling home never crossed his mind. Doing his homework never crossed his mind. He knew it was getting late only by the diminishing daylight and the chill in the air, but he didn't know what time it was. He didn't realize that he had missed dinner. He assumed the discomfort he felt in his stomach was caused by something else. Jake was a little tired, sure, but it was nothing compared to how he felt at the end of a baseball game. He felt he could ride his bike forever, and he would if the circumstances required it.

He had but one objective on his mind, and that was to find his best pal.

* * *

In their squad car, Sergeant White and Officer Markley drove slowly down a dimly lit residential street, passing the elementary and junior high schools and slowing further to look at the kids gathered in the school playground. It was late in the day, and a group of older kids was throwing around a football while a few onlookers sat and talked underneath a tree. None of them looked like the young O'Hara boy, whose picture stared at them from a plastic holder on the dashboard of the squad car.

The officers were three hours past the end of their shift. They had been in their squad car most of the day and on their current assignment for the last five hours. Sergeant White couldn't explain why if you asked him, but he felt he had to find this lost man and the boy. It wasn't a desire or even an order; it was a need. From the moment he left the O'Hara's home, he was connected somehow to the situation and to the family. Mrs. O'Hara hadn't said much at all, but maybe it was simply the look on her face and the despair in her eyes that had reached him.

If Peter had been there in the car, he could have told Sergeant White that he knew exactly how he felt. Melanie had an uncanny ability to make *him* do things—things he would never dream of doing—all without saying a word. Then again, maybe this was a different situation altogether. Maybe Sergeant White was just doing his job, a job he took as seriously as a heart attack. It was Sergeant White who suggested to his partner that they stay on the street a while longer, and with that, the decision was made. Officer Markley did whatever the Sergeant suggested, and no doubt he could use the overtime.

* * *

After several hours, Peter realized he was covering the same ground. He needed to change his tactic. The car was suffocating, and it seemed the air conditioning couldn't keep up with the heat generated by the engine. He had covered a lot of ground, but he still felt like he wasn't getting anywhere. He was spending so much time fighting traffic and trying to avoid an accident that he could have passed right by Jack without seeing him. Peter's car typically was his refuge, yet now it was all he could do to stay behind the wheel. He had to escape.

So he decided to hit the streets on foot. He parked his car in front of the library and took to Main Street with a strong step and a new vigor. It felt good to be out of the car, his prison for the last God-knows-how-many hours. He was better now, walking down the street freely and with a mission. All of the distractions were gone, and he could observe and interact. That felt good, felt promising. He hurried down the street, stopping passersby to show them a picture of Jake and Jack. Many of the people knew Peter and his family personally, but no one had seen Jake or Jack. If nothing else, Peter told himself that these folks would keep an eye out and call the police if they saw anything. To Peter, it seemed like he was at least making some progress.

* * *

Jack found himself over in what he thought of as one of the "livelier" parts of town. Neon signs blinked above a diverse assortment of establishments: Mike's Bar, Choochie's Diner, the Green Slate pool hall, and even South Side Ink, a tattoo parlor popular with the college kids. Jack was out of his element, to say the least. He'd been used to quiet for such a long time, and what he saw and heard on this street was at the opposite end of the spectrum. He looked around with a mix of wonder and confusion. The blinking lights reminded him of Coney Island, for some reason, which comforted him, yet the strangers lurking all around made him uneasy. He inadvertently bumped into a man who was walking in the opposite direction down the sidewalk, and it startled him. The man barked a comment, in a language Jack couldn't understand, and after staring Jack down, he barked more and continued on his way. Jack didn't hear.

* * *

Jake was near the high school, pedaling by a park where some older kids were in the midst of a pickup baseball game. He slowed, then stopped. Standing with his bike propped between his legs, he watched the game as he held himself and rubbed his arms. The oncoming darkness of night had brought with it quite a chill.

He looked out at the field at the players and sighed with worry. *Where could he be?* He could only hope that his grandfather was safe somewhere and in out of the cold. He tried to think of where that might be, but nothing came to him. He watched the batter, who held his bat up above his right shoulder as he waited for the oncoming pitch. When it came, the batter swung hard. There was a loud *crack* of the bat as the ball took off into the outfield, and the batter sped off to first base. The crack of the bat triggered something within Jake, and he instantly had a revelation. He hopped onto his bike, turned around, and pedaled away down the street with a newfound sense of determination.

* * *

Jack ended up in a wide alley that looked dark and desolate. There was a brick wall on one side and garbage strewn in all directions. Steel beams stretched above. He backed up to the brick wall and slowly slid down until his rump hit pavement. He sat against the wall, alone and still, an improbable character in that particular setting. There were two large dumpsters on each side of him that provided shelter and a hiding place, although he didn't realize he might need such cover. A chill ran through him, and he lifted up the collar of his jacket, zipping the front up all the way. He was tired and done for the day, settling in for the evening, alone and scared. His weary, aching body now relaxed as his heartbeat slowed and his systems started to shut down. He lowered his head, and his eyelids drooped to slits. The clarity of emptiness overcame him.

* * *

Melanie sat in the same chair she had been in earlier when the police were at the house. The characters had changed, and Jackie and Mike were there with her now. The story was the same, though. They sat quietly on the sofa, sipping coffee, worrying and wondering where the men of the O'Hara family were.

Peter walked in the front door and entered the living room, stopping just beyond the archway. The three of them rose to their feet and looked to him for confirmation that everything was going to be all right. Peter was looking for similar confirmation. He shook his head, and Melanie shook her head in response. It was not the confirmation they had been hoping for, and they deflated with disappointment.

Melanie ran to Peter and began to sob. She wrapped her arms around him and buried her face in his chest. He held her tightly but turned away. He couldn't look at her, or at anyone. He had failed in his search. He had failed at keeping his family together and safe. He had failed at taking care of his father and protecting his son, and those thoughts of failure tore at him. He nestled his face into her hair and tried to hide the emotions forcing their way out. The skin under his eyes, skin kept relatively dry throughout his adult life, took on a reflective sheen that he hoped no one would see.

11

As hard as it was to believe, the O'Hara family unofficially called off the search at eleven o'clock that evening, *unofficially* because the search would never end, not until Jack and Jake were back home and safe. But Peter needed a break. He had covered the town limits more times than he could count, and, by eleven o'clock, he was more likely to hurt himself or someone else on the street than to find his father or son. He was tired, distraught, and was lost himself. Fortunately, Sergeant White, who had just dropped his partner off at the station, pulled up alongside Peter at a stoplight. They pulled over to talk.

Sergeant White had nothing good to tell him, aside from the fact that they would keep searching through the next shift. He assured Peter that they would call him as soon as they found or heard anything. He suggested that Peter try to get some rest, but he knew that it was not realistic advice. He was a father himself and could only imagine what Peter and his wife must have been going through. He insisted that Peter go home. While it took some coercion, eventually Peter resigned himself to Sergeant White's better judgment. He realized that he needed to be home with his wife, where perhaps he could be more effective on the phone.

Now, Peter was in his office at home, sitting alone behind his desk and contemplating his anguish. He was alone by necessity, for he was not able to share his pain and the guilt he felt about his failure to finding Jake and Jack. It was simple. All he had to do was to take care of them and protect them. Yet he had failed.

Melanie was in the kitchen. Jackie and Mike had gone to a hotel after making endless phone calls and keeping her company for most of the evening. Peter had told her that he had his own calls to make to the surrounding hospitals, as it had been an hour since his last attempts. She knew he wanted to be alone, and that was fine with her. She needed some time to herself to worry and to work on chain-smoking the pack of cigarettes she picked up when she was out earlier. Given the circumstances, she found her cigarettes were the one thing keeping her on an even keel.

Peter's craftsman-style desk lamp cast an unnerving dim orange glow across the room. Irritated, he reached forward to turn the lamp switch and realized that the three-way bulb was at its highest setting. He looked around, almost in a daze or a dream, at the darkness of the room that engulfed him. He leaned forward in his chair and looked out the window at the shadows. Unconsciously, he rubbed his hands together. The developing raw skin would cause him further discomfort in the following days.

He had made three calls to hospitals and a call to Sergeant White. After that, he was wedged into paralysis. He couldn't think of anyone else to call and had never felt so helpless in all his life. He contemplated going back out to look, but where would he start? The thought crippled him further. He pressed his hands together, palm to palm, and closed his eyes. His lips began to move in a near-silent whisper. He wasn't a religious man, but he had no one else to turn to. Peter had never failed at anything in his life until today. He began to perspire, and his hair follicles tingled.

He was interrupted by the sound that indicated an incoming email message. It seemed this sound was constant in his life.

Whether he was at home, at the office, or on the road, he could never escape that *ding* that let him know that someone wanted or needed him. The sound annoyed him, grating on his raw nerves. He turned to look at the computer screen to find a message from Tim. The subject line read: FINAL REQUEST—REPLY IMMEDIATELY!

An animal rage from deep within Peter erupted, and his worry and distress morphed into unbridled anger. *Final Request? Who do you think you are?* His reaction happened so quickly, he didn't realize what he was doing. He reached across the desk for the computer and, while rising from his chair, violently slung the laptop off the desk. The computer bounced off the wall and hit the floor hard as it rolled back like tumbleweed. It rested against the wastebasket in two pieces connected by a tangle of frayed wire. The keyboard unhinged from the cracked video panel. A high-pitched hum rang out from the shattered remains with a sound that was foreign to Peter and suggested a failure of one thing or another.

The room turned tomblike. Peter looked around for bystanders, but no one was there. Only the shadows were watching. He listened for footsteps that didn't come, and all he could hear was the pounding in his eardrums that radiated throughout his skull. His heart raced, and while he tried desperately to calm himself, he just couldn't. The rage would not subside. He ran a hand through his hair and felt wetness as he turned to continue his gaze out the window, searching for a sign, for a guiding hand, anything. His left eye started to twitch uncontrollably, and he was breathing heavily. Peter clutched his chest with his hand. He fell back down onto his chair and wept. He reached down deep for all the remaining strength he could muster.

All that came was fog.

* * *

The town had gone to sleep, and only the late shift and trouble remained on the streets. The evening had cooled, and a storm front had rolled in, bringing a noticeable dampness along with it. The rain would be coming soon, joined by a certain level of violence. The wind picked up considerably and moved some garbage through the streets.

Jake was riding up a desolate and barren street, kept company only by the streetlights. He came to a stop across the street from the baseball stadium at the far edge of town and stood with his bike propped between his legs. He looked up at the darkened stadium sign, hoping for a message, but all it conveyed to him was *good night*. He waited for the traffic light to turn green, and he got off his bike to walk it across the street. Once up on the curb, he jumped back on and pedaled toward the stadium.

* * *

Melanie sat in the dark and empty kitchen, only the red ember of her cigarette visible. It pulsed with each drag. Peter was still in his office down the hall with the door closed, and she wondered if and when he might emerge. She was nearing the end of her strength, and she needed him. She had heard the crash earlier. It was a sound that alarmed and worried her. She went silently to his office door and listened for a moment but decided not to go in. Instead, she rapped on the door just once and afterward heard him say, "Everything's fine." She went back to her own solitude at the kitchen table. She was afraid, alone, and had no one to comfort her. She was afraid for Jack and for her little boy, but now she was afraid for her husband. Even more disconcerting than the crashing sound that came from his office was the look in Peter's eyes when he had walked into the house. She had seen a vulnerability in him that had never before presented itself in all the years they had been together. He was the strong one, or at least that was the front, the façade, always. This evening, she had seen a loss of control that sickened her and a defeat in him that she was not sure he could overcome. She could only sit and smoke and pray that everything would be all right.

Then, the phone on the counter rang, breaking the silence like a fire alarm. She jumped from her chair, fought off an instinctive reaction to flee, and instead hurried across the room to answer the call.

"Hello?"

"Mrs. O'Hara, this is Sergeant White. We found your son and father-in-law."

"You did? Where? Are they all right?" A wave of emotion came over her, and she began to cry.

"They're fine. I'm with them over at the north parking lot of the baseball stadium. Get here as soon as you can."

She was sobbing so hard she couldn't talk.

"Mrs. O'Hara?"

She took a deep breath and wiped the tears from her cheeks with her free hand. "All right. We'll leave right now." She swallowed hard. "Sergeant White, thank you."

She hung up the phone and turned to find Peter standing in the doorway. A certain light, a glow, could be seen in his dampened cheeks. She said, "They found them, Jack *and* Jake. They're over at the baseball stadium."

Peter looked at her with relief and a renewed sense of life. The hand that was still holding his chest relaxed, and his arm fell to his side. He stepped forward, wrapped his arms around her neck, and squeezed her tightly. He leaned back and wiped away more tears from her cheeks, and they both smiled. He took her by the hand, and they hurried out the back door to the garage.

* * *

They arrived at the baseball stadium and pulled up behind a parked squad car in the otherwise deserted parking lot. The lights flashed and threw shadows in every direction. Peter jumped out and ran around the car to grab hold of Melanie as she exited the vehicle. He realized they were at the back side of the stadium by the left field bleachers. He saw Sergeant White at the far end of the lot and waved to him. Hand in hand, they ran, and as they got closer, they could see Jack huddled between two garbage dumpsters. Jake was sitting by his side. Jake appeared fine, but Jack sat motionless, his glazed eyes in a blank stare.

They ran to Jake, picked him up, and hugged him.

"Jake, honey, are you okay?" Melanie said. "We were so worried. My God, are you all right? She looked at his big green eyes and the smile on his face, and she knew the answer.

"Mom, I'm fine, really. It's no big deal."

She hugged him hard. Peter said, "Take it easy. You're going to squeeze the life right out of him."

"Really, Mom, I'm okay." He turned to look over at Jack. "We need to help Grandpa."

Peter stepped away and knelt down in front of his father, who was sitting with his knees tucked up close under his chin, his arms wrapped around his shins. He was shivering uncontrollably and staring beyond Peter into the distance. He put a hand on Jack's knee. "Pop? Are you okay?" There was no response as Jack's eyes remained fixed. He gave Jack's knee a gentle shake. "Pop?" Again, there was nothing.

Sergeant White walked up behind Peter. "That's quite a young man you have there. Somehow, he tracked your father down here then went to get help. He flagged down a patrol car six blocks away from here and told the officers his name. They called me immediately."

Melanie brushed the hair from Jake's forehead and kissed him. "I'm so proud of you."

Peter took off his jacket and draped it around Jack.

Sergeant White said, "I called you first, but after I assessed your father's condition, I called for an ambulance. It should be here any moment."

Peter looked up at Sergeant White. "Thank you, for everything."

They heard the sound of a siren in the distance, and they all turned to watch it approach, willing it to come more quickly. As the ambulance drew closer, the sound intensified, like an echo of their call for help. The ambulance added its own strobe of lights to the display of the night as it pulled into the parking lot and up to where they were gathered.

* * *

Peter instructed the ambulance driver to take Jack to Shady Acres and provided Dr. Halper's contact information. Jack was admitted there close to midnight, while the inhabitants of the building were resting and asleep. He was back in his bed in Room 146 shortly thereafter. Peter, Melanie, Jake, Jackie, and Mike all stood at the foot of the bed, watching him rest and saying a special thanks to their individual wish-bearers for getting Jack and Jake back safely.

Dr. Halper was there with them, making a note on his chart.

"It's fortunate that Jack's room was still available," he said. "He's a creature of habit and routine, and being in the same room will be a comfort to him." He turned to look at Peter, waiting for a question.

Peter said, "So, what do you think?"

"It's really too soon to tell. He's had a pretty stressful day, and he appears to be in much the same condition as when he was here before. Let's allow him time to get some rest, and I'll look in on him first thing in the morning. At that time, we can discuss how we'd like to proceed."

Peter nodded his approval. No one else had anything to say.

Dr. Halper stepped away from the bed. "We'll take good care of him," he said as he turned and left the room.

The family remained standing around the bed with their arms around each other, comforting and consoling one another. They communicated only with touch. After a while they decided to leave as well. They took turns saying good-bye, Peter and Jake at the end of the line.

Peter stepped up and looked solemnly at his father. "See you later, Pop." He adjusted the blankets and looked around to make sure everything was in order. He had difficulty walking away.

"Go ahead, kiss him," Jake said.

Peter thought about it for a second, looked at Jake and smiled, then he bent down and kissed his father. He stepped around the bed and walked toward the door.

Jake hurried forward and practically jumped up into bed with his grandfather. He hugged him tightly and gave him a kiss. "Good night, Grandpa." He ran over to join his father.

As they left the room, Jake broke away. "Hold on," he said. "Just one more thing." He ran back over to the side of Jack's bed and looked at Jack. He leaned over and hugged his grandfather once more, this time harder, tighter, and longer.

"C'mon, buddy," Peter said. "We'll be back to see him tomorrow."

Jake rose slightly to look at his grandfather's face, which was cold, pallid, and distant. He studied the lines in his face, the calm of his expression and closed eyelids. He touched the gray stubble on his chin and was amazed at how soft it was. He looked back at Jack's closed eyelids and noticed his eyes darting around underneath with the faintest of movement. Jake leaned back down and whispered something into Jack's ear. He let go of his embrace and ran back to his father, who put his arm around him as they walked out of the room and down the hallway.

* * *

Outside the front entrance of Shady Acres, they said their good-byes to each other. Jackie hugged Peter, then Melanie, then Jake. She held Jake's face in her hands and looked down on him. "Jake, I'm very proud of you for what you did tonight. Thank you for bringing Grandpa back home." She kissed him on the forehead and smiled. Jake smiled back, full of pride. He looked up at his parents, who nodded in agreement.

Mike stepped forward, kissed Melanie, and shook hands with Peter and Jake. He tousled Jake's hair. "Good job, Kiddo."

Jackie said, "Good night," and she and Mike turned and walked to their car.

"Good night," Peter said. "I'll call you in the morning."

Peter, Melanie, and Jake walked hand in hand down the sidewalk to their car as the moonlight guided their way.

12

When they arrived home, Peter parked in front of the house. He didn't feel it was appropriate to immediately subject his wife and son to the darkness and destruction that was their kitchen. He would let them ease into it. Everyone got out, and Peter pulled Jake's bicycle out of the trunk. Melanie and Jake walked toward the front steps.

Peter said, "I'll be right in. I'm going to put Jake's bike in the garage."

"Don't be long," Melanie said.

"Yeah, Dad. Don't be long," Jake said, mimicking his mother and grinning.

Melanie put her arm around Jake, and they walked up the stairs and into the house.

Peter watched them go in and smiled. He thought for a moment about the simple fact that he hadn't smiled in quite some time. The thought made his smile linger. He walked the bike down the drive toward the garage, taking slow and unhurried steps to take in a little more of the night air.

The garage door was open, and it was dark inside. The neighborhood was asleep, save for the crickets that sang their late-night soliloquy. Peter walked the bicycle into the garage and reached for the light switch. The single bulb hanging from the ceiling illuminated the garage, and the light made him squint until his eyes adjusted. He lifted the bicycle up and set it on the rack at the far end of the garage. He turned to look at his workbench, which he hadn't used in years. It was littered with a mess. He turned on the radio, and a song came on that he recognized and liked, so he left it. He turned up the volume and started to clean up some of the scrap wood and paint cans on the bench. As he did, he contemplated a thought that was pressing on his mind.

He looked around the garage and noticed the chair that Jack had been sitting on after the fire. He stopped to remember the day, and his thoughts took him back in time.

A series of images flashed through his mind. He saw the bad images first: Jack sitting on the chair in the garage after the fire; Jack all alone in his room staring blankly out the window; Jack at the cemetery viewing the tombstone of his wife, his wife who had been alive the last time he had seen her; Jake and Jake among the dumpsters at the ballpark. The images and the associated feelings saddened him and created a knot in his stomach. But then the good images followed: the family at the dinner table laughing at Jack's jokes and being impressed at his magic tricks; hot dogs at the ball park; the Wiffle Ball games on the front lawn; Jack, Peter, and Jake with their arms around each other, carrying their fishing gear after a day at the lake.

Peter smiled.

He looked around the garage again and noticed an old baseball glove hanging on the wall. He walked over and pulled it from the nail, then held the glove in his hand and studied the leather, the creases, and the stains. The glove was small, but he put it on his left hand and turned the palm and pocket upward. He gently rubbed the aged and worn leather of the glove palm then he balled up his right hand and pounded his fist into it, like he had done so many times before when days were simpler. From a well-guarded vault, he summoned the thought of the last time he had worn the glove, and he slipped away to another time, another place.

* * *

It was thirty years earlier, and summer was coming to a close. It was a spectacular day; one touched by the gods. It was warm and bright, and the air smelled of dirt, grass, and children.

A little league baseball game was in progress, and there was electricity in the air. The simple metal and wood grandstands were filled to capacity with parents, relatives, and children of all ages, many standing and all cheering with eyes trained on a young boy who was stepping into the batter's box.

A baseball coach on the sideline shouted instructions to the young boy through a cupped hand. "All right, Peter! All we need is a base hit." The coach looked out onto the field—where both teams were in their defined positions—and assessed the situation further.

A young Peter O'Hara was at the plate, his bat resting on one shoulder and his free hand hitching up his pants. He grabbed the bat with both hands and tapped home plate while he dug his spikes into the batter's box. He had teammates at second and third, and they watched him and shouted words of encouragement, looking on with anticipation. One of the boys had a hand behind his back, fingers crossed as he exhausted his stash of accumulated wishes.

Peter dug in firmly and readied himself, adrenaline kicking in and taking control. He lifted the bat gently off his shoulder and watched the distant pitcher, waiting. The opposing team's pitcher, looming tall on his sand pedestal, wound up and delivered his pitch. Peter followed the ball for a second, fixed on it, then closed his eyes and swung the bat with every ounce of strength he had—and some he didn't know he had. The connection of body to bat to ball was direct, solid, and perfect. There was a *crack*, and the ball shot through the infield and into left-center field. The runner at third base scored, and the game was over, just as the coach had planned. Peter was the hero, and his teammates mobbed him with congratulations and cheers.

When the celebration ended and the dust had settled, Peter picked up his dusty ball cap and walked over to the sideline. His mother was standing there, young, radiant, full of life, and likely the proudest person on the planet. Next to her was his father, a young Jack O'Hara, dressed in a fine gray suit, holding his fedora in his hands. He rocked back and forth on his feet and strained to hold in his excitement. They were beaming, bursting at the seams and waiting with anticipation to congratulate their boy.

Peter approached them. He was surprised to see his father. "Pop, what are you doing here?"

Jack stepped forward and put his hat on his head. "Just like I taught you. That was one fine hit." Jack reached over and rubbed Peter on the top of his ball cap.

"I thought you couldn't make it, that you had to work," Peter said.

"The championship game? I wouldn't have missed it for the world. The work will always be there, or something else will take its place. But there's only one championship baseball game on this day, and my son just hit the winning single." He swallowed hard. "You know, I'm really proud of you."

The young Peter smiled, and it was indeed the happiest day of his early life. He said, "I can't believe you made it."

Jack bent down and held out his arms wide. "Come here."

Young Peter stepped forward and put his arms around his father. His father lifted him up and hugged him, spinning him around. His mother stepped forward and hugged them both.

* * *

Peter looked at the glove and smiled; his eyes were moist. He raised the glove up, buried his nose deep into the pocket, and smelled that long-ago summer day. The aroma and the memory stirred his emotions and filled him with a sense of longing and hope. He put the glove back on the nail and stepped back to admire it.

He pulled out his phone and dialed a number. The call was answered on the fifth ring. "Hello, Derrick. It's Peter, Peter O'Hara."

A groggy voice replied, "Peter? What, what's the matter? I haven't heard from you in years."

"I know. It's been a long time. Listen, I'm sorry to be calling so late, but I really need to talk to you."

"Now? It's the middle of the night."

"Yeah."

"What about?"

"How's the construction business?"

"Fine. Why?"

"That's good to hear. Listen, do you think you could come over and meet me at the house tomorrow afternoon? I've got a project that I'd like you to help me with."

"Uh, sure." The fog was clearing. "I could come by after lunch. How's one o'clock?"

"That would be great. Thanks. I'll see you then."

Peter hung up, and he passed a finger beneath each eye to

clear the dampness. He looked invigorated, determined, and ready to take on a new challenge. He breathed deeply and stood tall and confident. Turning off the radio, he switched off the light and walked out of the darkened garage toward the house.

An unplanned recollection had prompted a realization, which had provoked an idea and created a diversion that set a new plan in motion, a plan that would lead Peter down an unexpected path. He forgot about everything else that had transpired that day. Now, only a single thought remained. He felt like it was a new day.

* * *

Peter had trouble sleeping again that night, or morning, but for different reasons than the last several weeks. Surprisingly, the lack of sleep seemed only to invigorate him more. He was up at six o'clock, hung around until Jake left for school at eight, then made his way to the office, arriving at nine-thirty.

At the office of Jackson, Parker & Finch, the elevator doors opened, and Peter exited first from a large crowd. He looked sharp and fresh, like a new employee showing up for his first day of work. There was a flash of eagerness in his stride and a glint of inexperience in his eyes. The only odd thing about the scene was that instead of carrying a briefcase, as he normally did, he was carrying a plain brown shopping bag that contained two bouquets of flowers.

Instead of hurrying past the receptionist as he usually did, he walked right up to her and stopped. He looked at her with a boyish grin.

Kelly was a little surprised, to say the least, and she returned a similar expression. "Good morning, Mr. O'Hara."

"Good morning, Kelly. You know, you do a great job here at

the firm. I just wanted to let you know that."

She was taken aback. "Well, thank you, Mr. O'Hara."

He reached into the bag, pulled out a bouquet of flowers, and handed it to her. "Please, call me Peter," he said.

"I, I don't know what to say. Thank you." She examined the bouquet, a multi-colored assortment of wildflowers and lilies, and she pulled them close and smelled them while looking around to see if anyone was watching.

Peter smiled, turned, and walked down the hall toward his office. Kelly watched him as she smelled the flowers again and shook her head, like she couldn't make sense of what had just happened.

He continued toward his office at the far end of the aisle, stopping to say hello to everyone along the way. He was in a great mood and much more sociable than normal. People noticed and were happily surprised.

As he approached his office, he stopped at April's desk. "Good morning, April."

"Peter, it's great to see you," she said.

He reached into the bag again and pulled out an even larger bouquet of flowers. He handed the bouquet to April and flashed the boyish grin again.

Surprised, she said, "Peter, they're beautiful."

He said, "You're the best. You're the one person here who makes this place a joy to come to."

She set the flowers down on her desk. "I received your message this morning. Thanks for thinking of me. Let me know what I can do to help."

Still smiling, Peter dropped the empty bag into the garbage. He stopped for a moment outside his office door and glanced in at his desk but did not go in. He turned and walked down the hall.

* * *

Tim sat at his desk, lecturing. Marc sat across from him, squirming. Tim looked frustrated; Marc looked absent. There was a knock at the door, and Peter walked in with a confident, powerful stride.

Tim was startled at the interruption, and he stood up and barked, "Peter, where have you been? I've been trying to reach you since yesterday. I should be mad as hell that you never got back to me. I *am* mad as hell."

"It's good to see you too," Peter said.

With those words in Peter's relaxed tone, the tension dissipated. Tim looked at Marc, then Peter and said, "You're here now—that's what's important." He appeared to feel better about the outlook for the morning. "We'll let bygones be bygones. Listen, we've encountered some unexpected issues that Marc has been unable to solve, and Gattling is starting to get concerned."

Marc looked wounded.

Peter walked up to Tim's desk, upbeat and knowing that nothing, absolutely nothing, was going to change his mood today. He said, "I had some family business to take care of. Everything has worked out fine. Thanks for your concern."

Tim tried to speak, but before he could get the first word out, he was interrupted.

Peter said, "It's taken me a while, but I know now that I have my priorities in line."

"Well, that's great to hear," Tim said. "Have a seat, and let's see if we can't keep our client happy."

Peter reached into his jacket breast pocket and pulled out a long white envelope. He handed it to Tim.

"What's this?" Tim asked.

"I appreciate everything you and the firm have done for me. I do. But it's time for me focus on what's really important."

Marc looked back and forth between Peter and Tim. He was trying to process the words, but the meaning was elusive.

"What are you saying?" Tim asked.

Marc didn't have the first clue as to what was happening.

"I'm sorry for the short notice, but I'm resigning, effective today."

"You can't resign," Tim said, indignant. "What about the firm? What about the partnership?"

"I've got a new partnership and a new project that starts today."

"What? *Where?*" Tim looked like he had been sucker-punched.

"I'll be available to work with you and Marc for as long as it takes to facilitate a smooth transition."

"Are you kidding? That'll take forever," Tim grumbled.

Peter was undeterred. "You both have my home number." He turned and walked toward the door. Once there, he spun around, slow and thoughtful. "Please give my regards to Phillip and Victor. I'm sure they'll understand." He turned back toward the doorway and walked out.

"I never saw that coming," Marc said.

Speechless, Tim looked at Marc with contempt and renewed frustration and simply shook his head as he lowered himself down in his chair. He swiveled the chair around and looked out toward the horizon, thought about his predicament, and pretended that Marc wasn't there.

* * *

Peter walked back toward April's cubicle with a spring in his step. He walked like he owned the place, and in a way he did. She was standing there waiting for him, and he walked up and hugged her.

"You take good care of your father," she said.

"I will."

"And your family," she added.

Peter stepped back, nodded, and adjusted his suit jacket, looking at it like it was completely foreign. "I think it's time for a different type of uniform."

April said, "Don't be a stranger." Her chin wrinkled up and her bottom lip quivered as she tried desperately not to cry.

Peter smiled and walked away, maybe even strutted a little, as he made his way down the hallway. He got onto the elevator and, as the doors closed, got his final glimpse of the offices of Jackson, Parker & Finch.

13

That afternoon, Peter met with his old friend Derrick McKee. Peter and Derrick had been close friends in grade school and high school, *best* friends, each of them might have said. They did their best to stay in touch while Peter was away at college, but business and family made it more difficult. Eventually, they lost touch. Derrick had passed on college and instead joined his father's construction firm. Three years ago, Peter had seen an advertisement in the local newspaper about Derrick's new business venture and remembered being impressed by his entrepreneurial spirit.

It didn't surprise him at all—Peter remembered many of Derrick's early ventures, like the lemonade stand, the car wash, and the lawn service. Derrick now specialized in developing senior residential communities, a growing field given the country's rapidly increasing elderly population. Peter had sent him a note of congratulations and offered to buy drinks in celebration, but they had never found the time to get together. However, Peter had kept tabs on Derrick over the years.

Now they stood out on the lawn in front of Peter's house and reminisced about their early adventures. After a short time spent catching up on old times, the division of years of separation quickly narrowed. That's how it is with good friends. You can be out of touch, but you never really forget why you were good friends in the first place. They both believed that good friends were friends forever. It is that simple premise, not the critical and sometimes foolish differences people create or dwell upon, that makes a lifelong friendship possible. As they talked, they both realized they were very happy to still be friends.

Derrick's truck stood at the curb, a heavy-duty white four-by-four with 'DERRICK CONSTRUCTION" emblazoned on the side. Like Derrick, the truck looked ready for anything. It gave Peter a good indication of Derrick's professionalism and success.

Peter opened a set of blueprints to show to Derrick the project he had in mind. He said, "Melanie and I were toying around with this idea back when my father first got sick, five years ago. We've got that large side lot that would be perfect for an attached in-law cottage." He pointed in the direction of the side lot then turned a page. "It should fit perfectly on the lot, and the cottage floor plan we've designed should provide plenty of room for my father. We've also included room for a live-in caregiver."

Derrick examined the plans with interest and a careful eye. He noticed that the bottom of each page was titled, THE JACK O'HARA ESTATE. "Your design is pretty impressive," he said. "And your father is pretty lucky."

"So, how quickly do you think we can get this done?" Peter asked. "I'm kind of in a hurry."

Derrick wanted to say *isn't everyone*, but instead he just smiled. He studied the plans further and thought about the question. He made a series of mental calculations and planned out the necessary tasks and activities in his head. "What are *you* doing for the next three months?"

"Me? Nothing. My schedule just freed up."

Derrick thought that was a little odd, but he liked the answer and let the thought pass as he considered the plans further. "I can have a crew here starting next week. How does that sound? With your help and an aggressive schedule, we'll have it done in twelve weeks."

"How do you do that?" Peter said.

"What?"

"The estimating, the planning, and telling me we're going to get the project done with confidence and conviction, in twelve weeks?"

"It's just a knack I have, I guess. Plus, I've done this a few times."

"Well, it's perfect, and it's a deal."

Peter and Derrick shook hands, and they both grinned like schoolboys.

"You know, for some reason, I think we're going to have a good time with this," Derrick said.

"I think we will." Peter rolled up the plans and turned them in his hands. He watched as Derrick walked over to his truck. "Hey!" Peter shouted.

"Yeah?"

"It's good to see you."

Derrick acknowledged the sentiment and nodded. "You too." He smiled and jumped into his truck, pulling away as Peter turned to look at the open lot next to his house.

The plan was coming together.

* * *

Six weeks is a long time and more than enough to get lost in something. For those forty-two days, those one-thousand-and-eight hours, Peter immersed himself in his new project and his new career. He did so with a passion that he had not felt in a long time. It was good medicine for him. He had a new outlook on life and a new purpose. It was a fresh start, and he was in complete control.

Peter could honestly say that he had not thought about the firm or the Gattling Project since the day he stepped onto the elevator to leave his office for the last time. Though he had offered to participate in a transition with Marc and Tim to ensure the continuity of the project, no one at the firm had taken him up on that offer. He was a little surprised but not really. He knew Tim too well. If someone thought the firm wasn't good enough, he could go to hell; that was Tim's outlook. After someone left, Tim relied on everyone else to pick up the slack during the transition. No matter how he felt about his previous position, Peter knew that he was replaceable and that the firm would carry on. It always did. Peter didn't have to, but he felt a bit sorry for Marc, who would be responsible for keeping the Gattling Project on schedule. He remembered that Marc had said, "It's nice not being tied down" and felt amused at how things had turned out.

Peter didn't miss the firm or the life he'd had there. He had his memories stored away, safe and secure, and when the time was appropriate in some future year, he would recall them and reminisce. If you were to press him to think about it, he'd probably tell you that he missed April because she was the nicest person in the office and maybe even one of the nicest people he had ever met. She was loyal, always hard working, and only cared about getting things done. He respected those qualities.

He would also tell you that he missed Victor Gattling, his self-declared mentor whom he respected and looked up to more than anyone else. He felt Gattling was more than a customer, that he was a genuinely good person, and what stuck with Peter the most was the meeting when Gattling had inquired about his father for the first time. It was a simple gesture, a man taking a personal interest in another man's life, but through that gesture alone they had made a connection. It's not surprising that the basic qualities of a person are the things we remember and the things that matter the most.

As promised, Derrick was at the O'Hara house the week after Peter quit his job, and the project commenced with little fanfare. The crew and the excavation equipment showed up first, and they had the foundation poured by the end of that first week. The framing came next, and they were under a roof at the end of week three. Peter was there every day, putting in ten to twelve hours with the rest of the crew, and he welcomed the hard work. He looked forward to the fresh air and rejuvenating physical labor.

The new project, his very own personal design and dream, was coming to fruition before his eyes. Peter had spent years thinking about the possibility of making the dream a reality, and in a few short weeks the idea sprang up from the ground like a miracle. Seeing his father's new home take shape was, without a doubt, the most rewarding project Peter had ever worked on. His other designs were for customers, people he only knew at the surface. This design was for his father.

Only a short time had passed since Peter made his career change, but already he realized that it was the best decision he had ever made. It was a turning point in his life and in the lives of the people around him.

* * *

There are only a few careers that give you the opportunity to leave a legacy. Most careers simply take; few allow you to give. More often than not, you put in your time and collect your paycheck until you find that your days spill over, one to the next, and the end seems far off in the distance. It's easy to get caught up in your work. Weeks turn into months, months into years, and if you have the ability to look back, you find that all you have to show for your effort is a lot of meaningless *stuff*. Stuff really doesn't matter.

That's what Peter thought about as he sat on the roof of the new addition with his son Jake, showing him how to nail in a shingle. He had lost a lot of time, but at least he had his buildings, those already standing and those that were to come. And Peter had his family. He cherished every moment he had with them, but building things was in his blood. He was going to continue to pursue his passion, albeit with a different focus and motivation. He felt lucky to have a second go at it.

Jake held one end of a chalk line while his father measured twice. Peter put his tape measure into his utility belt and held onto the line as Jake pressed his end down firmly on the roofing paper. "Okay!" he said.

"Go ahead, give it a snap," his father instructed.

Jake reached over, lifted the taut chalk line, and let it go. The line snapped down onto the roof, and a fine, blue powder rose from the surface and drifted away, leaving behind a guideline for nailing the next row of shingles. "Cool," he said.

Peter wound the line as Jake carefully lined up a shingle and nailed it into the papered plywood. Peter watched as Jake did exactly as he had been taught. Peter thought it was a beautiful sight and that he could watch Jake work all afternoon.

The Jack O'Hara Estate was a family affair. Jackie and Mike were there as well. Mike was pushing a wheelbarrow containing some bushes, and Jackie was directing him to the area off to the side of the cottage where they were working on the landscaping. On weekends like this one, the crew rotated, replacing the paid craftsmen who *had* to do the work with the weekend warriors who were unpaid but *wanted* to be there. For the O'Hara family, the motivation for the project was simple: it was about family. It was about solving an immediate challenge, but over time it became more about bringing the family together. They cherished the time they worked together.

Melanie came out of the front door with a tray and set it on a makeshift table of plywood and sawhorses. "Lunch time!"

Jake finished pounding in a nail and sat back on his heels to assess his work.

Peter patted him on the back. "Great job."

Jake was happy with his accomplishment. "Maybe I'll be an architect, just like you."

"You can be anything you want."

"I know, but maybe I'll be an architect." Jake said.

"Maybe."

They left their tools on the roof, came down the ladder, and walked over to the table where they met with the others. They all gathered around for a family lunch.

"Just a couple more weekends, and it should be ready," Peter said.

"Do you think he's gonna like it?" Jake asked.

"I think he's gonna *love it*," Peter said.

Jake smiled. "Me too."

* * *

Peter sat across the desk from Dr. Halper, wondering how the day's discussion would proceed. Peter had been visiting Jack every other day since his return to Shady Acres and had met with Dr. Halper on a weekly basis to discuss his father's status. Together, they hoped Jack's condition would improve enough that he could leave Shady Acres once again, for good. But, so far, that hope was off in the distance. Their hope was based on nothing more than Peter's expectation. He *wanted* his father to be healthy and back at home. Unfortunately, though Dr. Halper had been treating Jack for years, he still wasn't sure how to address Jack's condition, especially since he was still trying to determine the specific nature of the condition itself.

Peter said, "After visiting with him today, it doesn't appear that there's been any progress. It's a little disappointing, as you can imagine. It's been almost three months."

"Unfortunately, that's true," Dr. Halper said. "As you know, we have him on the same medications he was taking before. We want to keep him stable." He looked around his desk for a folder. Finding it, he opened and studied it. "Peter, if we take the same approach as before, we'll likely get the same results; it's as simple as that. I don't think that's what any of us wants. I'd like to suggest that we include your father in a new study that includes a regimen of a brand new drug, one that has been surprisingly successful with patients experiencing a variety of brain function issues."

Peter had a different agenda. "Let's talk about that later. I'd like to talk about moving him into his new home."

Dr. Halper set the folder down. "The addition is ready?"

"We're just putting the finishing touches on it. I think it will be perfect for him, but I know there are a few details, big details, that still need to be worked out."

"You're thinking about hiring a full time caregiver to live with him?"

"Yeah. It's the only way."

Dr. Halper was distracted as he noticed someone standing at the door. "Excuse me," he said then looked to the doorway.

Standing in the doorway was Jerry, Jack's TV-watching buddy. He was noticeably nervous and reserved, shifting side-to-side from foot to foot. His hands were jammed into his front pants pockets, and he looked down at his shoes.

Dr. Halper said, "Hello, Jerry. What can I do for you?"

Peter swiveled around in his chair so he could see both the young man and Dr. Halper.

Jerry continued to look down. One hand came out of a pocket, went up to his nose for a swipe, and went back into the pocket. Timidly he said, "Sorry to bother you. It's just that I saw Mr. Jack's son come in this morning, and I thought . . ." He wiped his nose again and cleared his throat, never taking his eyes off of his shoes. He pulled both hands out, picked at a fingernail, and fidgeted.

Dr. Halper said, "It's okay, Jerry. You thought what?"

Jerry thought about the question for a moment then looked up, raising his head ever so slowly. He said, "I, I just thought we might be able to give Mr. Jack the red pill again."

Dr. Halper's reaction was instant, as he was no longer interested in his visitor and dismissively he said, "Thank you, Jerry. Why don't you go back to the Gathering Hall and watch television. I'll stop by, and you can tell me all about it later."

Peter turned to face Jerry and glared at him. "What red pill?"

Jerry looked back down at his shoes and didn't say anything.

Peter got up from his chair and walked over to him. "Hello, Jerry. I'm Peter O'Hara."

Without looking up, Jerry said, "I remember, from when Mr. Jack got better the first time."

Peter extended his hand to Jerry.

After a few seconds, Jerry raised his hand and shook hands with Peter. Peter shook his hand gently, careful not to break it. Jerry lifted his head and looked at Peter, gazing at him with a certain longing. "Mr. Jack is my friend. I'm glad he's back. He's the only person that will play backgammon with me."

Peter said, "Jerry? What red pill?"

"The one that made him better."

Peter turned around to look at Dr. Halper, who came around his desk and walked up to stand beside him. Jerry thought he had done something wrong, and he took a step backward out of the doorway.

"It's okay, Jerry. You can stay," Dr. Halper said. Jerry remained still. "Jerry? Did you give Mr. O'Hara some medicine?" Dr. Halper asked.

"No, not me. Nurse Benson—she's the one that gave it to him. I was standing right there. Two whites and one red, not two whites and one blue. Didn't think anything of it at the time."

"When was this?" Peter asked.

"It was the night before he got better."

Dr. Halper looked at Peter, thoughtful and suddenly nervous. "I better go check the dispensing records and talk with Nurse Benson." In a hurry, Dr. Halper stepped past Peter and Jerry and headed down the hall. Peter stepped past Jerry and started down the hallway to follow him. He turned back. "Hey, Jerry? It was nice to finally meet you."

"You too," Jerry said, happy about having made a new friend. They shook hands again. "Thank you," Peter said.

"You're welcome."

Peter turned and headed down the hall, and Jerry watched

him as he remained in the doorway. His hands came out of his pockets, and he grabbed hold of his pants at the front belt loops and pulled them up an inch or two higher than they were meant to be. He smiled proudly, like he had done a good deed to help his friend.

* * *

Dr. Halper stood in front of the nurse's station, which was at the end of the corridor and just at the edge of the Gathering Hall. He held a chart in his hands and studied it with a peering eye. A nurse sat behind the desk and studied the doctor. She looked worried and waited. Peter walked up and stood next to Dr. Halper.

Dr. Halper asked the nurse, "Can I see the dispensing log for May eighth, please?"

The nurse got up and walked back toward a row of gray metal filing cabinets that lined the rear wall. They stood six feet tall, a treasure trove of information, personal, medical, and historical. She scanned the row, magically found the drawer she was looking for out of the dozens to choose from, and slid it open. After ruffling through some file folders, she pulled out a single manila file with a color-coded tab and closed the drawer. She handed the file to Dr. Halper then busied herself with a stack of files and papers on her desk.

Dr. Halper opened the file. He flipped one page, then another and another, scanning the pages intently. Ten pages in, he stopped. He ran a finger down the page and paused halfway down, studying it for a long time.

Peter looked on. "Dr. Halper? What is it?"

"It seems that there was a mix-up on May eighth. That was the day you came to visit with Jake. On that particular evening,

Jack inadvertently received a pill that was supposed to go to Mr. Riley." He thought some more then said, "But that doesn't make any sense."

"What? What did you give him?"

"Nothing, really. The red pill was a placebo."

"A placebo?"

The lines on Dr. Halper's forehead deepened, and his eyes narrowed. He licked his lips several times, trying to overcome the dryness. "Yes, there are certain circumstances where patients react positively to a placebo, and that's been the case with Mr. Riley. Your father was part of test program three years ago, and there was no effect whatsoever. Your father's taking the placebo could not have resulted in any change whatsoever, and the pill the placebo replaced was of such a low dosage that I can't imagine there would have been any noticeable impact."

"Is it *possible* that there could have been an impact?" Peter asked.

"It's not possible. As much as I'd like to have a potential solution to your father's condition, we're not any closer today than we were yesterday or four years ago. Sorry." Dr. Halper pondered the situation a little more, his mind racing, sifting, and analyzing. "How did Jack react to your visit that day?"

"There was no reaction at all," Peter said.

Dr. Halper studied the chart further. A slight smile formed on his face. "It does give me an idea though. I don't know why I hadn't considered it before."

"What?" Peter said.

"Peter, I need some time to research a few things."

"What are you saying?"

"I'm saying I need some time to pore over some research data.

I have an idea, but right now it's just that, an idea." He handed the file and the chart to the nurse and started to walk away. "Peter, give me a few hours. I'll call you later." He picked up his pace and hurried down the hall, his white physician's coat fluttering behind him like a cape.

Peter was left standing at the nurse's station, alone and out of place. He watched Dr. Halper walk away and thought again that maybe it was time to start looking for another doctor.

14

Two weeks later, Peter pulled into the driveway of his home and stopped the car by the front door. He got out and walked around to the passenger side door. He opened it, and there was Jack. Peter reached in to give him a hand, and Jack playfully swiped it away. Invigorated, Jack swung his legs out and stood up with conviction. He looked ten years younger, seventy once more, and acted as though he had a new lease on life, again. With a hand on the open door, he looked around and took in the wondrous site. He breathed in the sweet, crisp air.

The front door of the house opened, and Jake sprinted down the steps, arms wide as he ran up to Jack and hugged him tightly. "Grandpa! You're home!"

"How's my boy?" Jack wrapped his arms around Jake and squeezed him. He held him like he didn't want to let go.

"I'm great, just great." He took his grandfather by the hand and pulled hard. "Grandpa, come on! We've got a surprise for you!" It was all Jack could do to keep from being pulled forward onto his face, but he maintained his balance, held back a little and shuffled along, closely following his pal.

Melanie, Jackie, and Mike descended the front steps, looking like kids coming down the stairs on Christmas morning. They all gathered around Jack, their one big present, and welcomed him home. They surrounded him, locked arms around each other, and hugged him in a family grip. They held him just a few seconds too long.

"Hey, cut it out, would you?" Jack said. "It's good to see you all, but stop making such a fuss. What'll the neighbors think?"

They loosened their grip. Jake took Jack by the arm and led him and the group as they walked along the new paver walkway toward the front of Jack's new home.

Holding Jake's hand, Jack stood in front of his new cottage, the new addition to Peter and Melanie's house and his new home. He also looked like a kid on Christmas, eyes wide in wonder and brimming with anticipation. He felt like a young boy again and thought about a day some sixty years ago when his father took him out back to show him the small but perfect clubhouse he had built for him. At the time, Jack thought he was the luckiest boy in the world. It was one of the times with his father that he cherished most dearly.

He hadn't thought about that day in what seemed like forever, and he was surprised how the memory came flooding back with clarity and vivid detail. He could smell the freshly cut lumber. That clubhouse was the source of endless neighborhood meetings with boys and girls alike, and it served as Jack's refuge until he was almost seventeen, the age at which his legs would no longer extend comfortably within the shrinking confines. The thought of that day flashed through his mind, and it gave him a chill of excitement.

He turned to Peter. "You did this? For me?"

"It's all yours, Pop. Go on in and have a look."

Jack grinned, and a soft but excited laugh began to rumble in his chest. It was more of a giggle that grew in intensity, and the others could hear and feel his excitement. He tried to take it all in, starting at the roof and bringing his gaze down slowly, admiring the care and craftsmanship that went into that beautiful building. His gaze descended to the flower bed in front under the bay window, and he noticed that it held the same flowers he had planted for Peter and Melanie in front of their house. It was a small touch that blended the two structures together, but, more importantly for Jack, it showed thought, care, and love that they had gone to such trouble. His eyes began to water. He broke away, pulling Jake behind him, and led the way into his new home. Everyone followed.

Peter was the last to go in, and just as he was about to step into the front door, he heard footsteps coming up the walkway behind him. He turned to find the mailman coming at him at a fast clip.

"Afternoon, Mr. O'Hara," the mailman said.

"Oh, hi, John."

"That's quite a place you built there."

Peter couldn't contain his own excitement and pride. "Thanks. It's time for my Dad to have his own bachelor pad."

The mailman smiled, admiring the place. "Here's your mail."

"Thanks," Peter said again as he took a bundle of letters from him.

"Yes, sir, that's quite a place," the mailman said to no one in particular as he continued down the sidewalk.

Peter rifled through the stack of letters. He spied a return address on an envelope, and it piqued his interest. He pulled it from the stack and ripped it open, then unfolded a single sheet of paper.

He read the letter quietly to himself:

Dear Peter,

When I heard of your resignation, it surprised me, but

not really, I guess. I'm disappointed that you won't be able to see my project through to the end, but I'm even more disappointed that I'll have to deal with Marc.

Peter smiled and continued to read.

I understand and can appreciate what you're doing. I wish I had your guts back when my father was still alive. Maybe I would have done the same thing. Maybe I would have had more time with him. I respect your decision and wish you, your father, and your family all the best.

When things settle down, give me a call. I have an idea for a project that would be perfect for you—maybe something for the new firm that you can start out of your home office. Given our experiences, it's likely we both have some ideas that need to be explored.

I look forward to hearing from you.

Sincerely,

Victor

Peter folded up the letter and put it back into the envelope. He stared at the return address and thought about those words and the man they came from. He really didn't need the confirmation, but he was glad he had received it, especially coming from a man he respected so much. Peter was convinced he had made the right decision.

Peter walked into the cottage and closed the door, leaving the past behind.

Epilogue

It was a clear and bright early autumn day. Rays of sunlight streaked through the trees like fingers reaching from the heavens. The sky was a magical blue, and the grass was a well-watered shade of green. Peter and Melanie and Jake walked through the town cemetery with a leisurely stride. There was no reason to hurry to their destination, for what they were going to do.

Ten years had passed since that memorable day when Jack O'Hara left Shady Acres for the second and final time and walked into his new home and new life with pride, vigor, and determination. It was a decade etched into history, the years enlightened, special, and memorable as a result of a unique turn of events that no one in the O'Hara family could have imagined.

Peter had his arm around Melanie, and she was holding hands with Jake. As they navigated the maze of headstones, they thought of the warmth of the day and the warmth in their hearts. They each knew, deep down, that they had made the most of the special opportunity they had been granted.

Jake was now a man, eighteen years old, towering and ready to take on the world. He was in the middle of his second semester at college, his major undecided. He was still considering all of his options. He was in an exploratory program that allowed him to get additional exposure to many of his interests and passions.

He lived on campus and was relishing his independence, but he came home frequently for visits, which made his parents happy. The visits made Jack happy, too. Jake was studying English, international studies, and architecture design, and he was excited about his future prospects and what the world had in store for him.

The additional ten years had given Peter and Melanie a look of refreshed maturity. They were each still on their second careers, steering their lives as their hearts directed them. Melanie had just released her fourth novel, this one a *New York Times* bestseller, and Peter was designing and building innovative homes with his friend Derrick to help keep generations of families together.

They walked between the various headstones, careful not to insult anyone by stepping on a grave. They came to a stop at a pair of granite slabs, one old and one new, and they all looked down to observe them, turning solemn. Melanie handed two long-stemmed red roses to Jake, and he stepped forward, bent down, and laid one rose on the ground in front of the old headstone. He laid the other rose down on the ground in front of the new one. He stood up and folded his hands, lowering his head.

Jake said a prayer for his grandmother and tried to picture her face.

With a slight turn of his head, he looked at his grandfather's headstone and could see himself reflected in the polished surface of the rock. He had some special words for his grandfather which he spoke quietly to himself:

> *Hey, Grandpa. I can still remember the day that Dad took me to visit you for the very first time at Shady Acres. It was a day I had anticipated for a long time and a day I'll never forget. Before that, I really didn't know who you*

were, but shortly afterward, we were best friends. It's hard to believe that it was ten years ago that you came back to us for the second time. You have to know how important those ten years have been: to me, to Dad, to everyone. I'm so grateful to have had that extra time with you to be friends.

Jake looked over to his parents and smiled. He continued:

I hope you don't mind, but I'm only going to say hello when I'm here. There's no need for good-byes. We're still best friends and always will be, and you'll always be with me, in my heart and in my life.

He stepped forward and knelt down in front of the new headstone. A close-up of the headstone revealed:

JACK O'HARA

Loving Husband, Father, and Grandfather

Below the two lines were the dates reflecting the eighty years that Jack had graced the earth. Jake ran his fingers over the carved numbers, not noticing the coldness of the polished granite.

He said to himself:

From that first day I visited you, Dad always believed that you could hear us.

He thought back to that first visit, of leaning in to hug Jack and whispering into his ear as he said good-bye. He thought back to the time when Jack returned to Shady Acres after he found him at the ballpark, and he had whispered into his ear in a similar way when he said good-bye. As he knelt in front of Jack's headstone, he rested his hand on top of it and said for all to hear:

"I know you heard me then, and I know you can hear me now. Grandpa, you're the best in the world."

Jake turned to look up at his parents and smiled again. He stood up and walked over to them, and they all embraced.

Hand in hand, they walked off into the distance.

"The future disappears into memory
With only a moment between
Forever dwells in that moment
Hope is what remains to be seen."

— Neil Peart, *The Garden*

Acknowledgements

Writing a book is a solitary endeavor. Publishing a book is a team effort. I would like to thank the following individuals who were such a critical part of my publishing team and who had a hand in making this book a reality. First and foremost, I want to thank my publishers at Eckhartz Press, Rick Kaempfer and Dave Stern, who are pursuing an evolutionary and refreshing approach to publishing in Chicago. It has been a pleasure to work with you and I will always be grateful for your dedication and unwavering support. I would also like to thank my editors, Kelly O'Connor McNees and Ashley McDonald, who helped me to polish and refine the words and sentences of my story. I do believe you can judge a book by its cover, and I want to thank Susan Rackish Janssen for painting such a poignant image, one that truly encapsulates the essence of the story. I also want to thank Siena Esposito and Vasil Nazar for their book interior and cover designs and for helping to pull it all together. I am so proud to be one of many published authors in Chicago, and I want to extend my gratitude to everyone who is involved in supporting our local writers. In particular, I want to thank Randy Richardson, President of the Chicago Writers Association, who has been a tireless friend and supporter of the Chicago writer. Lastly, I want to thank my wife and children for their endless love and total support of every new endeavor I pursue.